D1486028

MY FRIENDS FROM CAIRNTON

Books by Jane Duncan

★

CAMERONS AT THE CASTLE
CAMERONS ON THE HILLS
CAMERONS ON THE TRAIN
CAMERONS CALLING

★

MY FRIENDS THE MISS BOYDS
MY FRIEND MURIEL
MY FRIEND MONICA
MY FRIEND ANNIE
MY FRIEND SANDY
MY FRIEND MARTHA'S AUNT
MY FRIEND FLORA
MY FRIEND MADAME ZORA
MY FRIEND ROSE
MY FRIEND COUSIN EMMIE
MY FRIENDS THE MRS. MILLERS

MY FRIENDS FROM CAIRNTON

BY

JANE DUNCAN

MACMILLAN

London · Melbourne · Toronto

1966

Copyright © Jane Duncan 1966

MACMILLAN AND COMPANY LIMITED
Little Essex Street London WC 2
also Bombay Calcutta Madras Melbourne

THE MACMILLAN COMPANY OF CANADA LIMITED
70 Bond Street Toronto 2

PRINTED IN GREAT BRITAIN

With love to
AUNT KATE

'The Lord shall smite thee with madness,
and blindness, and astonishment of heart.'

Deuteronomy xxviii. 28

PART ONE

MONDAY, the 29th of November 1954 was a memorable day in my life. It is not often that a pin-point in place and time can be determined accurately as a turning-point in a life, for all our moments are such a fluid compound of echoes from the past, the tick of the present, and adumbrations of the future, that our time is as mobile as water and impervious, as water is, to the holding of a steady pin-point mark. But this day towards the end of November in 1954 holds such a mark for me and it is worth the record of memory.

Its morning was exactly like the morning of any other day at our house, Guinea Corner, on the sugar plantation of Paradise, in the West Indian island of St. Jago, like any other morning of the past year, that is, for all these mornings had been alike, because it was almost a year to a day since my husband had emerged from hospital after a serious illness. Quite suddenly, in the summer of 1953, it had been discovered that his heart and liver were seriously impaired. He had nearly died, but, after long treatment, he had come out of hospital, a matter of pride to his doctor and nurses, a man able, as they said, to live again.

But in cases like these, the words 'to live again' are deceptive. They do not mean 'restored to life as it was before'. They mean literally to begin living again in a new way, under new conditions and this is not a simple matter for a man in his mid-forties. It is not, either, a simple matter for his wife, I had found.

3

It is tedious to recapitulate the dreary routine of the days of that year. They were all alike, as I have said — the checking of the temperature morning and evening and the making of the entries on the chart; the swallowing of the pills morning and evening and the taking of the tonic after each meal; the arranging of the meals themselves to obtain some variety when so many items of food were barred and to give to the food some taste when salt was forbidden; the overseeing of the Negro servants to see that all the instructions for cooking were carried out; the constant furtive watching of the pulse in the neck, just under the left ear, when he came in from the office for lunch at twelve and again at the end of his working day at four. Looking back, the only days in that year that had in them anything that was different were the last Saturdays of each month and they were marked by a new peak of anxiety for, on those days, the medical chart for the month was rolled up, an elastic band put round it and we got into the car to drive to the hospital at St. Jago Bay for the monthly check-up. It was gratifying that over the year, by a process so gradual as to be imperceptible while it was happening, both heart and liver had improved. There was no doubt, Doctor Lindsay said, that the patient was better. Although he would never be entirely fit and would always need the greatest care, he was better.

I knew the patient by the name of Twice, a name that I myself had given him when I first knew him because his full name was Alexander Alexander, but it was a name by which everybody now called him because, in some fortuitous way, it was so apt that it was almost a summary description of his character — his character before this illness overtook him, that is. He had extraordinary tenacity, and when he was particularly interested in anything he would look at it, be it an object or an idea, and then his glance would intensify as if he looked at it again, the

4

sharpening of the glance or concentration being so marked as to be almost palpable, like the double blow of a blacksmith's hammer or the double line at the bottom of a balance sheet. A friend of ours, Sashie de Marnay, had once put this trait, which I had thought till then I was the only one to observe, into words by saying: 'Twice thinks it is a good idea because he did a twice-ness about it', and it summarises the whole complex result of his illness and the whole reason for my anxiety and unhappiness when I say that, at the end of a year after his emergence from hospital, this 'twiceness' had gone. The patient was better, according to the doctor, but, according to me, Twice was no longer Twice.

No relationship is a static thing and since Twice and I first met in 1945 — late in our lives, for we were both thirty-five at that time — our relationship had changed and modulated through many vicissitudes. People such as my family, my friend Monica and Sir Ian Dulac of Paradise, who thought they knew us well, would no doubt describe our relationship as a long and violent quarrel or a passionate upheaval punctuated by short intervals of peace and calm, but even the most intimate friends of two lovers have little conception of what lies between them. The noisy arguments, the bouts of near-fisticuffs in which pie dishes and minor items of household equipment had been known to be thrown, were mere surface storms between Twice and myself; they were the rains that watered, the heats that fertilised and the winds that winnowed the harvest of feeling that was engendered in us. Much of the reason, I now know, for the noise we indulged in and the violence of physical action which we displayed was that we could seldom find the words to say what we meant and neither of us was very patient, so that, instead of discussing some cross-current that had developed between us in calm and reasoned words, we would both begin to shout the first words that came to our rage-impaired tongues and then, becoming entirely incoherent, one of us — usually myself — would seize the nearest portable object and hurl it against the wall and the resultant noise would either make us both laugh or make me burst into tears or make Twice take hold of me and shake me, but, whatever the result, we would end with a passing difference settled and more closely at one with each other than we had ever been before.

But, since the illness, violence of word or deed was no longer permissible. There must be no emotional storms, nothing to make the heart beat faster or cause the blood to rush to the head. Twice, the patient, must live a calm life and I, his wife and nurse, must meet everything that happened with calm and patience, and this is how it had been for a year, a year when this enemy of illness in our home had never been discussed, because to discuss it might be upsetting; a year through which a calm routine had been pursued of day following uneventful day; a year, not of life, but of avoiding death. Death had come too close. In life, there should be no familiarity with death. It should not be one of the everyday contingencies, for its proper place is away in the distance, at the point where the horizon tips over into the unknown — it is the last contingency of all. But here at Guinea Corner, it seemed to be in the house with us. 'If he does this,' Doctor Lindsay had said, 'he will die. If he does not do that or if this should happen, he will die.' He did not put it exactly in these words, but that is what he meant. Death should not be as familiar as that, as familiar as going to the cinema or getting up in the morning. 'If I go to the cinema, I shall miss seeing Thelma this afternoon' and 'If I don't get up in good time, I shall be late at the hairdresser's.' Death should not be a contingency like that. It is not a part of life like seeing Thelma or going to the hairdresser. It should

6

always be in the far distance, an invisible sentinel standing at the very end of the road.

Although I was forty-three when Twice became ill, it seemed to me now that, until that time, I had always had to life the attitude of youth. I had always looked forward with the full confidence that tomorrow would be a lovely day and, during this past year, I had come to think that I had been too fortunate, that life, indeed, had cheated me, luring me on towards a tomorrow and tomorrow and tomorrow with golden promises until there came that tomorrow when Twice became ill, and life struck me down with the hard fact that the days to come not only had little golden promise but that the days themselves were numbered. For a year now, I had been veering between a sickly self-pity because I had been cheated and a bitter sense of shame that I had been so engrossed in the day-to-day that forty-three years of my life had been spent without my gathering the experience to meet this contingency which had come upon me; but, on this morning of which I write, I could no longer summon up the spurious comfort of self-pity nor the astringent spur of shame towards a better effort. During the last few days, I had left both self-pity and shame behind and had gone down into an acceptance of defeat. Life, as I recognised it, seemed to be finished. Twice and I, now, would go on through the days as we had come through the past year, with no point of contact between us except the chart where we marked down the number of ounces of urine each day, moving steadily, as we had done for the last twelve months, towards the last Saturday of the month when we would be afraid to speak to one another on the way to the hospital and too relieved to speak to one another on the way back, in case one of us would break out of tension into tears. We could not live any more, I had come to accept we could only spend our days in the careful avoidance of death.

7

At twelve noon, on this remembered Monday, Twice came home for lunch as usual, bringing with him the mail which had arrived at the sugar factory office during the forenoon.

'Quite a haul today,' he said, handing me the letters. 'The home mail is on schedule this week.'

While he poured himself a glass of iced barley water — exactly six ounces of barley water in the jug — I watched him covertly, counting the breaths as he drew them, studying the motion of the pulse at the side of his throat as I always did when he returned after even the shortest absence. As he turned round with the glass in his hand, I looked down at the letters in my lap, feeling guilty about this furtive observation of him, this obsessive thing that I could neither stop doing nor discuss with him, yet aware at the same time of astonishment that he had not already noticed it in me. A hurt, bitter astonishment, I should have said, because his intimate knowledge of me, before, had been so very acute that, eighteen months ago, I could not have watched him like this without his being aware of it. But that telepathic sense between us seemed to have been lost; the distance between us now seemed to be too great for it to span.

'Who are they from?' he asked as I turned the letters over.

He had no real interest in the letters, I knew. The question was asked merely to 'say something', to maintain a front of contact between us.

'Monica, Jock — one from Hugh Reid —'

'What has come over Hugh? He is a Christmas-only type as a rule. The end of November is a bit early.'

The strange thing was, I thought, that any observer, standing by the clump of hibiscus on the lawn, watching us and listening to us there on the veranda, would have thought that we were a most happy couple, middle-aged,

8

at ease with one another, reading our mail from our friends at home. To look at Twice, you would not know that he had ever been ill as he stood there, sturdy and stocky, tanned of skin and brightly blue of eye. Quite often, during the last few months, I had taken myself severely to task, accusing myself of imagining things, assuring myself that our situation was an all-too-common one of our times, for diseases of the heart are one of the marks of the twentieth century as surely as the Black Death was one of the marks of the Middle Ages. But none of this arguing with myself made any difference. I remained sure in my mind that Twice was now withdrawn from the world and from me, strangely detached, and I knew that this interest in the letters from home was a simulation, a faint echo of the warm and vibrant interest which used, once, to emanate from him on mail-days. It was as if he had decided that these letters came from people he would never see again, for we had been told that the Scottish climate was a risk that should not be taken, so that, already, they had lost reality for him.

'I suppose it is Hugh's Christmas letter, really,' I said, slitting the envelope. 'Maybe he has made a special resolution this year.'

I unfolded the letter and began to read it aloud because Twice had evinced a little interest in it.

'My dear Janet, Although it is really your turn to write, I shall forgive you this time if only for the reason that there is something I want you to do for me, but first I must say how happy I am that Twice is still going on so well. I have not met your Doctor Lindsay but I have read papers by him at one time and another and have every confidence that you could not have a better man. I am sending you someone who I hope you are going to like. She is a patient of mine, Lady Hallinzeil, the wife of the coal, steel, and shipping man, and she is going out to St. Jago to spend a month or two. She will be staying at the Peak Hotel, which is, I believe, one of the best in the island but I think you told me once that you know the owners of it. If this is so, I shall be most grateful for anything you can do to make things happy and comfortable for her. She has just recovered from an attack of flu but please don't get the idea that I am sending you an invalid. Physically she is quite strong but she has been very depressed of late. I have a feeling that a little of your company will be very good for her if you take to one another and you can spare the time. Above all, I do not want her to be lonely. Next week, I leave London for Switzerland—not to ski, but for a conference at Lausanne, but even although I am no winter sportsman, Lausanne will be preferable to London in December—'

'To the devil with Lady Hallinzeil,' I said, folding the letter when I had read to the end of it and putting it back in its envelope. 'I suppose it is a natural snag in living in a place that is a fashionable holiday playground, but I do think people at home are unimaginative. They seem to think that one has nothing better to do than drive up and down to St. Jago Bay to see that their wealthy friends aren't dying of boredom.'

'How does this name Hallin-what-you-said spell?' Twice asked. 'Is it German?'

I took the letter from the envelope again, spelled out the name, and added: 'For my money, it could be Siamese. Not that it matters. She will get along nicely down at the Peak without me.'

I picked up the next letter from my brother Jock, Hugh and his friend already dismissed from my mind. After a year of never going anywhere except perhaps to tea with Madame Dulac, the owner of the estate, the idea of leaving Twice alone at Guinea Corner to drive down to St. Jago Bay to call on a stranger was as foreign to me as the idea of stepping into a rocket for a trip to the moon. I had begun to slit the envelope of Jock's letter when Twice said: 'I think you should call on this good lady, darling. After all, Hugh is one of your oldest friends and he has never asked you to play island hostess before.'

Again, the watcher by the hibiscus clump could never have known what these few words signified. They sounded like the merest comment from a reasonable-minded husband to a rather ill-natured wife perhaps but, for me, they had all the significance of a peal of bells that announced some victory so long-awaited that hope had almost been abandoned. My hands became arrested with the half-opened envelope between them. I did not dare to lift my head and look at Twice. In a whole year — more, for he had been in hospital for some four months before that — this was the first time that he had ever expressed an opinion to me, the first time that he had ever indicated a preference for a certain course of action on my part.

At work at the sugar factory, I knew from Sir Ian, Madame Dulac's son, that he could be as didactic and opinionated about his views as he had ever been, although he now had a sedentary post as assistant manager instead of being the physically active engineer representing a British firm that he had been before his illness, and this was a thing that I had not been able to understand. According to Sir Ian, he was as 'bloody-minded' about engineering matters as he had ever been — and Scottish engineers are notoriously bloody-minded, the which word describes them more graphically than any other — and it seemed to be only with me that he displayed this cold, distant, disinterested, detached docility.

'Would you like me to call on her, darling?' I asked, not looking up at him.

'I don't want you to do anything you don't want to do, but —' he said and stopped.

He spoke very quietly and seemingly without a great deal of interest, whereas two years ago he would have been almost shouting: 'Dammit, it's the least you can do for Hugh. Lord love us, you've known Hugh for over thirty years and you won't even go and welcome a friend of his to the island when he specially asks you to!' I looked up at him now. 'Twice, I don't mind very much one way or the other but I'll go down and call on this old trout if you really think I should.'

He frowned and looked out through the mosquito screen of the veranda at the lawn and garden. 'I have no business shoving my oar in,' he said. 'She may be awful. She may be another Martha's aunt. But I just thought — sort of —'

Two years before, Twice did not ever think 'sort of —' Before he was ill, Twice thought very definitely and, where I was concerned, he said what he thought in terms so plain as to be beyond all misconstruing.

'What did you think, darling?' I asked.

'Well, I just sort of thought it would be nice for you to see somebody new. But not if you don't want to, of course.' He looked down at his hands that were holding the glass and frowned again as if what he had to say was of almost impossible difficulty.

'You see, since I've been ill, you have never gone anywhere except about the estate here and it must all be terribly dull. But I am not so ill now as I was?' The last phrase was tentatively questioning.

'Of course you're not!'

My voice was shaking and I was close to tears for this was the first time since he had left the hospital that he had ever said, in straight words 'I have been ill'. He looked at me, his eyes intensely blue.

'You don't like to talk about it, I know,' he said and looked past me and out to the bright garden and I felt that he was slipping away again, into that remote place where he now seemed to live.

'I think it might be better if we talked about it a little,' I said, trying to keep my voice calm and steady.

'You loathe illness and sickroom charts and everything,' he said thoughtfully, not looking at me but speaking as if he were saying over to himself something that he had said many times before. 'It is strange that a long-drawn-out illness like this of mine — a permanent disability like this — should have been visited on *you*, as if life had specially chosen the thing you hate most.' He sighed. 'You see, I can't get completely better the way you did that time you fell at Crookmill.'

'But you *are* better, Twice,' I said with a desperate wish to call him out of himself, to bring his eyes to my face and away from the distance into which he always seemed to be looking now. 'Darling, I know you will never be able to do the sort of job you did before, hopping by air from one island to another and to one engineering project after another and working impossible hours, but you are holding down a highly skilled job here and still keeping both of us in luxury.'

He still looked past me, away to the garden. 'But this is not what we had planned. If our plans had gone through, we would be back in our own country by now, among our own people. You have never really liked this island or its climate — you have never really been at home here.' He sighed again. 'But they say I can never cope with the British winter. I suppose they are right.'

'I think you are forgetting one thing, Twice,' I said. 'You seem to forget that my home is where *you* are.'

His eyes turned to my face. 'Is it still like that? In spite of everything?'

I was hurt by this and although I tried not to let it show, he became aware of it.

'Don't be hurt, please,' he said and his face was infinitely pleading. 'You see it is so terribly hard to believe.'

'But, Twice, why?'

'You have been so terribly — cheated. That is how it seems to me. I wanted to do so much for you, promised you so much, and I can't do any of it.'

'But that is not how it is! I don't want things done for me. I want us to do things together, just as we have always done, just as we are doing now.'

'You are doing most of it and it is all stuff you don't like to do.'

'That is not true, Twice. All right, I was always afraid of illness and sickrooms before — I admit that — but I am not now, especially when I see the results I am getting. Doctor Lindsay was *terribly* pleased with you last month!'

'I know.' He looked away over my shoulder again out into the garden and sighed once more. 'But he still says the British climate is out of the question. I asked him.'

'Twice, I think going back to work at home is an idea you have to give up. I thought you had accepted that, darling. I accepted it for good long ago — we can't risk another attack of bronchitis or any chest trouble. You know that. Quite honestly, I don't *want* to go back home.'

'Oh.' His eyes came slowly back to my face. 'This is something else that I don't understand, but I have never been able to ask you about it. Is it because Reachfar is sold that you don't want to go home, then?'

'Partly,' I said, but I did not want to talk about the sale of my family home. 'But even if Reachfar were still there to go to, I wouldn't want to go to Britain because of the risk for *you*, don't you see? You simply don't seem to understand that *you* are the important thing, darling.'

He smiled very faintly. 'It is difficult to feel important when you are mainly conscious of your nuisance value.'

'If you feel that you are a nuisance, it means that all my sickroom stuff hasn't been much of a success. You didn't feel a nuisance when Sister Flo was nursing you in hospital.'

'That was different. I didn't feel anything much at all at that stage, but nursing was Sister Flo's job. It isn't yours. I never intended to turn you into a sickroom attendant. There is a thing you and I tend to forget. We are what is technically known as lovers — you made no sacred promises in church about cherishing me in sickness or in health or anything like that. We couldn't get married but you loved me enough to join your life with mine. It seems to me that this last year hasn't been much of a love affair in any sense. What has happened is that you have expended endless love and care on a hopeless crock, that's all.'

'This is absolute nonsense, Twice Alexander!' I said indignantly, and I was horrified when a tremor as of fear crossed his face and he said: 'Try not to be angry with me. Words are terribly clumsy for what I have to say but I have to try to say it now I have begun.'

'Twice, I am not angry, but you are thinking about things in the wrong way. You speak as if I had expended love, as you put it, on something that isn't worth spending it on. Love isn't like that. One can't choose about spending it and if it is there, it has to be spent. Don't you see that?'

He smiled. 'Yes. I see it when you say it. I think that maybe you and I have not said enough to one another during this last year. Saying wasn't so necessary before, but we need it now and it is so difficult to say exactly what one means. Besides, we have had nothing very pleasant to say things about.'

'It has not been that so much. But Doctor Lindsay was so emphatic about your not getting excited or worried —'

'Is that —' he hesitated and seemed to make an effort of

15

courage before he went on '— why you have never talked to me about Reachfar being sold?'

'I did talk to you about it,' I defended myself. 'I told you about its being sold just after we came home from hospital.'

'Yes, you told me about its being sold but you didn't say about how you felt.'

It was my turn to look away, not to meet his glance. 'There didn't seem to be much point in talking about it. I wasn't sure what I felt. I am still not sure.'

'It was a dreadful thing to happen at the time it did. I have always wanted to tell you that I knew how dreadful it was but I didn't dare. I know it is a very private sorrow.'

'Not private from you, Twice. And it is not really a sorrow. It is like you being ill — it is a great big happening, something I have just had to accept in a blind sort of way and try not to think about or question. I am sorry you have felt shut out about it. I didn't mean it to be like that. I am glad you have talked like this today, darling. I am so glad I want to cry. You have stayed shut away for so long.'

'It seemed to be the natural thing to do,' he said quietly. 'It is difficult to believe that anybody could want somebody like me any more.'

I felt as if, physically, my heart were going to burst, but whether with sorrow or anger or mere hurt feelings, I did not know and I was almost afraid to speak in case I should display too much of what I was feeling, yet it was this very restriction of emotion that was making much of our difficulty.

'I think we must go and have lunch,' I said. 'We are fifteen minutes late now.'

'Talking like this is better for me than lunch, since that is what is worrying you,' he said. 'It is like getting rid of a great weight I have been carrying about. I don't want to be a bore but, somehow, when you are told that your heart and liver are different from the hearts and livers of other people, it separates you from other people. I suppose that is reasonable enough. Then you get into a habit of thinking of yourself as separate and a barrier builds up until it reaches the point when you can hardly see over it, even when you try, and much as you hate the barrier being there you keep on making it higher and stronger. It is partly that, and partly that you feel you are a nuisance, a failure, and a lot of things like that. Then you get to the stage of thinking that maybe it is better to keep quiet, stay behind your barrier and do what you are told for, after all, everybody is doing their very best for you and all you can do is shut up and be grateful.' The words were pouring out now, rapidly and as he spoke his hands moved with small impatient gestures if the word he wanted did not come at once to his tongue. 'But you can't live all the time just being grateful — at least, I can't. I am grateful for all you have done for me — don't misunderstand me — but I want more than that. I want us to be more like we were before — not just you looking after me all the time and me being grateful although I *am* grateful — Oh, hell, darling, I am in a hopeless muddle. Why can't I say what I mean?'

Somewhere between tears and laughter, because the impatience of the last phrases was something I had not heard for the last sixteen months and had been sorely missing, I said: 'Heavens, you never could say what you meant. There is nothing new in that and you can't blame your heart and liver for it. What you do mean is that you are feeling a lot better and you want me to stop fussing and cackling like an old hen and will I for pity's sake go out and visit this friend of Hugh's and leave you in peace for an afternoon.'

He smiled with a curious shyness. 'Maybe that is what I meant.' He paused for a moment. 'But I mean more than that. I mean that when you come back from visiting her, will you be truly glad to come back? Just to come back here and tell me about her because you would rather be here than anywhere else in the world?'

I got up and went to stand beside him and then, from behind, I put my arms round him where he sat. I did not want him to see that I was crying but my voice was unsteady when I spoke. 'If Doctor Lindsay knew about this emotional scene, he would be furious,' I said. 'Besides, you and I will soon be forty-five and that is a little old for plighting our troth all over again. But yes, I shall go and see this woman and I shall come back and tell you about her because I would rather come back here than to any other place in the world, even Reachfar.

He turned his head against me and looked up into my face. 'Even Reachfar?' he said on a note of wonder.

'Yes. Even Reachfar,' I repeated. 'Does that convince you that you are not just a sickroom nuisance?'

'Yes. But I shall never understand it.'

'That is something you will have to put up with,' I told him. 'There was a time when I thought that if I lived long enough I would come to understand everything, but I have got past that. I have got wise enough in my old age to discover that living is not just a question of getting to know more and more. And now I am going to wash my face and then we'll have lunch.'

'All right. And, darling, thank you.'

'You are,' I said, 'as Martha would put it, entirely welcome.'

Over lunch, in an absurd way, we were as shy with one another as if we were young lovers and further embarrassed, of course, by this very feeling of shyness, so that we discussed in a solemn, even sententious, way a few unimportant very mundane details connected with the sugar factory and the plantation. In truth, we were both longing, I think — I know that I was — to be alone to think over

18

what amounted to a rebirth of the relationship between us while, at the same time, unlike seventeen-year-old lovers who long to be alone and staring at the moon, we were old enough to be aware of our absurdity. Over the coffee, by which time we had exhausted the few mundane items of conversation that came to our fuddled minds, Twice said: 'So you think you will call on this Lady What's-her-name, Flash?'

'Oh, yes, I think so,' I said, and now I had to look down into my cup to hide what I felt must be showing in my eyes.

Twice had not called me by that absurd nickname for over a year, which was little wonder, if I thought of it calmly, for the name had reference to the flash-point of my temper which, in the early days of our relationship, he had reckoned to be too easy of ignition. For more than a year now this temper of mine had not shown a spark, much less a flash and it was little wonder that the name had fallen out of use but it was with difficulty that I kept my voice steady as I said: 'Oh, yes, I'll go. It will be good for me to shake out of my slovenly habits and get dressed up and go out. Just remember when you go back to the office to ring the Peak and find out when she arrives.'

'I'll remember. And that's another thing. There is another delay in the telephone installations around the estate. A letter came in to the office saying not for another three months.'

'Again? What a nuisance.'

About a year ago, Sir Ian Dulac had decided to install telephones in all the staff houses, a decision which had been influenced to some degree by Twice's health, so that a doctor could be called quickly, but at this time St. Jago was expanding industrially at a very rapid rate and industrial enterprises were given priority by the telephone company. Paradise, as an industrial concern, already had

19

four telephones—one at the factory office, one in the medical clinic, one in the Great House, and one at the estate manager's house—so that other telephones applied for, such as ours at Guinea Corner, were rated as of a social nature and low on the priority list. The lack of a telephone was merely one of the small anxieties that had fretted me, although not so much recently as it had done a year ago, when Twice first returned from hospital and the situation was so new and strange to me.

When Twice had gone back to the office, I went to sit in a bemused way in a corner of the drawing-room, wondering at the difference, now, in this day from all the days of the past year. Even the tropic light that beat on the garden beyond the shaded windows was different, just as the very shapes and colours of the familiar furnishings seemed to be different. They were brighter, more clearly defined, as if a grey mist had lifted and rolled away.

Twice's questions about the sale of my home, Reachfar, had gone to my heart, for this was a queer thing which, I felt, I would never be able to explain to him. Reachfar was a small farm, on poor marginal land on top of a hill in Ross-shire, with a small house and steading of rough, sturdy, white-washed walls under a slated roof and a few acres of low-grade arable land and a few more acres of heather moor where a few fir-trees grew. Reachfar was not much of a farm or much of a house or much of anything, but it was part of my very being, for the first ten years of my life had been spent there in a perfect unclouded happiness which is very rare.

Nowadays, when I thought of Reachfar, it often brought to my mind a quotation from Plato which had remained with me since my university days. 'Except in the case of some rarely gifted nature there will never be a good man who has not from his childhood been used to play among things of beauty and make of them a joy and a study.' It seemed to me that this quotation, modified by two words to read 'there will never be a happy woman' summed up the endowment that Reachfar had given me. I had played for the first ten years of my life among the things of beauty in which Reachfar abounded and I had studied them all in a loving detail because I was a child alone among busy grown-ups who had little time to amuse or distract me. This place had given me my capacity for happiness, but, paradoxically, it was that very capacity for happiness which had lured me on to the age of forty-three without my developing any capacity or philosophy for meeting life's ultimate sorrow. At this time, I saw Reachfar as my greatest friend as well as my greatest enemy.

In a way that, I think, may be unusual, this place had a hold on me which few places have on few people, and I cannot explain the origin of this hold although I can tell something of its nature. All my standards were based on Reachfar standards, for instance, and in times of bewilderment or fear I would return there in memory for guidance and the guidance never failed to come. When I could not sleep, even, I would go in memory to the moor or the old quarry at Reachfar and soon my limbs would cease to twitch, the flashing lights behind my eyelids would die away and I would fall asleep. When I was writing to friends, describing the island of St. Jago, I would tell them that the chief town of St. Jago Bay was some thirteen miles as the crow flew to the north-west of where we lived, but this orientation was made not on a mental map of St. Jago but on such a map, of a transparent sort, overlaid on a mental map of the landscape seen from the hill of Reachfar, which caused St. Jago Bay to fall on the lower slopes of Ben Wyvis. These slopes were some thirteen miles from Reachfar by crow flight, therefore St. Jago Bay was some thirteen miles from Guinea Corner. This was how my mind worked, while in my memory were a million pictures of Reachfar itself, Reachfar in winter sleet, in summer sun, in spring rain, or in the purple and gold of its heathery harvest time. Reachfar, to me, was something as eternal as its own infertile rocky earth or the wide sky that spread above it; it was, to me, something as much a part of myself as my arms and legs or the blood that coursed through them, and when I received the news from my family that they had sold it, it was as if I had suffered a sudden and terrible amputation, as if, in some hideous and grievous way, an essential part of myself had been torn from me.

In cold logical fact, the sale of Reachfar was a natural outcome of socio-economic and family factors. My brother was a scholar, with no aptitude or liking for farming, while Twice was an engineer and his and my paths lay where industry was, and my father, my uncle, and our family friend Tom were now too old to work a little farm which, in the mid-twentieth century, was of exactly the wrong size to be a profitable economic unit. With my mind I knew all this, just as with my mind I knew that Twice's illness was the logical result of years of overwork in a tropical climate, careless eating and drinking, and general strain, but it is possible to know things with the mind and yet be unable to accept them with the heart. And this is how it was with the sale of Reachfar.

There was, too, another factor in my loss of Reachfar and this is what made it impossible for me to talk to Twice without reserve about that loss. A strange thing had happened when Twice was so desperately ill in hospital. In the middle of the brilliant tropical afternoon, death itself had come into the little white room where he lay and in the terrible moment when I had seen the recognition of it in his nurse's eyes as she rang the emergency bell at the head of his bed, I had begun to pray, not aloud but with a desperate inner cry: 'Please God, don't let him die! I'll give anything—anything—' and as I prayed I felt about me the light wind that sighs in summer across the moor of Reachfar. Twice had not died, but on the day that I brought him home from the hospital to Guinea Corner the letter that told me that Reachfar no longer belonged to my family was waiting for me on the hall table.

'You told about it being sold,' Twice had said today, 'but you didn't say about how you felt.'

I would never, I thought, be able to say to him how I felt, for, as I had told him, this was something that I was not yet sufficiently sure about to put into words. Since that day, about a year ago, when the letter had come in, I had never ceased to be grateful that Twice was alive, but I felt, away deep in my heart, that the God who had heard my prayer that day in the hospital was the harsh God of the Old Testament, a God who drove very hard bargains. I would never say that I felt this, for, even if felt, there are some things that one should not tell, so that this silence about Reachfar, I thought, would always lie between Twice and me.

But the happiness of this great day could not be spoiled for me by the thought of this little silence when Twice and I had just broken through the thick sullen silence of this long year, and when I am happy I always want to share it in some way. It is only when I am unhappy that I want to be alone and silent and that is why, during this year of 1954, I had written so few letters.

In the course of my first few years in St. Jago, I had developed a very large correspondence with a wide circle of people at home but during this last year letter-writing, for the first time in my life, had become a burden, a tedious chore and I had neglected everyone except the immediate members of my family.

This afternoon, however, I looked across the room at my

23

writing-table, saw in it something of its former attraction and almost without conscious will I went to it, sat down, and began to write to Hugh Reid.

'My dear Hugh, Thank you for letting me know about Lady Hallinzeil. Since Twice was ill I have gone out very little, partly because I have not been much in the mood for social affairs and partly because the detail of his diet cannot be left too much to the servants. St. Jagoans are the kindest people and they cannot believe that a man must eat vegetables cooked without salt or that 'the Massa' must be restricted to the little bit of butter on the white plate. But I shall certainly make a point of visiting Lady Hallinzeil. Your memory for detail is almost as good as my own — could this be something that we both owe to our schooling at Cairnton Academy? Anyway, the owners of the Peak Hotel are indeed friends of ours as your memory told you and Twice is talking to them from the office this afternoon about Lady H. —'

When I had finished this letter, instead of going on to another as I had intended, I did something that I had not done for quite a year, which was to sit down in a chair in a corner and look out of the window at the blaze of colour that was my tropical garden. For the last year I had been hating this garden, with its luxuriant growth and its savage colours, for it had seemed to me to be typical of the riotous savagery of this violent country which had suddenly struck Twice down into illness. Even while I worked in the garden, tearing at the weeds, I had hated it, but I suddenly saw today that this hatred was false, a mere mental stamping of the feet in blind frustration and rage in the face of a situation that was beyond the control of my mind. This island had not been the cause of the illness. The illness was of long standing — it might even, Doctor Lindsay thought, date back for its origin to the attack of pneumonia Twice had suffered when he was a small boy of six. I tried to visualise Twice as a small boy of six. That would have been in 1916. It was strange to think that Twice was in the world then and I did not know of him. It seemed, now, as if I had always known him, as if he were part of me, like the arms and legs that had grown up with me. I felt that I knew more of Twice as a small boy than I knew of Alasdair Mackay, for instance, whom I had 'known' since I was six years old and before, and more than I knew of Hugh Reid, whom I had 'known' since I was ten. Alasdair and Hugh I knew only with my brain or my mind or my intellect, but Twice I knew with the brain, mind or intellect and also with my heart. My knowledge of Twice was a complete thing, a thing of blood as well as mind, and that was why this barrier that had risen between us was such a strong thing for it was born out of the revolt of the blood and minds of both of us against this limitation that had been forced upon us.

I became drowsy in the insect-buzzing, scent-laden heat of the afternoon, and in that borderland between sleep and wakefulness I began to think of those days so long ago when my world did not contain Twice.

*   *   *

Until I was ten years old, my world contained very little outside of Reachfar — Reachfar away on the summit of its flat hill with the moor to the south, and to east, north and west unlimited distance of sky, sea and hills — but this little world I knew with an intricate detailed intimacy. I knew the members of my family — my grandparents, my father and mother, my Aunt Kate, George, my uncle, and my friend Tom, who was our family helper — with that penetrating intimacy of which, I think, only children are capable, for they bring to their observation of the adults around them a detachment, a clearness of vision that is fuddled and clouded when age and experience overtake us. I knew the meaning, in relation to myself, of every tone of their voices and of every tremor of expression that crossed their faces and they, I think, affected permanently my attitude to human relationships. As I grew older, I found it more difficult to know people as intimately as I had known these people of my family, but I have always wanted to explore people in depth and it was because I knew Twice so deeply that, when this illness had interposed itself between us, I had felt such a sense of loss.

In the same way that I knew the people of Reachfar, I knew the place itself. I knew every stone of the rough East Moor, every cranny of the rocky West Moor and every tree and bush of the fir-clad Home Moor which was the winter shelter for the sheep. I knew where the different shades of bell heather could be found, from the palest pinky-cream to deepest purple. I knew which wild raspberry canes would be the first to show ripe fruit and I knew the trees that the wood pigeons liked best to nest in. I was not, as a child, consciously aware of the beauty of Reachfar, for this panorama of fields, hills and sea had been about me ever since I was born. It was something that I accepted as a part of life but I did not know, until I was ten years old, what an essential part of life, for me, this beauty was.

When I was ten there came in the life of our family one of these events that are cataclysmic, only to be likened to some dread phenomenon like earthquake, when the whole foundation of the earth heaves, shifts, and eventually sinks back into an entirely new and strange topography of hill and valley, river and sea. This was when my mother died in 1920 and my father and I left Reachfar together to travel to Cairnton, a little town near Glasgow, where he was to manage a dairy farm and I was to go to High School.

Until I travelled to Cairnton, I had never seen a train except at a distance of some twelve miles away on the other side of the Firth and I had seen only one motor-car at close quarters. I had heard, at school, of the Industrial Revolution; I could draw on an outline map of Scotland the positions of the main cities, the areas where coal was mined and the routes followed by the main railway lines. When I knew that I was going to Cairnton, I became interested in the Forth and Clyde Canal and memorised the route of that too, but all this was a minor matter of intellect and none of it was any preparation for the assault which Cairnton made on my senses when I first encountered it.

In another story which I have written about my friend Annie, I have told of my own personal life in Cairnton but now I have come to see the town in a broader light, a light which has accumulated over the years, a light, maybe, that is a little more kindly but this light is still not roseate and Cairnton, as seen by me or as described by me will never emerge, I fear, as a place of beauty, although I shall try to depict it truly as I saw it and still see it, very clearly, in memory.

Early in my schooldays, in the course of a geography lesson, it was explained to me that, very often, townships tend to grow up around a bridge or a ford, at the point where traffic could cross a river, and Cairnton was very proud of a very old bridge, in use at the time I knew it only for pedestrian traffic, called the Cairn Brig, which carried the one-time road over a little river called the Cairn Burn. Close to the Cairn Brig, there was a little old grey building, a ruin in the 1920's, which was still known as the Inn o' Cairn but although a ruin it had perpetual life in the language of the townspeople, who would say: 'That hat o' Teenie Gourlay's is as auld as the Inn o' Cairn.'

At one time, however, the Inn o' Cairn had been the centre of the township, as was proved by the close huddle of narrow wynds and little houses — slums in the 1920's — which clustered round it, but, with the coming of more roads, the railway and the cutting of the Forth and Clyde Canal, the focus of the town had shifted so that when I lived there it had no atmosphere of long history, but was a tight, hard clutter of late-nineteenth-century buildings of grey stone, built to house the workers in the stone quarries that surrounded the town and which had brought to it what is known as prosperity.

It was a prosperity which had been dearly bought, but it is useless to babble o' green fields and the people of Cairnton who lived in the grey cloud of quarry dust were well content with their bargain. Strangers, like myself, coming to the place for the first time from a clearer light and clearer air, saw this dust in a way different from the Cairnton housewives who seemed to see it as a beloved enemy, a thing against which they made constant war with scrubbing brushes and dusters but a thing, lacking which, life would be incomplete. They accepted too, without question, the constant clank and rumble of the stone-crushers and did not seem to hear, even, the thud and crash as one of the quarries detonated a blast that brought yet another green hillside rumbling down in a great avalanche of grey stone. They were a grim-faced, hard-working people, harshly thrifty, fiercely proud of their little grey homes and their tight little grey town, and very suspicious of and unwelcoming to any stranger within their gates. Hospitality seemed to have died in Cairnton when the Inn o' Cairn fell into ruin.

At my home in Ross-shire, our village of Achcraggan was split at that time into two factions — the people who lived by the land and the people who lived by the sea and this rift divided the men in the bar of the Plough Inn, the women when they met in the shops of the village and the children in the school playground. It was a cleavage that had in its depths the very substance of life itself, the business of wresting a living from the world, but it found its outward expression in religious symbolism. The landsmen claimed superiority because God had placed the first created man in a garden called Eden, and the fishermen claimed superiority because Christ had chosen His friends from among the fishermen who lived by the Sea of Galilee.

It was very interesting to me to discover that in Cairnton there were also two factions of a parallel kind, for, at ten years old, I had yet to discover that to split off into warring factions is a basic condition of the character of mankind. Where, at Achcraggan, there were 'the Village' and the 'Fisher Town', at Cairnton there were 'the Toon' and 'the Ither Side o' the Brig', but the Brig in this case was not the old footbridge over the Cairn Burn but the bridge across the Forth and Clyde Canal, for on the other side of the canal the dust of the quarries gave way to the blacker dust of the coal mines, the rumble and clank of the stone-crushers were replaced by the whirr of the shaft gear, and the hills pitted and scarred and turned eventually into hollows by quarry blasting were exchanged for the black man-made mountains of the slag heaps.

The quarry workers of the Toon were thrifty, cleanly, big-boned Scots, the miners of the Ither Side o' the Brig were thriftless, slovenly, under-sized Irish. The quarry workers were grim Presbyterians of hard, Covenanting hillstock, the miners were genial Roman Catholics from the soft green bogs of Ireland. The canal bridge was the boundary between two worlds, a boundary which could flare up into bloody war at any moment, but especially on Saturday, when the school-children were free to fight all day with some of the mothers to help them and warm up

29

the air for the real battle in the evening when the quarry-men came home from Glasgow by way of a public house or two after seeing the Rangers team play football, while the miners came home by way of another set of public houses after seeing the Celtic team play football. The battle of the year, naturally, was joined on the day that the Rangers team and the Celtic team played against one another. This battle began about a week before the match and quite often the most enthusiastic team supporters were in prison when the great day came along and did not see the match at all.

In Cairnton I had the great advantage — although at ten to sixteen years old it seemed to be more of a great loneli-ness than an advantage — of being outside both factions, for, although I lived on a farm a little way outside of the Toon, attended the academy in the Toon itself, and went with my father to the Presbyterian church, I was never accepted by Cairnton as one of its own, which I deserved, for I could not at that time accept Cairnton in any sense at all. I hated the place and it had every right to hate me in return.

The children of the miners had their own large Roman Catholic school, close beside their equally large Chapel, in their own territory on the Ither Side o' the Brig and, in passing, I ought to mention that another feature of Cairn-ton life was the exchange of hate-laden letters which appeared, almost weekly, in the columns of the *Cairnton Chronicle* and were written by the Roman Catholic priest and the Presbyterian minister of the Toon Kirk. Consider-ing in retrospect the venom of these exchanges between two men of God, it is remarkable that both of them were listened to, Sunday after Sunday, by devout congregations.

My home life at this time was very unhappy because of the rift between me and Jean Grey, a Cairnton native who was first housekeeper to my father and later became his second wife, and part of this rift between us was caused by my inability to take up what Jean deemed to be the 'richt' attitude to 'they Irish idolaters on the Ither Side o' the Brig'. Jean was of Cairnton quarry stock, Scottish, Presbyterian, and deep within the tradition of the Toon, and her attitude was thoroughly representative, but between the ages of ten and sixteen I could not understand it, for in spite of our Achcraggan factions of sea and land, we had had there something of respect on both sides for the other. In Jean's attitude to the miners there was nothing of this respect, and her condemnation of people she did not know — 'Ah widnae lower masel to set fit amang them' — and of Ireland, a country she had never seen — 'That bog o' sin' — and of a religion of which she knew nothing — 'bowin' doon tae graven images' — there seemed to me to be no reason, logic, or even human justice. I did not know then that ideas can be injected into a mind and become so solidified and petrified there that they become immune to the leavening of reason, logic, or human justice and that in Jean's case the solidifying and petrifying agent was the Cairnton code, which was as dead and inorganic as an accumulation in the brain of Cairnton's own quarry dust.

Because I was unhappy in my home, I spent as much time as possible outside of it and a great deal of my time alone on a green hill behind our house, a hill that was an infertile part of the farm my father managed and which, I learned much later from Hugh Reid, was eventually bought, after I left Cairnton, by the quarry owners and blasted into paving stones like so many of the other hills round about. However, in my day, it was still a hill, not a very high one, but enough of an eminence as a foothill at the edge of Scotland's central plain to see from its summit the oily windings of the canal, the steel snake of the railway, the tangled wires of the roads, the grey heap of stone that was the Toon, and the long molehills of the miners'

31

rows on the Ither Side o' the Brig in the shadow of the slag mountains. This was the view to the south. To the north, one looked towards more pastoral country, behind which the hills began to rise with, here and there, the large Victorian country mansion of some Glasgow industrialist showing its pepperpot turrets among its surrounding trees. In the main, though, I looked to the south for the other direction made me think of Reachfar and long for it, and even in those days, I think, I had learned the uselessness of yearning for a past that is behind and gone. I looked southwards and to the future.

When I first came to Cairnton I was not conscious of its tightly-closed hostility to strangers, for never before in what I called 'all my born days' had I encountered hostility of this kind, so looking south upon this new world I regarded it as a place to be explored. I did not make my first approach to it by an attempt to make friends with its children partly because I had hitherto lived in an isolated place and was accustomed to leaving other children behind when I came out of the village school, and partly because, in making friends with Hugh Reid on my first day at Cairnton Academy, I had made, from the point of view of all the schoolchildren and of all the Toon, the wrong sort of friend. Hugh was the illegitimate grandson of the old lady who kept a little sweetshop near the Academy, against whom the doors of the Toon had been closed since the day of his unrespectable birth and probably before. Nevertheless, I was not to know this and I made friends with Hugh, who piloted me round the big strange school and at my first lunch-hour I made friends with his grandmother too, hereby damning myself twice over in an unwitting way in the eyes of the rest of the community.

Outside of school time, however, I saw comparatively little of Hugh for he and his granny fought a constant battle for their bare living and in this battle Hugh, even at twelve years old, made his contribution by delivering the newspapers from the shop morning and evening and, on Saturdays, helping his granny with all the many other things that had to be done.

Just after our early breakfast on a Saturday in late September, 1920, I was on top of my hill at the back of our house, surveying the countryside that lay under the bright autumn sun, when I saw a remarkable thing down below on the canal bank. Walking along the path beside the water was a large grey horse, all alone, and some distance behind him, on the water, floated a big flat boat. After some minutes of observation it seemed indubitable that horse and boat were connected to one another in some mysterious way, and I at once began to run as hard as I could down the south side of the hill for never before had I made any mental connection between horses and boats. At Achcraggan, landsmen had horses, fishermen had boats and never the twain could meet. It was also more than a month since I had seen a proper horse and I had been missing Dick, Betsy, and Dulcie, our three horses at Reachfar, for, although this valley in which I lived now was farm country, it was all dairy farming and they did not use the big heavy Clydesdales that were one of the most beautiful features of the countryside round Reachfar. This fellow connected to the boat, however, even from a distance, looked to me like a 'proper' horse and helter-skelter down over the fields I went to intercept him in his slow and dignified march at a point about a mile to the east of the canal bridge.

Leaning on the fence I watched him come along, his big head nodding, his white mane silver in the sun, his big hooves making a soft clop-clop on the earth of the path. He was harnessed as Dick and Betsy would be for harrow-ing, but, instead of harrows being linked to the swingle-tree behind him, there were three ropes which after a yard

33

or two were spliced together into one thick rope which went away out over the water to the bows of the boat. I found the whole thing fascinating and when the boat came past I waved to the two oldish men who sat at her stern and very cheerily they waved back. This emboldened me to climb over the fence and follow the horse along the towpath towards Cairnton where the next remarkable thing of this exciting morning happened. As we approached the Brig which divided the Toon from the Ither Side the boat blew a loud horn and I noticed that the canal had grown much narrower until, indeed, the boat had nothing to spare as the horse pulled it in between the walls towards the bridge. Then the horse stopped, shook his head, and looked around him, and one of the men jumped from the boat to the wall and disconnected the now slack rope from the swingle-tree, coiled it up and threw it on board. Then, to my amazement, a man came out of a little grey house, went to a platform and began to turn an iron handle, and the bridge split open in the middle, the two halves rising into the air to let the boat pass through. Meantime, the man who had come ashore led the horse round from the towpath, up and over the main road and then down to the towpath again. I followed the man and the horse and the three of us stood waiting while the man on the boat had a conversation with the man at the bridge while they both edged the boat along the narrow walled channel with long poles with hooks on their ends.

'Is this your horse?' I asked the man beside me, who had a red face, a cap with a shiny black peak, and a thick navy blue jersey.

'Aye,' he told me. 'I suppose he is.'

'What's his name?'

'Hero.'

'Hello, Hero,' I said, looking up and the horse looked down and nuzzled my hand.

34

'He's needin' a piece,' the man said. 'Would ye like to gie him this?'

From somewhere under the jersey he produced a piece of bread and I took it and held it out for Hero, who accepted it with velvet lips from my palm.

'Say thanks for your piece,' the man said, and then Hero pawed the ground twice with his big fore hoof before pushing his nose against my neck and blowing in a pleased way.

'Ye're not frightened o' him?' the man asked.

'Oh, no!'

'Some folk is frightened o' him but Hero widnae hurt a flee.'

At that moment the coil of rope, thrown by the man on board, fell near our feet and the man with me found the three ends with the iron rings on them and began to link them to the swingle-tree, so I took one of the rings and linked it into place.

'Comin' for a sail?' the man asked then, looking down at me.

'Will you take me? Yes, please!'

'Come on then. Jump!'

I jumped from the wall across the two feet or so of water on to the boat and the man jumped after me.

'This is a beautiful boat,' I told them with genuine appreciation when we were seated in a row in the stern on either side of a pole that the other man was holding. 'I see its name is *Nancy*.'

'Aye, that's right,' my man said. 'And what's your own name?'

'Janet,' I told them. 'Janet Sandison. I live at Cairnshaws. It is a farm up the glen there. What are your names?'

'I'm Jimmie,' my man said and, pointing to the other one, 'and he's Robbie.'

'And do you two and Hero sail on the canal all the time?'

'Aye, we do that. Robbie here has been on the canal for thirty year an' I've been on it for twenty-five.'

'And what's in there?' I asked, pointing to the humped tarpaulin in front of us.

'A load o' pigs for the steel works.'

Up to this moment, I had thought these were two very charming men but I was disappointed that, after all, they were the sort who would invite one on to their boat and then try in an impolite way to pull one's leg.

'Don't talk nonsense!' I said in the stern voice my grandmother used when anyone was being silly. 'If there are pigs in there, I am a Dutchman. They would be squealing or grunting or something.'

The two men began to laugh in an uproarious way, loud laughter that echoed away across the now widening water, and their faces grew redder and redder as they slapped their knees in their mirth. I had almost made up my mind to ask in a dignified way to be put ashore when the one called Robbie collected himself and said: 'We didnae mean the kind o' pigs you mean, lassie. It's pig *iron* that's in below there.'

'Pig iron?'

'Aye. I'll show ye,' and he lifted the edge of the tarpaulin and exposed the long rounded lumps of metal lying tightly packed and stacked, side by side, in rows and layers, just like the young pigs at Reachfar when they lay sucking milk from their mother, the big white sow.

Everything became more and more interesting. Hero plodded along his path and soon we were round a bend and out of sight of Cairnton altogether and in very pretty country where the fields and woods came down to the water's edge, and at one place Hero stopped walking and began to graze while Robbie and Jimmie made tea in a black can on a little stove they had, and we all had thick sweet tea and bread and cheese. Then we called to Hero to go on and the rope became taut again and on we went until the fields and woods began to give place to houses again and soon I could see another bridge ahead of us.

'Noo, Jinnit, we're goin' to put ye aff at the brig here. This is Aucheninch. An' in a wee while Willie an' Andy will be comin' bye wi' a load o' scrap an' they'll take ye back tae Cairnton.'

'Oh. Thank you. What's scrap?'

I was not going to be caught out again over the loads that these boats called barges carried. By the time we had dealt with the scrap iron question, Hero had stopped at the Aucheninch Bridge and the canal was narrowing until soon I could touch the walls on either side of us.

'You know,' I said to Jimmie, 'there is no need for you to come ashore.' I had already become quite nautical in speech. 'I'll unyoke Hero and take him round and yoke him again.'

'That's very good o' ye,' said Jimmie solemnly, 'but I'll jist come wi' ye in case.'

He came, but he allowed me to detach the rope, take Hero by the bridle and lead him up, over the road and down to the towpath again and I also re-linked the yoke.

Jimmie jumped on board and, as Hero moved off, Robbie called: 'Noo, Jinnit, you stop near the brig here till Andy and Willie come bye.'

'Yes, Robbie,' I promised.

I was a little sad as I watched Hero make a strong initial pull and *Nancy* with my new friends sailed away towards the west, but I had another sail to look forward to and, while waiting, I looked about me.

There was not a great deal to be seen except a small huddle of grey houses under a layer of quarry dust, for Aucheninch was really an infant Cairnton which, nowadays I understand, has become joined to and absorbed in Cairnton itself by the spread of grey houses along the banks of the canal. All that my great voyage with Jimmie and Robbie had been, although I did not know it at the time, was a sail of two miles or so round the base of a low rocky hill and Aucheninch Bridge, as the crow flew and, indeed, as the road ran, was no more than half a mile from the centre of Cairnton.

The grey houses of the hamlet stretched away on either side of the road across the bridge and the gable of the house at the end nearest to me was covered with garishly enamelled tin plates advertising things like 'Mazawattee's Tea', 'Monkey Brand — Won't Wash Clothes' and 'Doan's Backache Kidney Pills'. I walked along to the front of this building to verify my idea that it was the village shop and just as I reached its door a girl came out, carrying a basket of groceries. She was a girl called Margaret Bailey, who was in the class above me at school, but she looked much older than even a Second Year person this Saturday morning, with the black purse in one hand and the basket of groceries in the other.

'Did I see you gettin' offa that barge?' she asked me before I could speak and in an angry grown-up way that was very like the manner of our housekeeper, Miss Jean.

'Yes,' I said proudly. 'All the way from the bridge at Cairnton I came.'

Her face became even less like the face of a schoolgirl and even more like the face of a scandalised Cairnton housewife.

'You won't half get it from your folk,' she told me, 'and serve you right. Sailin' on they barges!'

'Why?' I asked. 'It was very nice. The horse is called Hero and Jimmie and Robbie are very interesting.'

'Nice! Interestin'! They're *bargees*!'

'Yes, I know. The barge is called *Nancy*.'

38

'Decent folk has nothin' tae dae wi' they bargees,' she said. 'You'd better get awa' hame tae Cairnton. What you're needin' is a good leatherin'! Sailin' aboot wi' bargees!'

I began to feel very angry at all this grown-upness from someone who was only one class above myself at school and in a very poor grade of the class at that. How dare she say that I needed a 'good leatherin'' as if she were a grown-up person in some sort of charge of me, even if she *were* nearly fourteen?

'You shut your lip, Margaret Bailey!' I addressed her in the new idiom I had learned since I went to High School. 'I'll sail in the barges if I like.'

'Jist wait till your folk find oot. You'll no' half get a leatherin'!'

'I will not!'

'Then your folk are worse than you are. Bargees! I never heard the like!'

I do not know how long we might have quarrelled or how the quarrel might have ended had we not been interrupted by a loud blast on a horn. That sound was a new one I had learned that morning — the sound of a barge blowing for the bridge-keeper.

'Oh, fish-face flappy-mouth!' I threw at Margaret Bailey and ran away to the bridge, leaving her at gaze with her purse and her shopping basket.

Mary Barrie was just drawing in between the walls of the bridge and one of the men was leading a black horse with a white face over the road when I arrived on the scene.

'Hello,' I said. 'Did Jimmie and Robbie tell you about me?'

The man and the horse both looked down at me. 'Aye. So you're Jinnit?'

'Yes. Are you Andy?'

'No. I'm Willie. That's Andy on the barge.'

I reached up for the bridle rope. 'Let me lead him. What's his name?'

'Jock. Aw richt, here ye are,' he said, and relinquished the rope.

'Come on, Jockie, boy,' I said, and we clopped away down the little path to the canal side.

Willie and Andy were very interesting men, just as Robbie and Jimmie had been and we had a most pleasant sail back to Cairnton. It was very curious and interesting to observe the difference in the countryside as we sailed in the opposite direction and there were all sorts of new things to ask about that I had not noticed on the outward journey. When we came round the bend among the trees where Robbie, Jimmie and I had had our cup of tea, I saw on a hillside to the north the biggest house I had ever seen in my life.

'Mercy!' I said. 'That's the biggest house I ever saw in all my born days. Who lives in it?'

'That's Torrencraig, Lawson's place,' Willie said. 'An a' built oot o' scrap like that there,' and he pointed to the rusty load in the body of the barge.

'It is not!' I said indignantly. 'It's ordinary grey stone from the quarries! You can see it.'

'Willie means that the Lawsons made their *money* oot' o' scrap,' Andy explained.

This was a new idea to me, this conception of house in terms of the economic source that had led to its construction and large house after large house came into view, each more grotesquely baronial than the last, although none competing in sheer size with Torrencraig, I would say: 'There's another. What's it made out of?' and 'Coal' or 'Quarries' or 'Steel' Andy and Willie would answer, except for one house when Andy said: 'That yin? That's Hall o' Neil — Thomson's place. That's built oot o' ships!' and we all had a good laugh at the idea of a house made of a lot of ships all stuck together.

In fact, it was all so interesting and we had so many good laughs that I quite forgot about my meeting and quarrel with Margaret Bailey and when I was put ashore at Cairnton Bridge I just got home for dinner by running my very hardest all the way.

As soon as I had told how I had spent my morning, however, I remembered about Margaret and had to concede that to some extent she was right about what would happen to me, for Miss Jean made a tremendous fuss, said that I needed a good thrashing and that what I had done 'wisnae the thing at a',' sailing about with these rough bargees and what would people think, but after my father had talked to me about it a bit more when he and I were out for a walk together on Sunday, he said I might sail on the barges if the men would take me and as long as I did not make a nuisance of myself and get in their way, so from this time on I spent a great part of my Saturdays — more than anybody ever knew — sailing to and fro along the canal. I do not think I was ever more than four miles from Cairnton to east or west, but I came to know all the bargemen and no longer had to go to a bridge to be taken on board, for if I appeared anywhere on the canal bank, any barge would pull in to let me jump on.

This floating slowly along, almost on dry land, for one had little consciousness of the calm, narrow waterway beneath the barge, had a fascinating attraction for me, for one was completely detached from the fields and the trees and all the things of the earth although, yet, so close to them and the people on the barges seemed to have a similar detachment from the other people among whom they lived. They were a separate fraternity, with a tang of the sea about them although I believe that most of them had never seen salt water, as if they were semi-amphibious just as their barges were semi-amphibious only, dependent as they were on the land-bound horses on the earth of the towpath to pull them along.

I think that my liking for sailing on the barges was akin to my liking for spending hours along on the green hill above the house or in an old disused quarry that I had discovered, a place pleasantly overgrown with hawthorns and wild roses and which had a deep dark pool at its centre. This place had that air of melancholy which the eighteenth-century garden-planners tried to achieve by means of grottoes and sham ruins that they built. For me, the barges, the hill, and the quarry were places of escape from Cairnton itself as its grey stone seemed to close more and more tightly about me.

I was not an openly rebellious child and I was not demonstrative in any way, so that I did not make displays of temper or tears. Indeed, for much of the time, I think, I was unaware that I was unhappy and even unaware that I hated Cairnton. Children have no real awareness of happiness or unhappiness but accept what comes along and are endowed to meet life in a way that resembles the British infantryman's endowment for meeting the exigencies and discomforts of war. The child, like the infantryman, makes all sorts of curious shifts and throws up all sorts of clever improvisations to meet the moment, but both child and infantryman do this without the conscious mental process of: 'I am unhappy or uncomfortable so I shall do this and things will be better.'

I did, however, break into a short sharp open rebellion after I had been in Cairnton for about six weeks or so and the detonator behind this was Margaret Bailey, the same girl with whom I had quarrelled outside the little shop at Aucheninch.

It had been the family habit at Reachfar that some of us attended Achcraggan church every Sunday, and when my

42

father and I came to Cairnton after my mother's death, one of the first things he did was to become a member of the Presbyterian church in this new place. It was then discovered that, immediately after the church service on Sunday forenoons, a Sunday School was held and Miss Jean indicated that it would be the proper thing that I should be a member of this. I loved school. From my earliest days, the very word itself had held a magic, and the realisation of my first ambition, 'to be big enough to go to school' which took place when I was five, had in no way dimmed the glow of romance that the word held for me, so 'Sunday School', a new thing of which I had never heard before, developed a glow and aura all its own, vaguely golden, like the halo round the head of Jesus in the coloured picture at the front of my father's Bible.

On the appointed Sunday, when the church service was over, my father, in all good faith and probably glad that I was conforming to one aspect of the proper thing in Cairnton, put me in charge of the solemn-faced grey-clad elder who managed the Sunday School and set off for home. The elder asked me my age and then took me into a little room off the church hall where there were some fifteen other children like myself and told us to be quiet until the teacher came. Very shortly, Margaret Bailey came in and I obligingly moved along my bench a little to make room for her but she said: 'Quiet, everybody' in a very solemn Sunday voice and sat down on the chair in the middle of the floor, facing us all. My shock at the discovery that this girl was 'the teacher' is indescribable — I found it indecent and monstrous — and what happened next struck me as being more shocking still.

'The Lord's Prayer,' she announced in a commanding businesslike way and a boy at the end of the back row began: 'OurFatherwhichartinHeaven' to be followed by the next with: 'hallowedbethyname' and so on, each

43

rattling along as rapidly as they could enunciate until the girl at the end of the front row stuck, unable to remember the next phrase, whereupon Margaret Bailey snapped angrily: 'Hurry up, Tina Baxter!' and then: 'Oh, you go on, Elsie!' to the girl who sat next to the dilatory Tina. The prayer was finished by the time it came to my turn with no more to be said except the Amen which I pronounced.

'*You* don't say that!' said Margaret Bailey. '*I'm* the teacher. *Amen!* And now, Books of the Old Testament!'

'Genesis, Exodus, Leviticus, Numbers — ' the children began to intone in unison.

When this was over, we sang the hymn 'Jesus loves me', and then Margaret Bailey said: 'Now, texts.'

I could feel a queer emanation of uneasiness among the other children which I could not understand as they all produced from pockets or from between the pages of their Bibles little printed cards which they handed to Margaret Bailey.

'All right,' she said, sitting down on her chair again and looking at the back of the first card in her hand. 'Tom Grindlay.'

A boy in the back row stood up and began: 'Blessed are they that hunger and thirst after — after — '

'You haven't learned your text!' she accused him sternly. 'Here, get that learned by next Sunday!' and she handed the card back to him. 'Next, Walter Beveridge.'

After three or four attempts to recite these texts, some successful, some not, I came to an understanding of the rules of this game for Margaret, complimenting a little girl on a correct rendering, made a mark against her name in a blue exercise book and issued her a new card. There would be a prize, I decided, for the one who learned the greatest number of texts in a certain period and it should

44

not be a difficult prize to win because only about three people altogether were able to repeat their texts correctly, including the reference at the end 'Isaiah, Chapter 2, Verse 3', or whatever it might be. When they had all had a turn, Margaret took a card from her box, wrote my name on the back of it, handed it to me and wrote my name in her book. In those days, I had a mind like a rapid photographic lens and by the time she had licked her pencil and had slowly written my name in the book, I handed the card back to her and said: 'The Lord shall smite thee with madness, and blindness, and astonishment of heart. Deuteronomy, Chapter 28, Verse 28.' She had taken the card from me in an automatic way when I held it out to her and now it fluttered down to the grey wood of the floor while she stared at me, completely nonplussed.

'Make a mark in the book,' I encouraged her, 'and give me another one. All these other people have about six weeks' start of me in this Sunday School.'

This seemed to me to be quite a reasonable request in the face of this competition in speed and efficiency and I could not understand why all the other children began to titter and nudge each other. Margaret's face became red with rage and humiliation when she tried, without success, to silence them and she spat at me: 'Ye impiddent wee brat! I'll report ye to Mr. MacKinnon!'

It was my turn to be nonplussed. The other members of the class became quite uproarious, laughing partly at their teacher, partly at me and, in the end, Margaret picked up the card, thrust it at me and almost shouted: 'That's your text for *next* Sunday! Mind an' learn it!'

After what had happened, this was so ridiculous that the class got out of all control and I began to laugh too, largely from nervousness and lack of comprehension of the whole situation. Margaret then dashed out of the room leaving the door open and I went out through it, the 'text' crumpled in my hand, the laughter of the other children echoing behind me down the passage.

The next Sunday morning there was a scene in our house, for I announced point-blank that I was not going back to Sunday School. I knew before I made the announcement that it would lead to a scene, for the discipline in my home was of the kind that did not permit of me at ten years old making point-blank announcements of any kind. The scene was, however, a calculated risk on my part and I went into it with the consciousness that its sound and fury might obviate my having to explain my reasons for such a decision. The difficulty was that I could not explain my reasons. I had not the words to describe the desolation that the dreary grey room off the church hall, the combination of boredom and uneasiness in the other children, the meaningless recitations of the Old Testament books and the garblings of the 'texts', together with the petty self-satisfied arrogance of Margaret Bailey had induced in me. The scene was a loud and stormy one but, in the end, my father, in spite of Miss Jean's indignation, gave way and agreed that I need not attend Sunday School if the teacher was 'only a bairn' little older than myself especially as, since the age of four, I had been accustomed to attend the church service proper. There ended my Sunday School attendance and all I derived from it, now that I thought of it, was the lasting enmity of Margaret Bailey which persisted until she left school the next year, having attained the age of fourteen.

*　　*　　*

When Twice came home at about four o'clock, I was still sitting in the chair staring out of the window.

'What sort of afternoon?' he asked. 'Any visitors?'

'Not a soul, thank goodness,' I said as the tea came in.

46

'Very peaceful. I wrote a letter to Hugh and then I sat down here and I haven't moved since.'

'Very sensible. By the way, Hugh's Lady What's-it arrives on the seventh — that's a week tomorrow.'

'Fine. And listen, Twice, her name isn't this Hall-in-zeal thing that we have been saying. It is Halle-*neel*, with the first bit like the Halle in Hallelujah and the accent thrown back on the *neel* bit.'

'How do you make that out?'

'It is the name of one of the Victorian industrialists' mansions on the hills above Cairnton. I remembered about it this afternoon. I only heard it mentioned once, by a bargee, and I spelled it in my mind Highland fashion as Hall o' Neil until I saw it in print in the *Cairnton Chronicle* and realised that this Hallinzeil was my Hall o' Neil. I am sure this is right. It is like Dalziel being Dee-ell, you know.'

'You probably are right and its being a house near Cairnton would explain the connection with Hugh, I suppose. But tell me about this bargee. I didn't know you knew any.'

When I had told him of the *Nancy* and the *Mary Barrie,* their crews and their horses, he said: 'I can sort of see it all. I envy you that memory of yours, Flash — but memory isn't exactly the right word. It is as if you carry the people still alive in your mind.'

'But doesn't everybody do that with people they remember?'

'No. At least, I don't. A screen of time comes in between, altering the people in a subtle way. You seem to be able to go back through this screen. You must have experienced things more deeply than most children, I think.'

'I don't think so,' I said. 'I don't think it was a question of experience. I think I was fairly observant as a child—

yet the observation was limited to certain things only—and I have got a good memory. I always have had. It's a doubtful sort of asset, really. I remember not wisely but too well, as it were. Certain things, too well remembered, grow into meaningless rigidities in the mind, like this mental attitude I have to Cairnton and its people. I remember the impression they made on me as a child and it has solidified into a rigid mental image. I think it is probably false. As a picture, it is neither whole nor true. Until today, I had forgotten about the bargees altogether. I had forgotten all the nice bits of Cairnton because the beastly bits made the deeper impression at the time and they were what became solid in my mind down the years.'

'I wonder what made you remember the bargees today?'

'I think it was that name Hallinzeil—but in a subconscious way, a faint ringing of a bell. One's mind is such a jumble of associations and queer twisted connections.'

'It probably was,' Twice agreed. 'Words, just as words, quite simply in themselves mean more to you than they do to most people.' He paused for a moment, hesitating, and then: 'Today is like beginning a new life. It seems to be so long since we talked to one another. I don't mean only the time when I was ill. Even before that we were always embroiled with Martha's aunt or Cousin Emmie or somebody and jumping about mentally like fleas on a blanket.'

'And now it is Lady Hallinzeil,' I said. 'It is a sort of getting and spending we lay waste our powers and yet, it isn't exactly that. I have found out quite a lot about myself and about the combination of you-and-me through all the thought and rage I have expended on people like Martha's aunt and Cousin Emmie.'

'I suppose that is true but sometimes—in the afternoons when I have to go and lie on my bed, for instance—I have grudged, especially this last year, all the time and thought I have given to people like Dee Andrews because the thought and time would have been so much better spent on you.'

I laughed. 'But you were trying to sort Dee out and I don't need sorting out.'

'I know you don't. But there's a thing I'd like to ask, if you don't mind.' He was very grave, unusually hesitant.

'Go right ahead!' I said blithely, in an attempt to break the tension.

He looked down for a second and then sharply up into my face as he began to speak. 'Once upon a time,' he said, 'you wanted to write. It has occurred to me, especially during the last year, that by giving you the way of life I have, I haven't given you much opportunity to realise your ambition.' I attempted to speak but he silenced me with a straight concentrated glance from his blue eyes. 'I don't know anything about the art of writing, but it seems to me that the racket we used to live in followed by the sickroom routine of the last year are not conducive to the production of literature.'

I was acutely embarrassed. It was years ago that I had once told him of my early ambition to be a writer and the matter had hardly been mentioned since then. It was distressing to discover now that he had been worrying about this too during this long year.

'Darling,' I said, 'let's take this point by point: (a) given the most ideal conditions, I am certain that I could never produce a work of literature; (b) I am convinced that the person who is going to produce a work of literature will produce it no matter what the conditions; (c) as I have told you before, many youngsters of twenty think they can produce an epic poem but I am now old enough to know better; (d) as far as the racket we used to live in is concerned, that was more my fault than yours. Do I make myself clear?'

He grinned at me and it seemed to me that the grin

49

betokened a relief that was out of all proportion to what we had been discussing.

'Beautifully clear, my pet. I don't want to be a bore about myself and my cogitations during my year of self-examination but one decision I did make was that if ever I talked — really talked — to you again, I would be as honest as I could and I am going to stick to that decision. The only thing, I think, that I have ever been dishonest with you over is this business of your wanting to write. I pretended I was in favour of it. I am not. I never have been.'

This was a surprise and a shock to me and I tried very hard not to show this. I think I succeeded because Twice was looking down at his hands, his forehead wrinkled with concentration as he tried to find words of explanation.

'It is pure selfishness, of course. I know that. Having been faced with the rendering up of my soul to my Maker, as they call it, as a real contingency, I am a little ashamed of the smallness of what I have to render up,' he said after a moment. 'But there it is. I am mean and selfish of soul and it is as well to know it and admit it. If you began to write, you would get like Roddy Maclean — '

Roddy Maclean was a young man of our acquaintance who had written a highly successful novel and, at the mention of his name, I gave a loud derisive hoot of laughter, partly in protest against the almost indecent gravity of what Twice had been saying.

'For Pete's sake, Twice, you're out of your mind!'

'I don't mean you would start living as he does,' he told me impatiently, almost angrily. 'What I mean is that you would withdraw into this thing of writing, into art, if you like, and away from *me* and I don't want that. I have never wanted it. It is pure selfishness, as I said.'

'You needn't worry,' I told him. 'And anyway, Roddy is

an extreme case. I am sure lots of people write without living absolutely ruthlessly for it as Roddy does.'

'The writers who aren't ruthless about it aren't any good,' Twice said fiercely, 'and if you were going to do it at all I would want you to be good and that is why I don't want you to do it at all because if you did I would have to share you with it and I don't want that. It is utter selfishness, I know, but there it is.'

'You needn't get up such a head of steam about it,' I told him, 'a head of steam about something that is not going to occur.'

He expelled a long breath. 'I am glad I have been honest about the damned thing at last,' he said.

Twice and I had always tried to be honest with one another but in this moment I felt for the first time that we had been pursuing an unattainable ideal, that even in the closest relationships between two people there are some reserves. Twice now felt relieved that he had been honest with me but, paradoxically, during these last few moments, I had not been honest with Twice. I had not said in words anything that was not true: (a) given the most ideal conditions, I was certain that I could not produce a work of literature; (b) I was certain that the person who is going to produce a work of literature will produce it no matter what the conditions; (c) many youngsters of twenty think they can produce an epic poem but I was now old enough to know better. All these were true expressions of what I believed, but, in spite of that, I still spent most of my spare moments spinning ideas out of my head through the medium of my pen into words on paper. It was a thing I had done all the years of my life and a thing, I thought, that I would go on doing until I could no longer hold a pen. In spite of the racket in which we lived before Twice became ill, I had found opportunities for the exercise of this secret near-vice and during the long months of his illness, convalescence, and after, I had found more opportunities than ever. It had been instinctive with me all my life to keep my 'writing' a secret from everyone, instinctive for a complex of reasons which I am not going to try to disentangle here and, in a strange way, it was comforting to have this confirmation that to write was something that Twice had never wanted me to do in spite of his earlier protestations that if I felt I had a talent, I must try to exercise it. All I had was an urge to write words down on paper and all my life, from the time I had learned to write at the age of about four, I had gratified this urge at every opportunity. And I knew that I would continue to gratify it for the urge had no impetus towards fame or financial reward through publication. It was simply an activity that brought me the purest satisfaction that I had ever known. After today, I knew, I would indulge in this activity with an added sense of guilt because I was doing something that Twice did not like but I also knew that the guilt would not stop my indulgence. I would comfort myself, I was aware, with my friend Tom's dictum: 'What folk don't know won't hurt them', and as far as my writing was concerned, this would apply even to Twice.

'I wonder what Lady H. will be like?' I said as all this went through my mind. 'Having connected her with those Victorian baronial pepperpot turrets on those houses above Cairnton, one has started to preconceive her.'

'And how does she look?'

'There is a feeling of lots and lots of rather vulgar wealth. Cairnton and its district was peopled by a strictly money-society — I know all Britain is a money-society but it was more starkly obvious in Cairnton than I have ever known it at any other place. I think that was why I loathed Cairnton so much although I couldn't identify it as the reason at the time. I don't mean to convey that at home at

Reachfar we never thought of money or were above it or anything. We thought about it the hell of a lot, right down in the small units, among the pennies, but we were always conscious of a higher power — a power that could make the corn crop fail and there would be no pennies from it, or that could make the turnip crop fail and we would have to draw pennies out of the bank to buy turnips for the cattle. But in Cairnton there was no consciousness of a higher power. It was an industrial community and money was the top god. Everybody was graded by money standards from the people in the Victorian baronial halls on the hills down to the miners in the long rows of terrible hovels on the Ither Side o' the Brig. There was nobody like Sir Torquil Daviot at Poyntdale House below Reachfar. Sir Torquil was a neighbour of all the other farmers and crofters round about, interested in the land and animals as the others were and running the same risks of the weather and disease and so on. The people at Hallinzeil and Torrencraig weren't like that. They drew their incomes from the mines and quarries and things but they never came down among the miners and quarrymen and they didn't run any of the risks of mining and quarrying. They were distant, anonymous powers, dwelling like gods in the hollow hills — the hills they had made hollow by blasting out stone and coal.'

'But what about their weekly shopping?' Twice asked. 'Everybody eats, after all, even gods on hollow hills, human gods, anyway. Wasn't Cairnton the local town?'

'Not to them. They shopped in Edinburgh or Glasgow — they were about equidistant from both. They rolled through Cairnton in large cars. Sometimes they stopped at the Café Firenze, the Italian ice-cream parlour, to buy cigarettes if they ran short, but that was all. You are thinking of your genial little Border towns like Kelburgh with its recherché tailor and its lovely shop where they tie trout

53

flies for the Border dukes. There was nothing like that in Cairnton. There were no dukes either. If there ever were any dukes or their ilk in those hills, they died or ran away when big business hollowed them out. Getting back to Lady H. one preconceives a great deal of solid money and not much else.'

'She must be third or fourth generation out of the Victorian go-getter who built the baronial,' Twice said. 'She many have acquired quite a lot else by now.'

'I doubt it, although I am prepared to admit that this may be pure prejudice on my part. That was a very provincial area and proud of its provincialism in what I think is the wrong way — the sort of "here I stand and this is how I am and I am proud of it and I don't want to be different and anybody who is different is all wrong" attitude. They were all frozen into immobility by their sense of their own rectitude. And Cairnton had got on to the road to the money goal and could go on only in that one direction. It couldn't deviate into a more metropolitan attitude of mind or into an interest in the arts or into anything. I can't express quite what I mean. One had a sense, always, of a whole community being trapped in a blind alley, walled in by money, with a money wall at the far end that everybody was trying to reach without knowing why. When they reached the end wall they didn't know whether they were going to go over it into the unknown on the other side or sit on it and jeer at the others who had been beaten by them in the race. I think — and I think they knew it — that the wall at the end kept receding all the time as they advanced towards it and that they knew in a dull, dead sort of way that they were condemned to die in the harder and harder pursuit of more and more money, trying to reach the end of a blind alley that really had no end. The very rich are different from you and me,' I quoted and added: 'That phrase is a quotation from an

American novelist by the way. I would not like to claim as my own the words of a greater person. And the rich are not different simply in that they have more money.'

'No, money talks. But it can also silence,' Twice said. 'It can silence whole areas of thought. If you never have to think of where your next meal is coming from, that is three meals a day times three hundred and sixty-five days a year times seventy years of allotted span. That is quite a lot of non-thought when you put it statistically.'

'I had never thought of putting it that way.'

'Except that non-thought isn't right. The very rich must think about something in the time you and I take to think about where the next meal is coming from and it is what they think about that determines the difference between them and us.'

'Madame Dulac is very rich,' I said. 'And between meals she thinks mostly of her charities and whose business she can interfere in next. Then Martha's aunt was very rich and she thought mostly about nail varnish and hats for Martha's aunt.'

'These are two extremes of the thing. There must be an infinite number of mixtures and gradations of mind in between. It seems to me that there must be some unifying principle among the very rich, some one thing that's common to them all and differentiates them from people like us, like all the trees becoming coniferous above a certain line of latitude and beyond a certain line above sea level.'

'What is the unifying principle among people like us, then?' I asked.

'I think it is probably the desire to achieve the point where we *don't* have to think where the next meal is coming from.'

'So that people like us simply want to be like the very rich?'

'Probably.' Twice smiled at me, the gay mischievous grin which I had been missing so much lighting his face. 'Except that this is where you and I step out into a class by ourselves,' he added. 'You and I are out of the race now. If my health had held and we had maintained our rate of promotion in Allied Plant Limited, there might have been a chance of us arriving among — not the very rich — but the fairly rich. But not now. We have stuck at the point where I am assistant manager of Paradise Estates Limited instead.'

'And a very nice place to stick. I don't think I should have been much of a success as one of even the fairly rich. The habits of the thrifty poor are too deeply ingrained in me. And this is where I have to think of where our next meal is coming from for if I don't do anything about our supper, the servants surely won't.'

I left the room but I did not go to the kitchen as I had indicated I would do. Instead, I went along the passage and locked myself in the downstairs bathroom, stared at myself in the glass for a moment and began to cry, not out of sadness but out of keen joy. I did not know how it had happened but that little conversation about money was the first of its kind between us for a year and more and it was only now that I knew how much I had been missing these exchanges. Not the least important thing in the conversation had been Twice's completely natural reference to his own health : 'If my health had held —'. It had come out as something that had happened and had been accepted, an untoward accident that had changed the course of our lives, but there had been no overtones of ambition foiled or undertones of a sense of injustice and the silence of the last year had been filled with these barely perceptible overtones and undertones.

I could not understand what had brought about the change in him on this day. The logical explanation was

56

that its origin lay in the improved state of his health, that he had reached the point physically where the world had become real again for him but the change held for me something of the miraculous and, as I have said, I am a Highlander and we are a superstitious race. From that moment, Lady Hallinzeil became a symbol, a sort of luck talisman for this rebuilding of our lives. I could hardly wait for her arrival in the island so that I could serve her in some way as a demonstration of my gratitude and my only regret was that she would probably be in no need of any help that I could give.

PART TWO

PART TWO

ABOUT three days after Lady Hallinzeil arrived in St. Jago, I went down to the Peak Hotel and into the private office of my friends Sashie de Marnay and Don Candlesham, who were the owners.

'Darling,' said Sashie in his affected way, 'what bliss to see you after this long long time for it means that Twice is quite quite well and we *are* honoured that you should be hatted and gloved and all!'

'The hat and glovery are not for you,' I told him. 'I have come calling on Lady Hallinzeil.'

Sashie, who chose to defend himself from the world by this most embarrassing and affected manner, stamped a daintily suede-shod foot at me and said: 'Janet, one is extremely angry with you. As a friend, you should have told us of this unreasonable and quite illogical pronunciation of this name instead of letting us say Hall-in-Zeal and having to stand corrected by this so provincially middle-class person. *How* did *you* know how to pronounce it in any case?'

'It is the name of a place in Scotland.'

'That savage, absurd and illogical country again. One might have known!'

'And don't you be such a ridiculous little snob with your provincial middle-class persons,' I told him.

'There is no question of snobbery, darling. She is provincial and middle-class. To accuse one of snobbery for telling the truth, simply because the truth displeases you, is mere muddled thinking.'

61

'Sashie, don't be so quarrelsome,' Don said. 'Janet, sit down and we'll have some tea.'

'No, thank you, pet. I shall have tea with Lady Hallinzeil, I hope. And Sashie and I are not quarrelling. I don't think Sashie and I *can* quarrel. Total agreement is too deep-seated in us.'

'Dear me, yes,' said Sashie. 'Her ladyship is really quite harmless Janet but small, you know. I feel sure she collects those little coloured animals made of blown glass and has them on what she calls the mantelpiece, looking cute and sweet.'

'Sashie, you are a perfect wasp.'

'With a non-poisonous sting, darling. The companion, however, is a little macabre.'

'The companion?'

'Mrs. Drew, Lady Hallinzeil's companion,' Don explained.

'She has a companion with her?'

'Oh, yes, indeed,' said Sashie. 'A most odd creature—she has something of the look of those Belsen wardresses whose pictures were in that book — so very frightening— that that American wrote.'

'Sashie!'

'He is talking a lot of rot, Janet. Mrs. Drew is just an ordinary old housekeeper sort of thing.'

'But with an air of fanaticism, I insist upon that!' said Sashie.

'Look, get a waiter or somebody to take me to them,' I said. 'If I listen to Sashie any longer I shall take fright and run back to Paradise.'

'I'll take you out, Janet,' Don said. 'They are in the bungalow at the far end.'

The Peak Hotel was an old plantation house which had been converted and in addition to the rooms in the house proper it had a dozen luxurious little bungalows scattered about its grounds and connected to the main building by a network of pathways, all of which were covered by arbours of flowering vines. When Don and I reached the most remote of these, there were two women seated behind the screen of Pandora creeper that shaded the veranda and one of them, a little thin woman, her greying darkish hair drawn into a tight knot at the back of her head, rose to open the trellis door for us.

'Good afternoon, Mrs. Drew,' Don said.

The woman looked straight at us, but she did not speak nor did any flicker of expression cross her face and I had a sudden flash of memory of the grim-visaged suspicious housewives who lived behind the dark brown-painted doors of Cairnton.

'Mrs. Alexander has come to call on Lady Hallinzeil,' Don continued and at this a voice from inside called: 'Come in!' and, through the creeper, I saw the other woman rise from her chair.

Mrs. Drew still did not speak. She merely opened the door a little more widely, let me pass on to the veranda and then closed it behind me, shutting Don firmly on the outside.

'How nice of you to come,' Lady Hallinzeil said, holding out her hand. 'Sir Hugh Reid told me about you.'

I sat down in the chair that she led me to and she herself then sat down opposite to me. She was an ordinary-looking little woman with no remarkable features except a faded prettiness, and a vague air of a life unremarkable except for its lack of problems hung about her. She had soft plump little hands and on the left one there was a wedding-ring guarded by a half-hoop of very large diamonds — hands that looked as if they had never had to take a firm grip of anything. They were in precise contrast to the hands of Mrs. Drew, which had the knotted look of years of hard work and which, when performing some

63

light task such as the shutting of the frail trellis door, seemed to take upon it a grip that was unnecessarily firm and strong.

'Maggie,' Lady Hallinzeil said, 'will you go and order tea?' and, with a slight nod of her head, Mrs. Drew went out and away along the covered path. I began to wonder if she were dumb but felt that Sashie would have mentioned this if it were so.

'I am really very glad you have come to see me, Mrs. Alexander. It is nice to see somebody from home.'

'What do you think of St. Jago?' I asked.

'I don't really know what to think.' She looked out through the trellis at the sweep of green lawn that rolled down to the silver beach and the limpid blue sea. 'I am not a traveller. I have never been out of Britain before except to Paris. I decided on this holiday on a sudden impulse.' She looked round the veranda vaguely. 'It is all very strange now that I am here.'

I felt sympathy with her for I thought that I recognised something of what she was feeling, the disorientation that I myself had experienced when I first came to the island in 1948 and stayed for a few weeks in the exotic luxury of the Peak Hotel.

'It is all very strange at first,' I said. 'The tropics make a terrific impact on one's first encounter — the perpetual sun, the violent colours, the quite different racial spirit that dominates everything.'

She looked at me with a puzzled air. 'I didn't mean that,' she said. 'It is just that it is so odd to be away from the family like this, where I can't ring them up or see them or anything. Before I came, I just never thought of that somehow. I did ring up my daughter in London last night but it isn't the same. It's too far. I mean, you *know* all the time that all that sea is between you.'

I felt a little out of my element with this for I should

have never thought of telephoning London merely to chat even if I had had a telephone and I took refuge in the realm of strict fact.

'How old is your daughter?' I asked.

'Only nineteen and she is married and has a baby already,' she said with pride. 'And my sons are married too. I have two sons. And I've got five grandchildren altogether.'

'How lovely!' I said, because this was what she wanted me to say. 'And do they all live in London?'

Talking to me about her family, she seemed to be happy and all through tea she told me all sorts of details about her daughter's wedding and about how Michael, one of her grandsons, pronounced the letter R as if it were a W and in the telling of this she had an air of discovery, as if Michael were the first child that ever spoke thus, and her eyes contemplated the thought as if it were the first crocus to bloom in the spring. It made me like her because of its naïve pathos.

All the time that we were having tea and talking in this trivial way, I was aware of Mrs. Drew in the background. These bungalows were built on a rectangular plan, the veranda leading into a living-room, the bedrooms opening off the living-room and, behind them, the bathrooms opening off the bedrooms. This was one of the larger bungalows and had three bedrooms in all and from where I sat I looked into the living-room as at a stage and I was aware of Mrs. Drew coming out of one bedroom, walking along and going into another all the time. Unlike a stage, however, the light in the living-room was dim, shaded as it was on all sides by the veranda, the bedrooms, and the tropical vegetation as a protection from the fierce sun, and this dimness gave to the silent movements of Mrs. Drew a furtive secret air as she passed to and fro, to and fro.

'Sir Hugh Reid said he had known you since he was a little boy at Cairnton,' Lady Hallinzeil said when she had exhausted the subject of her family for the moment.

'Yes. Hugh and I met in our first year at the Academy. I was ten and he was twelve, I think. That was a long time ago.'

'When Robert — that's my husband — first had him as our doctor, we didn't know he had any connection with Cairnton at all. It was quite a coincidence.'

'Your name is connected with Hallinzeil House up above Cairnton, isn't it?'

'Yes. Hallinzeil was Robert's home. He took the name for his title.'

'You don't live there now, then?'

'Oh, goodness, no. You can't live in these places at home nowadays. Robert sold it. It has been turned into a mental hospital but of course it is not called Hallinzeil now. Robert would not allow that. They call it Cairnton North.'

'I see. Cairnton must be very changed. I have never been back there since we left it in 1926.'

'It is remarkable to think of a famous man like Sir Hugh Reid having been born in Cairnton,' she said.

I had an urge to laugh as I remembered, by one of those sudden associations in the mind, a history tutor at my university instructing us about the writing of a thesis on the Scottish Royal Burghs.

'Anyone who tells me that Mary Queen of Scots slept in a certain burgh on a certain night will have his or her paper returned as unacceptable,' he ended. 'Such facts are gossip, not history. The poor woman had to sleep somewhere.'

'I suppose famous men have to be born somewhere,' I said now. 'Come to that, Cairnton gave birth to a woman who is probably even more famous than Hugh — Kathleen

Malone, the singer, was born in Cairnton. Her father **was** an Irish miner.'

'Is she well known? Of course, I never go to concerts and things.'

'She is an international figure as a singer of religious music,' I said. 'Oratorio and the big masses and requiems and so on.'

'She would be a Catholic, I suppose? Did you know her?'

'Yes, as a child, and I have seen her a time or two since, but not since the war.'

'Are you a Catholic, then?' she asked and she was suddenly regarding me with suspicion.

'No. I am not anything in particular but my family religion was Presbyterian.'

'You mean you don't go to church?'

'I never go here in St. Jago because my husband works on Sunday mornings in Crop time — when the sugar factory is processing, you know — and I can't drive the car myself. Even if I could, I don't suppose I would attend church. I am not very good at doing anything as part of a crowd, especially a private thing like worshipping God. And then the Presbyterian minister we have here is very run-of-the-mill. He is not very interesting in the pulpit.'

'Interesting?' she asked with a puzzled air, looking as if she were out of her depth and at the same time disapproving of me for making her feel so.

'Yes. When I was a child, before I came to Cairnton, at home in Ross-shire we had a minister called the Reverend Roderick Mackenzie and he was a tremendous reverberating personality, just like the sound of his name and he was a great scholar and an inspired preacher. When he was in the pulpit, one really felt that he was a sort of channel between oneself and some higher power — that he could interpret God to you and you to God. It spoilt me for life, I think.'

She now looked merely embarrassed, as if I had said something that she found vaguely obscene. 'I always go to church. I have always gone,' she said. 'I have never thought of whether the ministers are interesting or things like that. I probably won't go here, though, because I am told that all the black people go too and that would seem terribly odd.... Were you in Cairnton at the time of that dreadful scandal about the minister?'

Her face was not of a very mobile or expressive type, but as she asked me this question there appeared in her eyes a gleam of malicious enjoyment. I had a sudden conviction that this was where she was at home — gossiping about her neighbours — just as she had been at home when telling me with so much satisfaction about her children and grandchildren. 'Small', Sashie had said and for perhaps the thousandth time I paid silent tribute to his acuteness.

'No,' I replied to her question. 'That happened shortly after we left. I remember reading bits about it in the newspapers but I don't remember the details.'

The last phrase is typical of the things I say almost involuntarily in order to see what will happen next. In this case, what happened was exactly what I expected. Lady Hallinzeil took a deep breath, licked her lips delicately and began to recount the whole sordid story of the minister's fall from grace, a story quite uncommonly obscene but the telling of it did not embarrass her in the least.

'Just think of it,' she ended, 'he was carrying on with these two women and that Catholic girl from the miners' rows as well and there is no doubt that that child the girl had was his — the court granted a paternity order and everything. Men really are the limit. It was a terrible thing for Cairnton.'

I laughed. 'Cairnton was a terrific place for scandals,' I said. 'It simply bred them — it was natural enough, I suppose.'

'What do you mean?' She was a little indignant.

'Well,' I said apologetically, 'it was a terribly repressed community — all its codes were so rigid. You can't repress people like that without the odd one blowing up in some way.'

'I don't see that at all. Most of the Cairnton people lived decent hard-working lives.'

'I suppose they did, but I always found it rather an unhappy place — the actual town anyway — but then I came to it as a stranger. If it was your home you would see it in a different way.'

'Oh, my home wasn't in Cairnton!' she said. 'My home was up in the hills at the back but we used to drive through Cairnton all the time. I always thought it was such a nice clean homely little town with all the white lace curtains at the windows and all the little houses so well kept and everything. I always looked forward to coming to Cairnton on the way out from Glasgow, especially when I was a little girl. Daddy used to stop the car at the café in the High Street and buy me chocolate.'

Having talked a few more trivialities while the silent Mrs. Drew went to and fro in the background, I got up to take my leave and said: 'If you feel like driving out to Paradise any day, Lady Hallinzeil, I should be delighted. If you have never seen a sugar estate it is quite interesting, and you might like to go over the factory perhaps.'

'I usually leave things like factories to the menfolk,' she said, 'but I'd love to come for a cup of tea some day and we could have another talk. It has been so nice meeting you and having a chat about home.'

'Then please do come.'

'When? Some day next week? I can hire a car at the hotel here at any time.'

I had not imagined that she would want to visit me so soon but I said: 'Splendid! Shall we say on Wednesday? I shall ask one or two other people.'

'Wednesday will be very nice, but don't invite anybody else. It will be nicer just to be by ourselves.'

I felt that she meant to compliment me but I have always found the word 'nice' difficult to accept in such a way. I was relieved, however, that she did not want other company for I would rather organise any function other than a tea-party.

When I arrived back at Guinea Corner, Twice was sitting on the veranda drinking barley water and wearing an expectant look on his face.

'Well? How was Lady H.?'

'Nice, I suppose but very dull, I am afraid. I sprang at Sashie in his office before I met her for saying she was provincial middle-class, but that is the trouble with Sashie, he is nearly always right. She just is thoroughly provincial middle-class — not that that would matter if she were not so dull. I mean, Madame Dulac is provincial middle-class but she is not dull.'

'In what way is this woman so dull?'

'Every way. She is so dull that there is nothing about her that one can even describe and there is nothing that she said that one can quote with any hope of amusing anybody.'

'How was she dressed, for instance?'

'In something expensive and nondescript. All I noticed about her was a hideous ring — a great half-hoop of diamonds all as big as peas.'

'What did you talk about?'

'Her children. She has a daughter and two sons, all married and she has five grandchildren. She talked a lot

70

about them all, but none of it was remarkable. The two sons and the son-in-law are in what she calls "the business" and one of her grandsons can't pronounce his R's yet. She even made the grandchildren sound dull although she is obviously fond of them. Then we talked about Cairnton. Her husband's home was Hallinzeil House but it's a loony bin now.'

'You must have loved spending an afternoon talking about Cairnton,' Twice said, 'knowing how you dote on the place. Stay there. I am going to get you a little whisky and water. You certainly deserve it and there is no reason why you shouldn't have something you enjoy just because I can't have it.'

'Cairnton doesn't seem so bad at this distance of space and time,' I said when he came back with my drink. 'Only it was a bit pointless to talk to Lady H. about it. It was like talking to somebody about the earth who had only seen it from the moon. She was one of these people I told you about who rolled through Cairnton in big cars. She thought it was such a nice clean homely little town, she said. She had seen only the white lace curtains at the windows and the outsides of the houses. But she became quite animated when she got on to the scandal about the minister. I have told you about it long ago but I pretended today that I didn't know about it and —'

'Why?'

'Just to see what she would say.'

'Why?'

'Well, it's mostly by what people say and how they say it that you get to know about them, dammit!'

Twice laughed. 'All right. What did she say and how did she say it?'

'She recounted every detail of the whole sordid story with the greatest enjoyment and yet, there was a queer thing.'

'What?' he asked, while I paused, thinking.

'She seemed to see the minister's fall from grace as a thing all by itself, an event detached from every other event. He was a bad man because the court had decreed a paternity order against him on behalf of the Catholic girl. The other two soi-disant respectable Cairnton ladies that he was sleeping with she had no blame for. And then when I suggested that the atmosphere of Cairnton might have something to do with the affair, she became quite indignant. That minister was just a bad man and that's all there was to it, but it seems to me that, given his potentiality to be bad as she calls it, he has also to be granted the time and the place to be bad *in*.'

'You mean that if he had been minister of any other parish but Cairnton he might never have been bad at all?'

'That is possible, but what I am really trying to say is that, since he was bad in Cairnton, Cairnton is part of the badness. You can't condemn the man and absolve the women and the place and all the other circumstances, but Lady H. is a bit like that about everything. She seems to see only the surface of everything — even her grandchildren — and she is content with that. And she sees everything standing by itself, detached from everything around it. I think that is what makes her so dull.'

'They don't live in Cairnton now?'

'No. London. That's another thing — she had never heard of Kathleen Malone. I shouldn't have thought it possible to live in London and not have heard of Kathleen Malone, would you? It's like living in London and never having heard of the Albert Hall.'

'Maybe she doesn't know about the Albert Hall either. It could happen, I suppose. I am sorry the thing was such a flop, darling, after I persuaded you to go.'

'It wasn't a flop, chum. It was a mad success, it seems. She has invited herself here for tea next Wednesday.'

'You had better rustle up a few of the ladies from the Compound.'

'No. It is to be a tête-à-tête, just the two of us, and we are to have a nice talk, like today. To tell the truth, I think the poor thing is homesick and I don't know what she is doing at the Peak at all.'

'It must be pretty dreary all on her own.'

'Oh, that's a thing, Twice. She is not on her own. She has a sort of maid-companion with her, a frightful-looking creature called Mrs. Drew.'

'Frightful in what way?'

'Sort of haunting. About fifty, iron-grey hair in a tight bun, and very silent. Sashie says she looks like a Belsen wardress and, tediously enough, he is about right. She lurked about in the background all the time Lady H. and I were having our nice talk. I felt she was keeping an eye on me to see that I didn't pinch the half-hoop of diamonds.'

'What a fool you are. Oh, well, I take it that there isn't much point in looking forward to Wednesday?'

'Not much, unless Lady H. has the most unsuspected hidden depths. However, I can write to Hugh now with a clear conscience and say that we are doing our best.'

The next forenoon I wrote to Hugh Reid again, telling him that I had called at the Peak and in the course of the letter I said:

'We talked quite a bit about Cairnton. She mentioned Cervi's café in the High Street and I had a nostalgic memory of the evening of our dog chase when Paddy and Fly scared those hooligans out of their wits. I suppose that in your life you have had lots of triumphs, but I think that moment when we stood in the middle of the street and watched them run must go down to history as one of the most triumphant moments I have ever known.'

*   *   *

If Miss Jean, who was a fair representative of public opinion in Cairnton, disapproved of my voyaging with the bargees, she disapproved still more of my next sortie into friendship. Very early in my tactless career in Cairnton, but after the time when I made friends with the barge-men, I started a campaign at home to be allowed to 'do the papers' with my friend Hugh Reid on Thursday evenings, which was the night of the week that all the periodicals taken in Cairnton blossomed into print and Hugh's load for delivery was at its heaviest. Hugh, I should mention, was a cripple who had been born without a left arm, and with the disability and the fact of his illegitimacy, he made a fine target for the name-calling which was a prime amusement among the Cairnton children and adolescents. Having 'ask-ask-asked' my father in my persistent way into permitting me to go on the paper round, I went on to 'ask-ask-ask' him to have my collie bitch Fly sent down from Reachfar, because I felt that since Hugh had a mongrel dog called Paddy, every decently equipped paper-deliverer had to have a dog.

The older I grow, the more I tend to believe that dogs tend to take on some of the character of their masters or mistresses, for Paddy, with his sad face and drooping ears was, in the streets of the town, an underdog just as was Hugh his master. My dog, Fly, was a different proposition. She was no mongrel but a well-bred, well-trained Shetland collie who had been my nursemaid since the time I learned to walk and I first learned to walk on the ground of Reachfar, ground that belonged to us Sandisons, who

74

had never been underdogs and after whom no rash person called names for the second time.

The big evening of my first paper delivery came. Hugh and I set off with papers and dogs, the name-calling began in the High Street and, as I have told in another story, I set Fly on the name-callers with highly satisfactory results. I have never seen so many male and female bullies between the ages of fourteen and seventeen running so fast, or heard howls of terror such as theirs as they tried to get away from two small dogs for Paddy, taking quick courage from Fly, put his ears up, peeled his lip back and was in the forefront of the chase. Out of all Cairnton, only three people were completely delighted about this débâcle. One was Hugh's granny, the second was Mr. Lindsay, the rector of the Academy and the third was Mr. Cervi, the Italian owner of the Café Firenze, pronounced Caff Fire-eens. My father was fairly rueful, I was a little overcome by the storm that was raised by the parents of the bullies who had been chased, and Miss Jean was absolutely scandalised. Probably that was why I saw fit to make no mention at home of the ultimate sequel to the dog-chase.

Mr. Antonio Cervi was of a type to be found in every small Scottish town and in numbers in Scottish cities in those days, an Italian who had brought with him from Italy the ability to make ice-cream in summer and fried fish and chips in winter, a flair for business and a great capacity for sheer hard work. His café was situated at what was known as the Top o' the Toon, for the Cairnton High Street rose over a hump and then ran downhill again towards the canal. It was in front of his plate-glass windows and round his door that the group of bullies congregated in the evenings after school, pushing and shoving at one another and on several occasions one of his windows or the glass panel of the door had been broken in the course of

75

the horseplay. On the evening of the dog-chase, as the scandalised townspeople popped out of their doorways on to the pavements, Mr. Cervi, with true Italian éclat and abandon, expressed at the same time his foreignness and his lack of sympathy with this grim place that was so unlike his native Italy by rushing out on to the pavement in front of his café, bouncing up and down like a rubber ball and shouting: 'Chase-a dem from ma door! Das *nize*! Alla time rounda door make-a da rude-a noise! Bite-a dem, dag! Bit-a dem good!' and then, when it was all over, he invited Hugh and me and the dogs inside and gave us all sweets and chocolate biscuits.

Cairnton did not approve of the Cervi family any more than it approved of anyone else from outside and, indeed, approved of them even less for they were so much 'no' like ither folk' as to be utterly damned in Cairnton eyes, but an atmosphere of the near-uncanny hung around them for it was beyond all doubt that the Cervis were rich, and wealth in Cairnton had a value that was unassessable. It was a sort of ultimate of desirability, of respectability, of achievement.

It did not seem to occur to the townspeople that the Cervi wealth derived from themselves through the industry and unfailing politeness and obligingness of the Cervi family behind the counters of the café and in the gaily painted pony-carts that carried the ice-cream to a radius of ten miles from the town centre. In some miraculous way, they seemed to think, the Cervis had 'got on and got up in the world' and Cairnton looked on this side of them with holy awe. On the other side, however, the Cervis were 'incomers' and worse than that for they were 'Tallies', people so foreign that they were almost not of the human race at all, and as a further corollary to this thing of being Tallies, there was the fact that they came from the very country where the Pope lived and were idolaters and worshippers of graven images just like those damned souls, the Irish miners on the Ither Side o' the Brig. The Cervis presented Cairnton with an anomaly. In the eyes of the Toon, idolaters should be a sub-race which had to grovel for its living in the bowels of the earth and live in the long black rows of hovels that were less sanitary than the cow byres of the farm my father managed, but idolaters should not be rich like the Cervis, live in a big two-storey house above the Caff where there was a grand piano, several violins, a 'cello, and a gramophone, and they certainly should not drive to their idolatrous mass at their chapel on the Ither Side o' the Brig on wet winter Sundays in two big Ford cars with canvas hoods while respectable God-fearing Cairnton folk walked coldly to the Kirk along the wet grey pavements.

After the incident of the dog-chase, Mr. Cervi became a good friend of Hugh and myself and each time we passed his café on our rounds he would give us sweets or toffee or samples of some of the other wares that filled his well-stocked shelves.

In my mind, in those early days, the Caff, as I called it like everybody else, was confused with Aladdin's cave, for never had I seen a place of such glitter and gilt and sparkle and splendour. All the walls were of looking-glass and on the shelves against this stood the glass bottles and jars and boxes of different-coloured sweets, while the woodwork of the place was dark and shiny and decorated all over with squiggly curlicues of embossed gilt. Along one side was a series of booths with high-backed seats with tables between them and on the wall above these, here and there among the panels of looking-glass, were gilt vases which sprouted great bouquets of artificial flowers from a land where the roses were blue and the willow catkins magenta and six inches long. The foliage of the plants of this wonderland was gold, so that the trails of ivy that hung down were

77

gold and gold again, reflected in the looking-glasses. Mr. Cervi did not trade in the penny slabs of candy or the penny toffee-apples which Hugh's granny sold to the school-children. No. Mr. Cervi sold chocolates by the half-pound box to courting couples on their way to the pictures, half-pound bags of Mint Imperials for the worshippers of the Toon to suck in the kirk on Sunday and he was ready to fill the luxurious requirements of holidaymakers passing through in their cars to Stirling or Edinburgh or even further away.

He was a round dapper little man and for the mere reason that he was short of stature I learned with astonish-ment that he was a grandfather, for the men of my family all ran to physical size and it was therefore my idea that to be a grandfather a man had to be 'big'. I remember dis-tinctly the day I made this discovery about Mr. Cervi. It was a Saturday afternoon in spring or early summer and I had been sent by my father with a letter to the station-master at the railway station which was at the canal end of the town and, as I came up over the hump of the High Street on my way back, I overtook a girl pushing a perambulator with a baby in it. I thought she must be about my own age or a little older, but she was much smaller than I was and very delicately made and coming up the slope she pushed hard at the perambulator, her head down, her bottom sticking out behind.

'Can I push too?' I asked.

'If you like,' she said and moved to one side of the bar so that I could take a hold.

The baby inside had dark curly hair and a pink face and was sleeping very hard.

'What is the baby's name?' I asked.

'Antonio,' she said and the name had a fluid musicality on her tongue. I thought for a moment and some vague connection with my Latin lessons came into my mind.

The name ended with an 'o' so probably the baby was a boy.

'Is he your brother?' I enquired, all ready to tell her about my own small brother at Reachfar.

'No. My nephew,' she said and I decided that she was one of these people who could not help telling lies and that I would not tell her about my brother after all. We had now reached the top of the slope and by common consent we stopped to have a rest.

'I am Janet,' I said. 'Janet Sandison.'

'I am Violetta. Violetta Cervi.'

'Mr. Cervi at the Caff is your father?'

'No!' She laughed as musically as she spoke. 'No. He is my *Gran*' papa. My papa he works at Kildyre at our Café Napoli there.'

'Café Napoli?' I repeated, trying to imitate her accent on the words.

'Yes. Like this in Cairnton is our Café Firenze.'

Although I was learning French at school, I was so astonished that the word 'café' painted in curly letters above Mr. Cervi's shop was not 'caff' and that the full title of the establishment was not 'Caff Fire ecns' that we rolled the perambulator the few yards down from the hump to the shop door in silence.

'We'll put Antonio round the back,' said Violetta, then, opening a door in the wall, 'hold it open for me.'

I held the brown-painted door and she pushed the baby through and I followed her.

It was a real 'Open Sesame' sort of door for no one, I thought, could have suspected, walking down the grey High Street, that there was a place like this behind the Caff — Café, I corrected myself. We crossed a cement-floored yard with stables on one side but the ponies were all out, a cart-shed on the other, but of course the gay little carts were all out too, a shed on the third that was full of

79

big boxes and crates of lemonade bottles and went on through another door in a wall into a big, terribly untidy, but very attractive garden. It had no neat rows of vegetables or gravelled paths and the poles that supported a clothes-line were all askew and off the plumb in a way that my father would never have tolerated, but it had a swing and a see-saw, a doll's house in a corner and in another corner a very fat lady in a bright red dress, asleep in a deck-chair and snoring so that the newspaper that had fallen over her mouth blew up and down in little gusts. 'Who is the lady?' I whispered to Violetta when we had parked the perambulator.

'Gran'mamma,' said Violetta in quite a loud voice, not in the least afraid of disturbing her. 'Would you like to have a swing?'

We had had several swings, several longish periods on the see-saw, and had taken all the furniture out of the doll's house and had put it back in different places when a window opened on the first floor of the house, a dark curly head came out and a voice called: 'Vyol-*ett*-a!'

'Mar-*ee*-a?' said my friend, looking up.

'Supper!'

'Come and have some supper, Janet,' Violetta said to me, with which, in the idiom of Cairnton, I 'nearly faintit'. I would never have dared to invite a friend to our house at Cairnshaws for a meal in this casual way and, at Reachfar, my grandmother would have issued the invitation with a: 'Violetta, Janet, come in! It's supper-time.'

'Is it six o'clock already?' I asked. 'I have to go home.'

'No. Only four. We have supper early on Saturdays before the evening rush. Coming, Maria!'

I noticed as we went into the house that Violetta spoke very much as the Cairnton people did except when she spoke her own name or the names of any of her family or the names of their shops. And, of course, there was a difference too in the titles 'Gran'mamma' and 'Gran'papa'. And the other people inside the house spoke in a similar way, all except the old lady in the red dress, who put 'a's' on the end of everything and called me 'Janet-a' just as Mr. Cervi always did.

Never in all my born days had I seen so many people of one family sitting round a single table and never had I heard so much fluid fluent speech and so much laughter. And the astounding thing about it was that this crowd could be only about half of the Cervi family, for all those little pony-carts were out driven by Cervi men and the shop down below was at this very moment staffed with Cervi women. I now began to revise my opinion about Violetta having lied when she said the baby was her nephew, for the pretty lady who kept going to the window to look down at the perambulator had introduced herself to me as Violetta's sister, but I pushed aside all thought of trying to sort out the Cervi family for the present. Their home — and the supper — were much too interesting.

High in a corner of the room, in what looked like a miniature corner cupboard of white-painted wood, there stood a gold cross and on a little shelf below it lay a tangle of several chains of beads with various crosses hanging from them. Before Violetta took her place at the table, she went to this corner, made a little sort of curtsey and then a sign with her hand over her face and breast. I suddenly realised that I was in the presence of 'idolatry' but, in a queer way, the word did not sound right as a description of what I had seen. What Violetta had done gave me the same feeling that I had at home when, before meals, we bowed our heads and my grandfather at Reachfar, my father here at Cairnton, said: 'For what we are about to receive, Lord, make us truly thankful. Amen.' This that Violetta had done was her different way of saying Grace, that was all — just as Sir Torquil Daviot at Poyntdale did not use quite the same words as my grandfather and father did, although he went to Achcraggan Church just as we did.

Then there was the supper. At home we had 'high tea' as all the Toon did, but in this house we had soup, then long white things with red gravy that had tomatoes in it and was very good but which I found very difficult to eat until the one called Maria showed me how to twirl the long white worms round my fork with the help of a spoon. After that, I ate up every bit and everybody laughed like anything in a very pleased way when I said: 'Yes, please' when they offered me some more. Then Violetta and I were given an orange each and sent out into the garden again.

Mr. Cervi, of course, had been at supper and a little while later he came down to us in the garden and said: 'Janet-a must-a go home-a now. You tell your papa you eat-a spaghetti, Janet-a? Das *nyze*! An' come again anotha day, play-a with Vyol-*ett*-a!'

I obediently went home over my private route by the fields to Cairnshaws and I still had plenty of appetite left to eat my home supper, but I did not see fit to mention the Cervis, Violetta, the spaghetti, or the idolatry. In my opinion, there had already been quite enough of a fuss about the bargemen, the Sunday School, Hugh, his granny and the dog-chase, but in the course of time I told my father in private that I had been to the Cervi home and he did not disapprove, it seemed, so I had quite a clear conscience when I was invited there again.

It is easy when recounting a story which centres round certain people to give the impression that these people were the only ones in life at that time, but this was not so of the bargemen, Violetta and her family. Most of my time out of school in those years was spent either by myself or with Hugh Reid, but Violetta and her Italian family were so strange and kind and interesting to me that they made a deep impression which, forgotten down the years, came back now in full colour, as if the Café Firenze had been excavated after thirty years of burial and its golden curlicues and blue roses had begun to shine again in the light.

I probably did not visit the house more frequently than once a month and never did I achieve a catalogue of the Cervi family in my mind. There always seemed to be a Gina over for the day or a Tino home for the weekend, often with their husbands or wives respectively and their children to add to the laughter and noise round the big table and in her large chair in the corner, Gran'mamma always seemed to be nursing and singing to a different baby. That was the dominant thing about the Cervi house —everybody could sing and they sang all the time. And everybody seemed to be able to play the piano or the fiddle or some instrument and even the little ones, boys or girls of only four years old, could sing and play real tunes on mouth organs, on which I and the other children I knew could make only a breathing-in-and-out sort of noise. In addition to all their fiddles and melodeons and the piano, the Cervis had a gramophone, one of the very expensive kind called a 'cabinet gramophone' which had no horn and a lid that shut down over the record so that you would never have known it was a gramophone at all. On this, they played the music of their own country and there was one very beautiful record which, although I did not know what the words of the song meant, always made me think of Reachfar. It was called *Ai nostri monti* and was a duet and often, after they had played it, the sister called Serafina would play the air again on the piano and Maria and her brother Alfredo would sing, which I thought even more beautiful than the record.

It was natural, I suppose, that the Cervis should think that I could sing too for I believe they had the idea that this gift for music was a common thing, but although I could hum an air and derived great pleasure from listening to music, I had no voice and no aptitude for any instrument. It was difficult to convince the Cervis of this for they thought that I was merely shy, so that, one evening, I was driven into a corner and said: 'Please, I truly cannot sing but if you have a record of a strathspey I could dance the Highland Fling for you.'

The brown eyes sparkled, they all clapped their hands, but they had no record of a strathspey. However, the word was written down by Violetta with, behind it in brackets, 'Marquis of Huntly's Highland Fling' and the next time I went to the house the record was there. They were kind enough to be delighted with my contribution to the programme, which was made for the first time on the evening of the 'feast' of some member of the family and on that occasion even more people were present. With the exception of myself and two others, all were Italian and spoke English of varying proficiency in the accents, I think, of nearly every district between Cairnton and the Scottish Border. The first of the exceptions was the old handyman who looked after the Cervi stables, a pleasant drunken old Glaswegian who had been christened William Brown, who was known to all the Toon as 'Wullie Broon' and whom Mr. Cervi always addressed with all ceremony as 'Meester Wulliebroon' under the impression that this was the old man's surname. It is this pleasant idiosyncrasy of Mr. Cervi's that has enshrined Mr. Wulliebroon in my memory, for I seldom saw the old man, but the other exception who attended the party has remained in my memory for different reasons.

She was a schoolfriend of Violetta and aged about fourteen at the time I met her, for she was about two years older than myself. I had been living near Cairnton at this time for a little over two years, but this girl, Kathleen Malone, was the first inhabitant of the Ither Side o' the Brig that I had ever met socially. It did not take long for even my slow underdeveloped wits to discover what was the bond between Violetta and Kathleen Malone or why Kathleen was welcomed to this musical house, for she had the voice of an Irish angel, warm and glowing and able to soar on wings in which the air vibrated as on the strings of a harp. In stature she was small as all the children of the miners tended to be, but already her chest was developing as was Violetta's and, as they stood side by side, singing Schubert's Ave Maria which Father Duffy, their priest, had taught them, they were like two happy young angels who sang this sad pleading prayer not because they were unhappy, but because Mary was unhappy and they thought that it might comfort her. Although I was younger than they were and much less developed — although academically I think I was more advanced — and although I did not understand fully the sense of the Latin they sang — and neither, I am sure, did they themselves understand it — I have always remembered the air of innocence about them while their voices — as trained by their priest — sent their prayer upwards as if it came straight from their hearts and was pulsing with their suffering blood. Even then, in a fleeting way like light coming and going upon water, in a way for which I could not then find words, I saw them both as channels through which something more powerful than themselves was being transmitted.

*   *   *

When I was thirteen, a quarrel had taken place between Hugh Reid and his grandmother on one side and me on the other. I put this in this passive way because that is how it was. We did not actively quarrel but life in general and the malicious gossip of the Toon in particular drove a wedge between us and for three years we did not, in Cairnton idiom, 'speak to' one another. The time came later when this breach was healed and the three of us were ashamed that we had ever allowed it to open but that is another story. What is relevant here is that from the age of thirteen until the age of sixteen I was deprived of my friend Hugh and consequently saw a little more of other people although I still spent much of my time alone.

I began to see less of my bargemen friends, for I was too old now for sailing on the barges: I continued to see Violetta and her family about once a month, or perhaps a little more frequently, but of Kathleen Malone I saw a good deal. At home, Jean, as I now called our housekeeper, disapproved more loudly and often of this friendship than she had ever done of any other for this was 'worse than a' else' and I was 'richt ower on the Ither Side o' the Brig' and 'amang they Irish scum', but if Jean was louder, I was older and less prone to listen to her than I had ever been. My father, to begin with, was a little doubtful, for vociferous public opinion is a strong force and, besides, he had in himself much of the Scottish prejudice against the Irish, that prejudice that talks about idleness, shiftlessness, thriftlessness and, above all, dirt. My father was a gentle kindly man but he was somewhat under the influence of Jean for, as I have said, he married her later on.

Sometimes the arguments in my home about my friendship with Kathleen seemed to me to resemble a struggle for the domination of the mind of my father between Cairnton tradition in the person of Jean and the Reachfar tradition in the person of myself and I think that in this struggle I had the advantage. The argument I remember

86

most clearly was the final one in which the final remark was mine.

'You know, Dad,' I said, when Jean had vociferated herself into breathless silence for a few seconds, 'when Cairnton talks about the Ither Side o' the Brig, it sounds exactly like Doctor Johnson talking about the Highlanders when he toured the Hebrides.' After that, there was never another word of any import in the house about my friendship with Kathleen, although Jean, for whom read Cairnton public opinion, continued to disapprove of it.

Kathleen was the youngest child of a family of eight and, like Violetta Cervi, very much the youngest, coming five or six years after the sister before her. At the time I came to know her, her three sisters were already away from home and in domestic service, and her four brothers were already working 'down the pit' with her father. The family lived in 'Number Two Row' which was the second of the seven parallel rows of some fifty houses each that were built as close to one another as possible, to take up as little space as possible and to contain more human beings than should have been permitted to be possible. They were built of brick, these rows, but it seemed that very soon after their building the coal-dust had got the upper hand of whatever the original colour of the brick had been, for they were black. And the ground around them — what little there was of it — was black too, trodden black with children playing there, with women sweeping out there the coal-dust from their houses, with coal that fell from the men's clothes as they came home from the pits.

Each home in these rows consisted of two rooms and that was all. There was no scullery, no lavatory, no wash-house or any form of sanitation. The lavatory was a row of small wooden cubicles with wooden seats with, underneath, a sloping slab of wood that led out to the ashpit behind. This pit was about five yards across the 'drying green' — a patch of soot-caked earth with poles and a clothes-line — from the door of the house, on the other side of it was a narrow lane and then there rose the black walls of the next row of houses.

The ends of the rows were towards the road and often I had walked past the seven low black gables, but I had never, of course, been 'down' the rows for the narrow lanes that separated them came to a dead-end at the railway embankment. But many times, before I knew Kathleen, I made a point of walking out that way on what was known as the Edinburgh Road, as opposed to the Glasgow Road at the other end of the town where the Toon took its walks, because it seemed to me such a pleasant way to walk on a fine evening. What made it so pleasant was not the scenery but the fact that the miners who were 'off shift' congregated in the evenings at the ends of the rows beside the road, all dressed alike in navy serge suits and grey tweed caps, and there they squatted in the position to which they had become accustomed at the coal-face, in a wide circle, and they talked or gambled at Pitch-and-Toss or argued about football or they sang and played melodeons or concertinas or mouth-organs. Mostly they sang and they sang beautifully. It was a wonderful thing on a summer evening to come through the grey High Street of the town where a few malicious gossips exchanged venom beside their whitened doorsteps or behind their prim lace curtains, cross the bridge over the canal and go down the slope on the other side to be greeted with all the colour and glamour of the March of the Toreadors from *Carmen*, sung by fifty or sixty male voices and played on a dozen melodeons. *Carmen* was a favourite opera with the miners — did they find in it the sunlight and colour of Spain? — and I have often wondered if the touring opera companies that came to Glasgow to perform it ever realised how great was the proportion of their audiences made up of miners and their wives, up on the spree from Cairnton and other mining communities.

Kathleen's home in Number Two Row was 'a double', which meant that the Malone family had two houses instead of one, or four rooms instead of two and this meant that the four girls, when they were all at home, slept in one room, four boys in another, Mr. and Mrs. Malone in a third and the whole family washed, cooked, and ate in the other. I never was in any room in the house except this last and I did not ever see it with the whole family in it, which I regret, because without having seen it, I can hardly believe that it could contain them all and yet I know that it did. However, I did not ever see all the Malones at home at one time, but on many Sundays I saw the parents, the four boys, Kathleen and myself in it and we made it very full for, in addition to eight of us, it contained a trestle with two big wooden tubs which served for both clothes- and body-washing, a large table and upright chairs to seat ten Malones, several other things and a battered upright piano. There was a small black coal-burning range, too. Yet I thought it a much nicer place than our well-polished living-room at Cairnshaws. It was a very bright sort of place in spite of the 'pit togs' which hung in two black rows of trousers and coats from pulleys on the low ceiling. The black range and steel fender always shone, the big black kettle was always singing and above the mantel there was a picture of the Holy Family with their donkey on the Flight into Egypt — a garish reproduction cut from some magazine but I liked the deep blue of Mary's cloak, the bright red of Joseph's and the brilliant yellow halo round the head of the Child. On the window-sill sat the pride of Mrs. Malone's soul, a red geranium with a carpet of green shamrock about its roots, the two growing and thriving behind the sooty panes in the dim light in defiance of every natural law, and on the end of the mantel was Mrs. Malone's secondary pride, a brass bracket that carried the oil lamp, which had a round brass bowl and burned a circular wick. The brass of bracket and lamp, the pair of brass candlesticks and the two brass trays, which sat on the mantel against the wall on either side of the Holy Family, always gleamed with polish and reflected back the flames of the fire and the light from the circular wick. Even the mournful banners of the dangling 'pit togs' could not darken the brilliance of the brass.

Mrs. Malone was a small, round, bright-eyed woman who was always busy and who sang all the time. I did not ever go to the house with Kathleen when she was not busy, washing or ironing or cooking, but I liked best of all when we found her ironing, for then she would be singing something slow, like 'Oh, Danny Boy', while she made long sweeps with the iron over her menfolk's Sunday shirts.

If I was invited to spend the evening there — I never went unless I was invited because it was a complicated household with the men, sometimes, working on three different mine shifts — I always went straight from school, which meant that I arrived at Number Two Row about five in the evening, after having met and had a chat with Violetta on the way. Mrs. Malone's working day went on until six-thirty when the men on the day shift had their one good leisurely meal of the day, but when that meal was over, Kathleen and I and whatever boys were at home did the clearing up while 'Mam', as we called her, had her evening sit-down across the hearth from 'Paw'. Even then, though, she continued to be busy and would knit socks, humming a little to herself while Paw read his evening newspaper. I used to wonder how this legend of Irish idleness and shiftlessness had come into being.

But, after the table was cleared, the dishes washed and all stacked away in the cupboard in the wall beside the fireplace, she would look up from her knitting and say: 'Well, what about a song, now?' especially on evenings when all four of the boys were in the house, as sometimes happened.

At the Cervis' house, as I have said, the music was mainly in the Italian operatic tradition, but on the Ither Side o' the Brig the nostalgic ballads of Ireland were being ousted by jazz, much to the annoyance of Mr. and Mrs. Malone. Their home, it seemed, had always possessed the old piano, an older concertina and an even older fiddle, but it was during the time of my visits there that a new ukulele and a second-hand saxophone were imported. Mr. Malone who, from long practice, could read the racing and football news in his paper in spite of any noise around him said little, merely looking at the two instruments as if they were strange animals before returning to the racing form, but Mrs. Malone, at first, was voluble in her disapproval. However, her nature was such that she could not be disapproving of anything for very long and when Clancy, the eldest boy, said: 'One, two!' and began to thump out 'Alexander's Ragtime Band' on the piano and Terry (saxophone), Mike (concertina), and Pete (ukulele) joined in, very soon her toes were tapping on the hearthrug as gaily as Kathleen's and mine. There was one thing, though, that she would not allow. If Kathleen as much as ventured to hum a bar of one of these noisy jazz pieces, Mrs. Malone's face would take on a mask that was really stern and which sat oddly upon it.

'Don't you tax your voice with that rubbish!' she would say. 'Stop it now or I'll tell Father Duffy on you!'

Towards the end of the evening, when the boys had played all the latest hits, the tunes of which they seemed to pick out of the air, for wireless was not yet very common and had no place in the miners' rows, Clan, as the eldest boy was called, would ripple his hands up the key-

91

board and say: 'Right, Kathie, what's for Mam an' Paw the-night?' and then Kathleen would sing one or two Irish and Scots folk-songs, while the mother dropped her knitting into her lap, the father folded his blackened hands over the paper and they both looked into the fire.

One evening in November of 1925, after something of a battle-royal with Jean, I set off for Number Two Row, for this evening had long been arranged and had been accepted as an engagement in my home until Jean discovered the full enormity of what was to happen. Father Duffy, who seemed to be more musical than even his musical flock, was arranging a special Mass for Christmas and Kathleen was to sing several of the solos. The Father was coming that evening to the Malones' house, bringing with him the score of Kathleen's part, that he might explain it to Clan, who would play for her at practice. When Jean discovered that I was to spend my evening in company with the priest, she decided that I had gone over to Rome and perdition, taking herself and my father with me, but as soon as supper was over my father said: 'All right, Janet. Off you go and be home by ten, remember!' and off I went.

I ran most of the way over my short cut in order to miss as little as possible of the very beginning of this great triumph in Kathleen's life, and it was not yet seven when I tapped at the door and let myself into the house as I now had the privilege of doing. Closing the door, I stopped short and leaned back against it, still panting from my run over the fields and down over the bridge. There was nobody in the house except Mrs. Malone on one side of the fire and Kathleen on a little stool by her feet, no Father Duffy, no Mr. Malone and no boys, but the most frightening thing of all was that Mrs. Malone was not doing anything. Her knitting was not even in her lap. Her hands lay idle, folded on her blue-grey apron, her grey shawl drooped about her shoulders and, as I stood there, she turned her eyes to my face — strange eyes with no light in them — and said: 'Come in, Janet. Pull in a chair.'

'What's wrong?' I asked. 'Mam? Kathleen? What's wrong?'

Kathleen got up and came over to me. 'There's been an explosion in Number Eleven. Clan an' Pete were — they were down with the shift.' She swallowed. 'Sit down there beside Mam. I am going to make her a cup o' tea.'

I did what Kathleen told me. I am always numbed by disaster and am grateful to be told what to do. I sat down on the little stool and put my hand on the mother's knee. She covered it with one of her own for a moment, then took the poker and stirred the fire into a blaze. Kathleen made the tea. The cheap little alarm clock that stood under the picture of the Holy Family ticked on. Suddenly, outside, there was a wild scream from a woman and Kathleen hurried out while the mother and I waited. When Kathleen came back, she said: 'They've brought up Tim Murphy an' ould Pat — they're both — ' She stopped speaking and shook her head.

'God rest their souls,' Mrs. Malone said quietly, crossing herself.

'Who is with Mary Murphy?' she asked.

'Her mother's there, Mam. Take a little more of your tea.'

We were sitting by the light of the fire, the blind not drawn over the window and there was a moon and some light coming out from the other houses in the next row. There was a constant traffic of people past the window, as scraps of news came up from the mine shaft and were passed on down the rows. The little clock went on ticking but time had lost meaning now. We did not speak. We simply sat, staring at the fire and sometimes our eyes

93

would be drawn to the window as somebody came down the row and went past. It went on like this for a long time and then a curious silence fell, a silence that seemed to be listening to the footsteps of a single person walking down the row. Mrs. Malone stiffened in her chair, straightened her back and said: 'That's the step o' Father Duffy! Light the lamp, Kathie,' and, putting her hand on my shoulder, she levered herself to her feet as the door opened. In his long black cassock and little biretta, the tall priest stood there, his face gradually becoming visible as the light travelled round the circular wick of the brass lamp.

'We have got both Clancy and Peter up, Mrs. Malone,' he said. 'They are both all right.'

He shut the door. Mrs. Malone and Kathleen dropped to their knees on the rag hearth-rug and I kneeled down too. I did not understand the Latin prayer that they spoke with the priest but silently I prayed: 'Our Father, which art in heaven — ', which was the only prayer I knew.

Father Duffy did not stay long. I think he had come to us first because we were an easy assignment in his long task that night, for deep in Cairnton Number Eleven nine men had been killed and twenty-three seriously injured. Clancy, Peter, and two others had been 'safe' in a little pocket behind part of the fallen roof.

In a little while, Mr. Malone, Mike, and Terry came in and said that Clancy and Peter had been taken to the hospital to have a few scratches dressed and that they would be kept there for the night.

'It's so as they'll be handy for questionin' in the mornin',' Terry explained. 'They yins up there on the hill are no' gaun' tae get it a' their ain road this time. The Union men's been doon at the pit-heid since seeven a'clock an' they're doon at the hospital noo.'

I did not understand much of this but I knew that 'they yins up there on the hill' were the owners of the mines, the people who lived in those houses whose pepperpot turrets showed above their surrounding trees.

'All right, laddie,' Mrs. Malone said placatingly. 'Come to the fire an' Janet an' Kathie will make ye some tea.'

We had just made the tea when I heard a sound outside that was very foreign to these miners' rows — the slow, deep Highland voice of my father.

'Gosh!' I said. 'What time is it?' and when I looked at the clock I saw that it was nearly two in the morning. I rushed to the door and opened it. 'Dad! Dad, I'm sorry!'

'That's all right, Janet,' he said and, stepping inside, bowing his head under the low door-frame, he took off his cap. 'This is a terrible thing,' he said slowly, looking at Mr. and Mrs. Malone, who had risen and stood beside the fire. 'Is —' He looked at Terry and Mike. 'Are — your boys — ?'

'Two o' them was doon there,' Mr. Malone said, 'but they're right enough. Only scratched. Ye'll take a cup o' tea, Mr. Sandison?'

'Thank you,' my father said. 'That's very good of you.'

He sat down on the chair that Terry placed for him and I suddenly realised that the room was very low and small, a room specially built for people who had to make do with cramped quarters and who grew to the size that these quarters dictated, but I was terribly glad that I had stayed out late and that he had come to fetch me and I felt more glad still when we were leaving and he said: 'And I have to thank you, Mrs. Malone, for your kindness to Janet,' for it made Mrs. Malone smile for the first time that night.

'Janet is aye welcome, Mr. Sandison,' she said. 'I'm sorry we forgot the time and made ye anxious.'

On the way home to Cairnshaws, my father was very

quiet for a long time until he said: 'It is a hard and terrible way of life that these miners have — just as treacherous and dangerous as the life of the fisher folk at home.'

'Yes, Dad.'

'It's funny, us living little more than a mile away and I never knew about that terrible disaster until after I crossed the canal tonight. There was not a word about it over here.'

He walked on thoughtfully through the darkness and I walked beside him, wondering about what he had said and then I took courage.

'Dad, I don't think it's right that people — people should be all separate from each other like they are here in Cairnton, do you?'

'I don't know what to think,' he said. 'Irish and Scotch people have always been separate and Catholics and Protestants have always been separate —'

'But they don't *have* to be!' I broke in. 'They don't have to be. I am not separate in this Cairnton way from Mrs. Malone and Kathleen.'

'No. That's true. The little wifie said you were welcome in their house and she seemed to mean it —'

But now we were at the gate of our own garden and the subject dropped. It would have dropped anyway. I was too young and incoherent to find words for what I felt and my father, I now know, had never developed the faculty for putting his deeper thoughts into words. We went into the house and went to our separate rooms.

*   *   *

Lady Hallinzeil arrived at Guinea Corner at about half-past three on the Wednesday afternoon and stayed until nearly seven, leaving only when I asked her if she would like to have supper with us. Twice, who had come home about five o'clock, thus had some two hours of her company and as soon as she had driven away, he said: 'Bless my soul, she *is* pretty dull, isn't she?'

'That is how it seems to me,' I agreed with him. 'It's this thing of knowing exactly what her opinion is going to be before she gives it — you know it is going to conform exactly to the standards of her class. She never seems to have thought about anything. I wouldn't say that you and I are a couple of brilliant, scintillating minds, but she has a way of making me feel like an idiot hitting his head against the wall of a padded cell. I resent it. I am not brilliant or scintillating, but I am not an idiot, either.'

Twice laughed. 'She seems quite definitely to be home-sick. I wonder what she is doing out here at all.'

We went on wondering this silently and aloud for some weeks while Lady Hallinzeil kept popping in to visit us every other day. We learned a few more facts about her, such as that her London home was in Sloane Street, that her husband was at present on a business tour to Australia and was returning by the Pacific and the United States some time in April, and that her youngest grandchild had cut her first tooth.

'But,' I complained to Twice, 'you can't call it knowing a person.'

'It is not your sort of knowing,' he said, 'but I think it is hers. She feels she knows us intimately, I think, now that she has got our historic facts sorted out, like my being born in Berwickshire and you in Ross and you spending six years in Cairnton and my never having been there at all.'

'Mary Queen of Scots slept here! That isn't even gossip, much less knowing a person. We both had to be born somewhere.'

'But you go in for knowing people with your heart, Flash. Lady H. knows them with her head and it is not a very intelligent or demanding head, either. It is content with the most meagre little facts. It is a pity she is such a bore for she seems to be determined almost to live here. Is she driving you nuts?'

'No. She doesn't bore me and she doesn't irritate me. It is more that I bore and irritate *myself* about her. I keep feeling that there is something pathetic about her and catching myself being sorry for her and that's just plain silly.'

'Your heart feels sorry for her and your head says it is silly.'

'It *is* silly. What reason is there for me to be sorry for a woman like that? If she is homesick out here, why doesn't she charter a plane and go home? She can afford it. She has everything in the world — wealth, a madly successful husband who writes to her every week, three children, five grandchildren and one of them has just cut a tooth! Why should I feel that I want to be sorry for someone like that? Do *you* feel sorry for her?'

'Not me, but then I don't see as much of her as you do. Maybe that is just as well. If I saw a lot of her, I think I'd get sorry for *me*. She is preposterously dull and I was the one who saddled you with her.' He looked rueful for a moment and then added: 'My intentions were good, of course. I felt that you had had a bit too much of my undiluted company.'

'You can't call meals and a few hours in the evening your undiluted company. You've been out at the office all the rest of the time.'

'Yes. Leaving you on your own. It is a queer thing. You are not gregarious and yet you do need people. They stimulate you. You feed on them.'

'You make me sound like a cannibal.'

98

'I put it badly. You give people something as well. That woman wouldn't come here day after day if she weren't deriving something from it.'

'But what? I am not conscious of giving her anything except a cup of tea, literally. There is no exchange of ideas or anything like that. She doesn't read. She is not a bit interested in the island or its history or exploring it. She doesn't seem to be interested in anything except her family and she makes even *it* sound dull. She seems to love all her children and all her children-in-law and all her grandchildren equally, for instance. That's dull. You would think she would have a favourite among them or simply loathe one of her daughters-in-law or something.'

'She may hate some of them or loathe the whole bunch but is too discreet and polite to say so.'

'Oh that! But one would know if she did. These things emerge. One would hear it in the tone of her voice or see it in the look of her eyes but she just doesn't. They are all her dear dear family. It is all so absolutely perfect that one simply can't believe in it.'

'What in the world do you mean?'

'I don't really know myself,' I admitted. 'But I wish some of those sons or daughters-in-law would come out here. I should like to see her *en famille* among all this perfection, but they won't come. I bet they are glad she is out of the way for a bit or something like that.'

'I think you are just making a compensating drama about her because she is so dull,' Twice said sensibly. 'You must take her round to call on Madame some day. Sir Ian was on about it again today.'

'I know. But she doesn't seem to want to go anywhere except here. But I shall make a definite thing of it and force her to come to the Great House.'

'I think you should. It's pretty dull for Madame these

days. Flash, have you thought of how enormously this place has changed in our few years here?'

'Often. It isn't like the same place at all. Of course, the change isn't really in the place — the island is basically the same — the change is in all of *us*. We are all older, we see it through different eyes and Madame is blind and doesn't see it at all now, poor old lady.'

'I know all that, but when I think of that Christmas play we did the first year we came out, it seems like a hundred years ago. What energy we all had!'

'And what fools we all were!' I said. 'Remember that awful nonsense between Don Candlesham and me? This island really went to my head, Twice. Now, that's a thing about Lady H. Nothing goes to her head. She is a bit like old Cousin Emmie in that way — the island, the climate and all the strangeness have no effect on her at all.'

'You yourself have changed basically very little, Flash, in spite of everything.'

I smiled. 'I notice you are calling me Flash again,' I said, for I was less shy about this now than I had been on that day in November. 'You didn't call me that for about a year. I thought it just as well. It is a youngish name for a forty-four-year-old. Why have you started using it again?'

'Because the flash seems to have come back a bit. It was in abeyance for a time.'

'It probably was and the ability to see it was in abeyance in you, too. Vision works both ways, I think. Perhaps I see Lady H. as dull, for instance, because the dull background of Cairnton colours my vision of her.'

'But Cairnton wasn't as dull as all that if you do it justice, what with having produced Hugh and Kathleen Malone and let us not forget your friend Annie and the minister with the love-life.'

'That's true. But anyway, dull or not, I have an affection

for Lady H. She marked a very important moment in my life and I shall always be grateful to her and she can spend *all* her afternoons here if she likes. And I know none of that is reasonable but there it is. Life is not all that reasonable anyway.'

PART THREE

ONE day, about the middle of February, much as I disliked going to St. Jago Bay, I went down to do some necessary shopping, travelling with Sir Ian Dulac, who was attending a meeting in the town that day, and we arranged that when I had finished shopping, I would go to Lady Hallinzeil at the Peak Hotel to wait till he could call for me. It was about tea-time when the car dropped me at the Peak and went away back to the Town Hall to wait for Sir Ian and, having called at the office of Don and Sashie only to discover that they were both out, I went along the covered walk to Lady Hallinzeil's bungalow. On the veranda, an ironing board was set up, a large number of dresses, blouses and skirts hung on hangers hooked to the trellis, and Mrs. Drew was engaged in the pressing of a mauve evening dress.

'Good afternoon, Mrs. Drew,' I said from the open doorway.

She looked at me, her dark eyes fiercely bright. 'Oh, so it's *you*!' she said.

It was the first time I had heard her voice and the flat accent of Cairnton did not surprise me, but the tone did. It was ill-mannered to the point of insolence. I am told I have a fairly quick temper and I felt a hot flash inside my head.

'Is Lady Hallinzeil at home?' I asked.

'No she's *not* at home!' she snapped at me in a pleased and triumphant way.

'I see. Very well. Perhaps you will tell her that I happened to be in town and that I called.'

I had turned away and was about to go down the steps when she began to speak and her voice arrested me, making me turn round to look at her. Both her hands were clenched on the handle of the electric iron on the board and she was leaning forward, her gripping hands looking very hard and knotted among the froth of stiff mauve lace of the dress she had been working on.

'Very high an' mighty, aren't you?' she said, and I noticed that her Cairnton accent was very marked now. Her face was a thin black-and-white mask with no life in it except the frightening blaze of the eyes. 'Don't think I don't know you! Coming here hobnobbing with my lady as if you were an equal. You're Janet Sandison and your father was nothing but a farm-hand at Cairnshaws. *I* know you all right. You and your R.C. Tally friends and your low scum from the Ither Side o' the Brig. I know you! You that came to Cairnton an' took all the school prizes away from the Toon folk!' She leaned even further over the ironing board, her fingers working and writhing on the handle of the iron among the delicate mauve material which was now gathered into a crumpled heap in front of her.

'But you'll not take *my* lady away from *me*, I'll warrant you that!'

'Mrs. Drew,' I began, 'this is —'

I was going to use the word 'monstrous' I think, but what I meant was 'madness' for there was little doubt in my mind that the woman was indeed mad but before I could say any more there was a small hiss and the heap of mauve material on the ironing board burst into a sheet of flame that rose between the woman and myself in a split second, but in that second I saw the white distorted face being engulfed and blotted out in a blaze of fire. On a table near the door there was a large bowl of flowers and, seizing it, I threw water and flowers at the ironing board.

The flames died down as suddenly as they had come up—they were dying before the water even reached them—and all that remained of a no doubt expensive dress was a mass of gummy substance that drooped in long gluey festoons like black chewing gum, over the edges of the board.

'It must have been some sort of synthetic,' I heard myself say before I came to myself and jerked the plug of the iron out of the wall socket.

Mrs. Drew had collapsed on to a chair on the other side of the board, her white face blackened, the front of her greying hair singed, and she was like a crouching animal as she glared up at me with her dark eyes.

'Are you all right?' I asked stupidly.

'Look at my lady's dress!' she said venomously. 'That's *your* doing! Coming here to come between my lady and me!'

'Mrs. Drew—'

'Don't you Mrs. Drew me! Clear out! Get out of here and don't come back!' She was screaming and I thought it best to leave her. 'And you can tell my lady about this if you like!' she shouted shrilly behind me. 'She'll not believe you. She'll not believe a word you say once I tell her who you are and who your friends are. Oh, I'll fairly put a stop to your uppishness, taking my lady away out to that place all the time! Just you wait—'

I backed down the shallow veranda steps, leaving her there crouched in the chair with the smell of burning all about her and the gluey festoons of synthetic material stiffening into a crazy network about the blackened ironing board.

I hurried along the path to the main building, let myself into Sashie's office and asked the waiter who answered the bell I rang, to tell Sashie when he returned that I was there.

107

By the time he arrived, I had achieved some semblance of calm and was sitting in his revolving desk chair smoking a cigarette.

'I came in the hope that Lady Hallinzeil would give me tea,' I told him, 'but she is out so I have come to you instead, if you don't mind.'

'Darling, delighted. Her ladyship has gone to have her hair done and to the dressmaker,' he said, 'and she won't be back until about six-thirty so that is simply splendid. How is my dear Twice?'

When the tea had been brought and the waiter had gone away, I said:

'Tell me, Sashie, have you noticed anything odd about that Mrs. Drew?'

'Darling, one told you the very day she arrived, practically, that the Drew was a macabre little woman.'

'All right. So you told me. Now tell me more.'

'Keeping a hostelry of this sort teaches one a great deal about humanity,' said Sashie sententiously. 'One knew right away that there was a little something that had to be watched about the Drew but it is no more than that same trifling old trouble.'

'What old trouble? Stop being so bloody affected.'

'Drink, my sweet. Booze. Alc. In the Drew's case, gin.'

'Sashie!'

'Fact, darling. She knocks it back as if it were her dear mother's milk.'

'But does Lady H. *know*?'

'Dear me, I shouldn't think so. Her ladyship is a very innocent — not to say stupid — sort of person, don't you think? Oh, no, I shouldn't think she knows. She would be horrified if she did.'

'But you can't live with a person in that small bungalow and not know, can you?' I asked. 'Sashie, are you sure you are right about this?'

'Don't be insulting, my sweet. I have seen so many sorts and conditions of drunks that I can no longer miss. I was a little slow in the uptake about the Drew because the stern John Knox façade put me off. Drink seemed to be the *last* thing, don't you know, but I knew there was *some*thing. I thought at first it was change of life as they call it and that's probably in it too, at her age, but the gin is *certainly* there. She buys it by the bottle at the wine-shop in the patio — she seems to be unaware that the shop is part of the hotel, poor thing. She carries it away in a large plastic handbag.'

'Sashie, it's awful!'

'Not really. A thing so usual doesn't inspire awe. Have a piece of cake. But *why* did you ask? Had you noticed a little something?'

'I went along to the bungalow when I arrived. She seemed a little queer — over-excited, sort of, you know.'

'Sort of. Yes. I know. Never mind. She will have calmed down by the time her ladyship gets back. At the Drew's age, the excitement doesn't last long. And then, of course, they are *very* cunning and her ladyship, as one said, is a very — unsuspecting sort of person.'

Sir Ian called for me and took me away before Lady Hallinzeil came back so I did not see Mrs. Drew again that evening but when I arrived home I told Twice of what had happened and of what Sashie had said.

'But he can't be right,' I ended, 'in spite of all his chapter and verse about the wine-shop in the patio.'

'Even without the chapter and verse, I'd lay odds that the little wasp is right,' Twice said. 'He has an eye like a gimlet for people and their failings. That is why he is such a successful hotelier. Darling, you know he is right.'

'But Lady H. must know about it, then. She can't be living that close to the woman and not!'

'You'd be surprised. Lady H. has probably never *thought* of such a thing, as she would say, and has probably never seen an alcoholic in her life. She probably thinks they only happen in books.'

'She doesn't read, she told me,' I said thoughtlessly, 'except for the odd magazine in a train or an aeroplane,' and then I had to think back over what I had said to discover why Twice was laughing.

'Then she probably doesn't know that drunks exist at all,' he said.

'One ought to tell her, I suppose.'

'I don't know that I would. What is the point? If she is happy and the Drew is happy, why spoil things for them? Only I don't think you should go back there without making sure first that Lady H. is at home and the Drew is sober. I confess to being very interested in the Drew now. Who is she?'

'What do you mean who is she?' I asked irritably.

'Well, she knew you at Cairnton it seems. Don't you remember her?'

'No. I haven't a clue. You see, all Cairnton knew me with winning that silly scholarship and all that, but they had a way of looking all alike to me except for Hugh and Kathleen and Violetta and a few odd ones. Mrs. Drew is a sort of apotheosis of the Cairnton housewife as I remember her — thin-lipped, shrewish, spiteful, rather like Jean, but most of them were skinnier and uglier than Jean. I haven't an idea who Mrs. Drew is and I didn't stay to ask. Lord, she was terrifying, especially when that dress blazed up and she looked at me through the flames. It was like looking into hell. In a way, it is a relief to know that it is only drink that is wrong with her. I thought she was a dangerous lunatic.'

'People can get that way on drink, remember. It goes for some people's brains the way it went for my liver. As I said, don't go back there unless Lady H. is there, Flash. There's probably a touch of religious mania in it too with all that stuff about your Roman Catholic friends. I think religion to a manic degree is far worse than drink anyway. History tells you that. Look at the Inquisition and things. You learn it at school, as Sir Ian says.'

'Religion really was a queer sort of mania with the Cairnton people when I think of it. A lot of them were of Covenanting stock and the Covenanters were a pretty maniacal lot when you think of it. The religious side of Cairnton was frightening, Twice, the Presbyterian part, I mean. The Roman Catholic part was different. They had their faith and that was that. But with the Presbyterians, it wasn't faith — it was a sort of confidence that they were in a conspiracy of judgment with the Almighty against the rest of the world. It is because of Cairnton that I never became a member of any church. When I was sixteen, I dug my heels in and just wouldn't become a communicant because of the horrible letters this minister used to write to the newspaper about the Roman Catholics and the next year there was this fine old scandal about him. After that, Dad did not say any more to me about becoming a member of the church and the whole matter dropped. But I took against religion as practised in Cairnton when I was ten.' I went on to tell him of my one-day attendance at the Sunday School. 'I ran home across the fields and when I got to the old quarry I discovered that I had this card with the text on it crumpled up in my hand. I had a spasm of horrible loathing for it and I tore it into little bits and threw them into the quarry loch. It was a horrible text, a proper Cairnton text. I can remember it still. "The Lord shall smite thee with madness, and blindness, and astonishment of heart." Deuteronomy, Chapter 28, Verse 28.'

'What an extraordinary thing to want a child to learn!'

Twice said. 'We didn't have those cards at my Sunday School.'

'I don't suppose they were peculiar to Cairnton but they might have been. But they were typical of Cairnton — that meaningless repetition of the printed word week by week, the text taken out of its context and nullified. There was nothing of the spirit of religion in Cairnton, only the dogma, as if the words had become petrified by the quarry dust so that they were preserved but fossilised and utterly dead.'

'That is one of the most terrifying things about the thoughts of great men, like the thoughts of the Old Testament prophets and even of Christ Himself. Down the ages they either become bastardised through misinterpretation or they become fossilised in peoples' minds into meaning-lessness. The spirit of the man who thought them gets eroded away by time and use. And the queer thing is that it is a two-way process. If a present-day mind gets filled up with these lifeless fossilised bits of dogma, it loses the power to think and so it accepts all the bastardisations and misinterpretations that are thrown into it. Great thoughts, like the gospel of Christ, are for minds that are alive and clear and able to take it in and give it forth again, giving it a fresh inspiration of life in the process.'

'That's it!' I agreed. 'That is what the old Reverend Roderick at Achcraggan used to do. He would prepare his sermon and preach it on Sunday and you would feel the thoughts coming over to you as if they were newly minted, as if they had been told to him all fresh, just before he entered the pulpit. I think that all the true religion I have I got from the Reverend Roderick. No. I got a little from Kathleen and Violetta too. I still remember Violetta making the sign of the Cross before she sat down to supper, and Kathleen and her mother praying with Father Duffy on the night of the pit disaster that Lady H. doesn't even remember, in spite of the High Court case and the mine-owners having to pay compensation of a kind that had never been known before.'

'Talking about Lady H. and fossilisation and that,' Twice said, 'I think she is a victim of another kind of fossilisation. Money and social form can be dogmas too. I think if you live by them entirely, the cells of your brain can get clogged up with them so that you can't think or see or hear in any other terms. That brings us back to the Drew. Lady H. won't see that she is a drunk because the social dogma Lady H. lives by doesn't have a chapter on drunks.'

'Maybe,' I said, 'but I am sick of Lady H. and sicker still of the Drew this evening. Let's not think of them any more for now.'

But, of course, I did think of them, especially of Mrs. Drew and, the next morning, as I went about my household jobs, I found myself searching back through my memories of Cairnton for some trace of her.

*   *   *

In March of 1926, I turned sixteen and was still attending Cairnton Academy, but was to go on to Glasgow University in the autumn. About this time, too, Hugh Reid and I made up our quarrel of three years' standing but Hugh had been at the university for two years now and I saw comparatively little of him. My main friends in Cairnton now or, at least, the friends of whom I saw most, for Hugh and his granny were still the principal ones, were Violetta Cervi and Kathleen Malone, but, of the two, Kathleen was by far the more intimate.

Both girls were about two years older than I was and the difference between sixteen and eighteen years old can be considerable, especially if the sixteen-year-old is as slow of development as I was. I was still a schoolgirl, but Violetta was a very gay and beautiful young woman who was causing a lot of anxiety to the respectable parents of the Toon as she flirted from behind the counter of the Café Firenze with all their sons. She had not grown very tall but she was beautifully proportioned and she had a colourful warmth that glowed like a jewel against the hard grey stone of her Cairnton setting. Her dark curly hair sparkled with life, her golden skin flushed to a tawny rose colour over her cheek-bones, her long-shaped dark eyes laughed constantly while the dimple in her chin came and went as she coquetted behind the bottles of coloured sweets and the boxes of chocolates among the gilt-scrolled mirrors that reflected her on all sides.

Cars, rarer in the early days, were now a commonplace and all sorts of gay blades found their way to Cairnton and to the Café Firenze to sit drinking coffee or ice-cream sodas and gaze at Violetta while she, her eyes full of dreams, looked anywhere but at them and mostly away to the sky beyond the windows while she hummed, in a pensive way, a bar or two of 'O Sole Mio'. Being slow-witted and a slow developer, as I have said, I used to think how kind it was of Violetta to turn away from all these young men who wanted to talk to her when I went into the Café. I did not realise that Violetta was born to the art of coquetry as surely as Kathleen was born to the art of song; that Violetta had an instinct for flirtation, knowing the effect of every glance and every turn of the head, just as Kathleen seemed to know instinctively which muscles of her throat to use and how to control her breath to make a note sound joyous and leaping with love or desolate and dying to the grave.

Already, in 1926, at the age of eighteen, Kathleen was on her way in the world of music and, strangely enough, the thing that helped her most in her amazing career was a national event which was in most ways a disaster, the General Strike of that year which is part of Britain's social history.

In Cairnton, especially on the Ither Side o' the Brig, May and June of 1926 was a terrible period, for it will be remembered that after the General Strike was over, and other workers, such as quarrymen, returned to their posts, the miners decided to stand out on their own. Whatever the political issues may have been, whatever the rights and wrongs, the stand made on the far side of the canal bridge at Cairnton, as I saw it, was a stand made in the grim face of utter starvation. The people of the Toon simply did not look that way. The miners, in their view, 'had aye been thriftless shiftless idolaters' and if they chose to remain on strike when 'ither decent folk' had gone back to work, that was their affair. If they were starving, that was their own fault — 'ither decent folk' had saved something against a rainy day while 'they idolaters had been gaun tae Glesca tae the opera'.

In spite of Jean, who was now my stepmother, saying that it was 'dangerous forbye bein' no' decent' to go over the bridge these days, I continued to go to see the Malones and I saw in the rows neither danger nor indecency. In some places there was rioting at this time, for a hungry man tends to be an angry man, but there was no rioting in Cairnton, just a dumb quiescent waiting which must have been based on some sort of faith in the outcome. The men, more of them than ever before, still squatted at the ends of the rows, but there was no Pitch-and-Toss now, there was no arguing about football, there were no renderings of operatic airs by voice, mouth organ, and melodeon. All the time, now, they wore their holiday clothes of navy serge suits and grey tweed caps but they had not a holiday look. Their faces were peaked and too clean. They had looked healthier when black of face except for whites of eyes and red of lips, with the 'pit reekies', the little oil lamps that they used down below in those days before the time of the safety lamp, hooked on to the fronts of their dirty caps. The men were listless and quiet, the women were anxious, trying to find a means of achieving a meal a day and the children, looking smaller and more stunted than ever, spent their days raking about in the slag heaps, trying to fill baskets and buckets with odd lumps of coal that had been thrown there by accident, that their mothers might have fire to cook the few potatoes or whatever they had been able to gather together to make a meal.

The Malone house was one of the fortunate ones, for all except Kathleen had been working and some money had been saved but it had been saved mainly that Kathleen might have singing lessons and Mrs. Malone grudged every penny that had to be withdrawn from the bank. Then, she could not eat herself and feed her own family with starvation showing on the faces of all around her and she would rush off, on her way home from the bank with the precious money, and buy bread and potatoes and bones from the butcher and start distributing them on all sides from her baskets as she made her way home. She became more and more cross and unlike herself as Kathleen's singing lessons lost ground day by day in the face of hunger.

Clancy, the eldest boy, idle like all the rest of the miners, sat brooding beside the piano for about three weeks until one day he put on his best suit, begged a pound from his mother and went off to Glasgow with a folded copy of the newspaper in his pocket. When he came home, he brought with him the piano score of a recent dance hit, set it up on the piano and said to his brothers: 'Come on. Get your stuff out.' They fetched their instruments and Clancy began to thump out the waltz tune on the piano.

I was there, in Number Two Row, that night and the sentimental tune, echoing among the silent black walls round about, sounded indecent. Mr. and Mrs. Malone, one on either side of the empty grate, looked with startled eyes at their eldest son and then at his brothers as their instruments picked up the air and seemed to wish to make some protest but they did not. I could understand, too, why they kept silent. Clancy had a strange wild look as he modulated to a different key and snapped out: 'Cut it, Mike an' Pete. Leave it to Terry an' the sax.'

Kathleen, who could do no wrong in Clancy's eyes and was unafraid of him even in this wild mood, stood behind him and looked over his shoulder at the cheap song-sheet and, as a new chorus began, she began to hum and then, as it came near the end, her lovely young voice rang out in full volume:

> *'All I ask is this one favour —*
> *Lay my head beneath a rose!'*

Clancy stopped playing. The other boys stood round him, holding their instruments and Kathleen kept her hand on his shoulder as he turned on the backless chair that was his piano bench to face his mother.

'Mam,' he said, 'I've put us in for a competition — Terry an' Mike an' Pete an' me. It's a new dance hall in Glasgow. They're lookin' for a band. We've to play a onestep, a tango, a foxtrot an' a waltz. Mam, I want to ask you somethin'.'

'Yes, son?'

'Mam, would ye let Kathie come with us, just to sing the chorus o' the waltz? Would ye, Mam?'

'No, Clancy,' said Mrs. Malone, using his full name to emphasise the negative.

'Aw, Mam! It would get us in — for sure it would!'

'No, Clancy.'

'Aw, Mam,' Kathleen now began.

It was a long argument.

'But listen, Mam,' Clancy said at last, 'if we could just get our feet in, we could get another singer. Wee Molly Gurney would jump at the chance in a month or so. It's just to get us a *start*, Mam!'

'Just for a month, Mam,' Kathleen pleaded. 'Mam, listen, if the boys get a start in Glasgow, they'll never have to go down the pit again. It's just a question of a start. And *I* don't want to sing in dance-halls! Aw, Mam, go on. Paw, make Mam see!'

'Mam, if we get a chance we'll get in,' pleaded Peter, the youngest of her sons and, I think, her favourite child.

In the end, after Father Duffy, who was still in charge of Kathleen's voice, had been consulted, the Malone boys got their chance. Mrs. Malone, while muttering every hour: 'Three months o' Kathie at the very outside, the Father says', drew some more money out of the bank, bought some stiff green silk and made a beautiful dress for Kathleen. 'Three months o' Kathie at the very outside —' she muttered again and bought new ties for the boys. 'Three months o' Kathie —' she muttered every few minutes as she pressed their suits and ironed their best shirts for the great night. By this time, 'The Malone Minstrels' were through the first heats of the competition and hot favourites for the permanent position on the dance hall's platform.

I was not, in spite of my most eloquent pleading, permitted by my father to attend the competitions on the five different nights at the dance hall but I attended every rehearsal at Number Two Row and can still sing — if what I do with my voice can be called singing — a soulful rendering of 'Lay my head beneath a rose', but two nights before I left Cairnton at the end of June to go home to Reachfar for my summer holidays, I was allowed to attend the

118

celebration party for the Malone Minstrels being elected, by popular vote of the patrons, to be the permanent band of the Blue Lagoon Palais de Dance.

Each year, since I had come to live in Cairnton in 1920, I had gone home to Reachfar for the months of July and August, the school summer holiday period, but in this year of 1926 I was not returning to the Academy but going on to the university where my classes did not begin until about mid-October. Mentally and spiritually, I have always belonged to Reachfar. No other place on the earth's surface has ever been as real for me and Cairnton in particular had never taken any hold on my mind or even on my affection. I can best, perhaps, bring home what I mean by saying that, after each summer holiday, I returned to Cairnton under the necessity of 'picking up the threads' of life there all over again, whereas when I went to Reachfar after ten months spent at Cairnton, I was never conscious of the threads of life at Reachfar having been dropped and consequently I never had to pick them up.

In 1926, having been at Reachfar for the months of July, August, September and the early part of October, there was a lot of picking up to be done when I returned to Cairnton, but I did not take it very seriously, for the place was already sliding out of my mental landscape. My father had decided to leave his post at Cairnshaws and was going back north to make his home in Achcraggan and I was to go to a village on Clydeside, to stay with some distant relatives as a paying-guest and travel from there daily to my classes at the university. I had no regrets about leaving Cairnton and very few, even, about saying good-bye to the few people I liked. I was only sixteen years old, after all, and at that age good-byes and departures seem to have no real permanence. There are plenty of tomorrows for the renewal of past ties. Life stretches ahead, long and full of wondrous possibilities and I think my feeling was one of joy to be leaving Cairnton and most of its people behind while those I liked, such as the Malones and the Reids, I could see at any time in the future that I chose. At sixteen, the whole world of choice seems to lie at one's feet.

From my chief friend, Hugh Reid, I did not feel that I was parting at all for he was already at the university and we had all sorts of plans as to what we would do together when I arrived there too and, in addition, Hugh had been writing to me while I was at Reachfar so, on my return to Cairnton, one of my first visits was made to Number Two Row, for Kathleen did not write letters. Neither did Violetta. Letter-writing is an idiosyncrasy which some people have and some have not.

The strike had now been over for some months and I understood that the miners had gained a point or two and some hope for the future by it, but the long black rows looked just the same and the inside of the Malone's double presented just as cheerful a contrast to the drear blackness outside—more of a contrast than ever, indeed. The boys were now living in lodgings in Glasgow, close to the Blue Lagoon and the little house seemed to be big and spacious, now that their pit boots were no longer in a row near the fire-place and their black pit togs no longer hung from the pulleys and only Kathleen and her parents were at home.

'I didn't really expect to see you,' I said to Kathleen. 'Friday is a big night at the dance hall, isn't it? Aren't you going up tonight?'

'The Lagoon?' she said. 'I've never been there since they shut down at the beginning of August for the holidays.'

'You don't mean the boys have left it?'

'Och, no,' Mrs. Malone said. 'They went back at the first o' September but Kathie didnae have to go. Violetta's singin' with them now. Violetta Cervi.'

'Oh. Were you sorry go give it up, Kathleen?'

'I was not!' said Kathleen with emphasis. 'I hated it. I hated everything to do with it. I only did it for Clan and the boys. It's different for boys — men — a place like that, but I think it's awful for a girl. They don't care, the men who come there, whether you can sing or not. They're not there for singing.'

'Does Violetta like it?'

'She loves it but you know what Violetta is — the way she could handle them in the Caff and that.'

'And Violetta isn't a singer anyway,' Mrs. Malone said. 'Her voice is good enough for a place like that, likely, but the smoke and the dust won't do it any harm or it won't matter much if they do. I'm glad Kathie's away from it, anyway.'

'But you are pleased about the boys, Mrs. Malone?'

'Och, aye, it's grand for *them*! They're making good money and well—' she looked up at the nearly empty pulleys '—it's fine to think they're oot o' the pit. I just hope it's for ever.'

'I'm sure it's for ever!' I said.

She smiled. 'You are like our Clan, Janet. My, you should hear the plans *he* has. By this time next year, he says, Paw will be leavin' the pit as well and we're to go to Glasgow to keep house for him an' the boys an' I'm to get a fur coat an' Paw an' me is to get to the theatre every Setterday!'

Mr. Malone shook out the football page of his newspaper and laughed.

'I doot I've been a miner a' my life an' it's a miner I'll aye be,' he said.

But I have always been on the side of the happy dreams. Even if they do not come true, there is no harm in dreaming them and if, by some unlikely chance, they do come true, you are the wise bird that 'sings its song twice over' and you have the dream as well as the reality.

'I bet you you won't, Mr Malone!' I said. 'I bet you finish up in a house near the Celtic football ground where you can watch the matches from your window, sitting at your own fireside.'

He stared at me over the newspaper and then said: 'That beats a'thing! You've got an even fancier imagination than our Clan.'

'But you havenae heard our big news, Janet,' Mrs. Malone said next. 'Kathie's startin' her real singin' lessons at the beginning of November.'

'Goodness! Where? Who with?'

'In Glasgow, with an Italian lady called Madame Pagliari,' Kathleen told me.

'Did Father Duffy find her?'

'No, but he's awful pleased. No, it was old Mr. Cervi,' Mrs. Malone said. 'She is some sort o' cousin o' the Cervis. These Eyetalians seem a' to be related to each other. I've never been so frightened o' anybody in ma life. Father Duffy an' me went up wi' Kathie for her interview — Madame Pagliari'll no' take any pupils except them she wants to take. I'm glad I'm not Kathie.'

'Och, away, Mam. She's nice!' Kathleen said.

'Well, she fairly frightened the life oot o' me,' said Mrs. Malone, 'but she's supposed to be one o' the best teachers in Scotland an' she's takin' Kathie.'

'Kathleen, I'm so glad. How often do you go?'

'Three times a week to start with — oftener later on if things go all right.'

'Where does she live? Do you go to her house?'

'Yes. It's out past Charing Cross.'

'But that is near the university. We'll see each other!'

'Maybe. But I'll just be up for my lessons and back down here again. I'll be working at Cervi's Caff in between whiles.'

Kathleen walked part of the way home with me and as

we passed the Café Firenze I said: 'Are the Cervi's pleased about Violetta's job at the Blue Lagoon?'

'I don't know. I suppose they are. Violetta's pleased anyway. Janet, Violetta's the limit in some ways.'

'What do you mean?'

'She's such an awful flirt. I don't think she thinks about anything much except boys. You should see her at the Blue Lagoon. She'll finish up by getting into serious trouble.'

I was two years in age behind Kathleen and a long, long way behind her — and behind most girls of my own age, indeed — in general knowledge of life. 'Trouble' for me, in the voice in which Kathleen had pronounced it, meant, for a girl, only one thing, the thing worse than death, an illegitimate child or the taking to a career of prostitution. At this time, Cairnton was just recovering from a major scandal which had kept the Toon talking for weeks. A local girl, the only child of highly respectable parents, who had been presumed for years to have had an office job in Glasgow had suddenly been discovered to have been pursuing a highly lucrative career as a prostitute ever since she left school, and the indignation of the Toon at finding this on its very doorstep, coupled with its fury at having been gulled by the young woman for years, had to be heard to be believed.

'You mean,' I said or whispered, rather, 'Violetta's going like Annie Black?'

'Oh, no!' Kathleen was vehement. 'No. Violetta isn't like that. But you know how bonnie she is and she's got so much personality —' In the nineteen-twenties 'personality' meant 'sexual attraction' in most vocabularies, ' — I mean, she's got what they call IT. Up at the Lagoon, there's dozens of men round her all the time — a lot of them *come* to the place just because of Violetta and well, you never know who they are or whether they're married

123

or not and I just hope she doesn't fall in love with the wrong one and land herself in trouble.'

'What does Clancy think?' I asked.

'Clan says she is pretty good at looking after herself, but I don't know. I don't want Clan to lose her because she is good at the job and she's nice to work with. The band boys all like her — there's eight in the band now, you know. But sometimes I wish she would get married and settle down.'

'But she is only eighteen!' I protested.

I felt that Violetta was my contemporary and to me the idea of getting married at this stage was ridiculous and, indeed, vaguely indecent. I thought of marriage as something, if it happened to me at all, that was far far in the future, when I was 'grown up'.

'She's old enough,' Kathleen said. 'Violetta isn't like you and me. You want to go to the university and I want to be a singer. Violetta doesn't want to be anything or do anything except flirt about with the boys. There's one of them up there at the Lagoon that I feel kind of sorry for. He's a real toff. He's got a big racing-car but it's not just the car — you can see he is the real thing and not used to places like the Lagoon. It's pretty rough, you know, especially on Friday and Saturday nights. He just comes because of Violetta and I think he is really in love with her.'

'But how did he come to the Blue Lagoon in the first place if he is such a toff?'

'Because of Violetta, I am telling you! He met her down here when she was working in the Caff.'

'Oh.'

'Then there's another fellow from Aucheninch that's engaged to a girl out there. *He*'s in the Lagoon every Saturday night after Violetta and I'm sure he can't afford it forbye anything else. And Bobbie Andrews from down the Station Road is always there and Tim Gallacher and goodness knows how many more. She is a proper vamp, that's what she is.'

'I don't see why you should worry, Kathleen. If Clancy's not bothering, you shouldn't.'

'That's true. And Violetta's all right — I mean she's not like Annie Black — but I wouldn't like her to get unhappy or anything because I was the one who got her in there. I hated it so much I was nearly going dotty and it was worrying Mam and Father Duffy because of my voice but I didn't want to let Clan down and then I was talking to Violetta one night and, well — she said she'd like to try it and there it was.'

'You've got too much conscience. If Violetta is going to flirt she'll do it anyway. She was doing it here at Cairnton before she ever saw the Blue Lagoon,' I pointed out with what I thought was considerable aplomb the fact that only in the last few moments had come to my slow wits.

'That's true. She was at it even before she left school,' Kathleen agreed. 'I suppose it's just the way she's made.'

I did not see Violetta before I left Cairnton to go to stay with my relations on Clydeside but I heard a great deal about her, mainly from Jean. When Violetta came down from Glasgow on her weekly visits to her home, it seemed, she never came by train or bus as suited her station in life but came by car, squired by some smart young blade, usually a different one each week.

'She's jist anither Annie Black,' said my stepmother and all Cairnton public opinion.

Very soon, however, it was the same car that was seen outside the Café Firenze — a blue Lorraine-Dietrich with leather straps on its long bonnet — every Wednesday afternoon, and there were numerous conflicting reports about the size, shape, age, and degree of handsomeness of the man who went through the door in the wall and up into the Cervi house with Violetta until, one day, the blue car was sitting at the curb and another big black chauffeur-driven limousine pulled in behind it and a gentleman got out and went in through the door in the wall. There was another outburst of conflicting reports, each more dramatic than the last. The gentleman was another admirer and a modern-day duel had been fought at the top of the Cervi stairs. The gentleman was the enraged father of the admirer in the blue car who objected to his son taking up with a Tally heathen idolater dance-hall singer. The gentleman was a high-up detective from Scotland Yard and the man in the blue car was in the white slave trade and had been arrested while trying to get away over the Cervi's back wall. The gentleman in the second car was the owner of the Blue Lagoon and had come out to sack Violetta for neglecting her work to run after the men. There was an infinite variety of speculation but the blue car was seen no more in Cairnton and neither was the black limousine, but Violetta continued to come home on one or sometimes two afternoons a week always squired by an admirer and she would appear, gay and flirtatious as ever behind the counter of the Café Firenze to give her sisters a helping hand. The males of Cairnton would flock in for cigarettes while the females, tight-lipped and watchful of eye, whispered around their doorsteps, wrathful at the injustice of life and God that did not bring Violetta to the bad end that they felt so vehemently she deserved.

With my departure from Cairnton to Clydeside, a phase of my life came to an end. In lodgings in the comfortable home of the courtesy-titled Uncle Jim and Aunt Alice, I was out on my own, separated from all my immediate family in a way that I had never been before and rejoicing in my freedom, managing my small monthly allowance of pocket-money, discovering the world of the university. I was very happy and very glad to put Cairnton right behind me. Now and then I would remember it, as on the occasions when I met Kathleen and we had a cup of tea together but only in a fleeting unreal way, for Kathleen was not of the Toon and the background I saw behind her was the bright, kindly Malone home on the Ither Side o' the Brig. And, of course, I saw Kathleen less and less frequently for she was deeply involved now in the world of music, a world of which I was completely ignorant, a world in which she was so much at home that she could not make it comprehensible to someone outside as I was, for Kathleen's gift was for song, not for the cold explicit words of explanation.

I think the last time I saw Kathleen in Glasgow was in 1927 and, thereafter, Cairnton dropped entirely out of my life for about a year until one day I was in a crowded teashop in Sauchiehall Street, after spending the afternoon in a big library near Charing Cross and before going home by bus to my lodgings. A young woman, very soberly dressed and carrying a vast amount of shopping came and shared the table where I sat and after a few moments, she said to me: 'You're Janet Sandison, aren't you?' I stared at her. She was an unremarkable young woman, with dark-brown hair under a plain brownish felt hat, a young woman like hundreds of others, and I was not aware of having ever seen this particular one in my life before.

'Yes,' I said, 'I am, but I am afraid I don't know you.'

'I'm Margaret Bailey from Aucheninch,' she said. 'I knew you right away.'

I felt embarrassed, as one does in such a situation, and, feeling that I had failed in politeness in not recognising her, I became almost gushing, as one tends to do, especially since I could not understand why she had troubled to recognise me at all.

'Margaret! How nice to see you. How are you?' I raked desperately about in my mind for facts about her, con-

127

scious that I had not given her a thought for about eight years. 'How are your people?'

'Very well, thanks.'

'You seem to have been having a day's shopping.'

'Yes, I have.' She looked very pleased with herself. 'You see, I am getting married. Next month, it's to be.'

I knew now why she had made herself known to me. I was one more person to tell of this achievement of hers, an unexpected dividend after her day of wedding shopping. But now conversation was easy. She was very proud and happy in her engagement, a little superior and patronising about my child-like student state, as she told me all about her young man and the wedding arrangements and described in detail the going-away outfit which she had just been buying.

'And where will you live after you are married?'

'At Aucheninch. Jim works at the big house, like me. He's chauffeur to Mr. Thomson. Of course, I won't be working after I'm married. Some of them go on just the same but Jim said to me: No, he said, I want my wife to be my wife and nothing else, and so that's that.'

'I think Jim is quite right,' I said, not because I had given the matter any thought but because I knew that this was what she would like me to say.

'You look just the same,' she said next, 'just like you always did. Of course, you're not very old yet.'

'I am eighteen. I'll soon be nineteen,' I said, for after all she could be no more than twenty-one herself even although she *was* about to be married.

'And still at school!' she said. 'Well, the university, but it's still school in a way. Do you like it?'

'Yes. Very much.'

'*I* wouldn't. I was glad to get away from school when I was fourteen. We're going to have quite a time of it at Aucheninch these next few weeks. The second gardener's getting married, then Miss Mary's getting married, then me!'

'Goodness!' I said.

'Miss Mary's will be a lovely wedding.'

'She is Miss Mary Thomson?'

'Of course!' She stared at me and I had the impression that she thought the university ought to make people like me more intelligent or go out of business. 'At the Buchanan Church here in Glasgow it's to be and the reception at the Grand Central. Five hundred guests there's to be and *ten* bridesmaids. All red roses they're to carry, except Miss Mary—her booky is to be white lilies, of course. She'll be a lovely bride.'

'I hope you will both be very happy.'

'I'm just having the two bridesmaids and it's to be in the Kirk at Cairnton. But you don't live there now? I heard you'd left. Your father got married, didn't he?'

On the whole, it was not for me a happy or a comfortable meeting. There were too many weddings mixed up with it and I was at an age when I was somewhat confused about weddings and matrimony in general. It is difficult at this distance of time to formulate this confusion of mine and this distrust that was in me of the pageantry of the bride with her white lilies, surrounded by a bevy of bridesmaids with their red roses which were a symbol in my mind of 'roses, roses all the way', a symbol which my mind, even out of its very limited experience, rejected as completely false. I was aware that, among the people I knew, I stood alone in this distrust of the pageantry and the whole attitude to matrimony, for even my hard-headed grandmother and my sensible aunt at Reachfar always greeted the news of an engagement with a dewy-eyed pleasure that sat strangely upon them, and seemed to set great store by the form and ceremony of the occasion, down to the last detail of the trimming on the bride's going-away hat. I had not the courage to question a thing so firmly established, even had I been able to find words to express the distrust of it all that I felt, so that all I could do was to go along, as I was going along now with Margaret Bailey, seeming to participate in the accepted view, but this had the effect of making me feel hypocritical which only made my inner confusion the greater.

'Roses, roses all the way,' I thought.

I could not visualise the future of Miss Mary Thomson, for she belonged to a class and background that I did not know, but I could see very clearly and, I think, truly the future of Margaret Bailey in her little cottage with her chauffeur husband. She would be a typical Cairnton housewife, washing on Mondays, ironing on Tuesdays, turning out the parlour on Wednesdays, growing more harassed and haggard as each baby came along and it seemed to me grossly unimportant if, at the initial ceremony, she carried sweet peas or thistles or whether her honeymoon nightdress was of crêpe-de-Chine or sackcloth. It seemed to me at this moment, as we sat in the crowded teashop, that Margaret's mind was fixed on the wrong thing and fixed on it in the wrong way, for she seemed to think that this ceremony that she was about to go through with her Jim was a final thing, that after it was over they would be fixed in their relation to one another for all time and that they would always, henceforth, be the two people who had stood in the church during the ceremony but welded together, body and soul, as if they had been sprayed with a coat of fixative varnish which would hold them for ever in the mental attitude of the moment of the ceremony. But, as I said, I could not at the time find the words for all this, even to clarify it in my own mind. I merely distrusted Margaret's attitude, felt hypocritical because of my own response to that attitude and, becoming more and more fidgety, I longed to get away.

'In fact,' she went on to say, 'we hope there'll be a fourth wedding at Aucheninch before too long. Master Robert is going a lot to Torrencraig these days.'

'Torrencraig?' I said vaguely, putting on my gloves.

She looked at me again in that sharply impatient way as if I knew nothing of any value or importance. I think this is why I remember the meeting so distinctly, for this attitude of hers was so typical of the Cairnton community, this outspoken confidence that Cairnton affairs, conventions, and beliefs were of the first importance and that all the rest of the world came a long way and very uninterestingly behind.

'You must have heard of Miss Lawson of Torrencraig?' she said to me, her voice rising shrilly in her indignation at my ignorance.

'Her photo was in the *Bulletin* again last week!'

'Oh, yes,' I said vaguely and feeling cowardly.

'They say she's the richest heiress in Scotland!' she went on, charging at the ramparts of my encompassing ignorance.

'She must be quite rich, then.' Conscious of inadequacy, I got to my feet.

'Of course she's rich!' In an impatient way, Margaret began to gather her parcels, putting her fingers through loops of string until both hands were festooned. 'It would be a wonderful match if only Master Robert would settle down and behave himself.'

We now began to make our way out into the street.

'Doesn't he behave himself, then?' I asked, trying to be intelligent and co-operative.

'You know what young men are like!' she said. 'Oh, there's a yellow tramcar!' She ran along the pavement, her parcels joggling.

'Cheerio, Janet!'

'Good-bye!' I called thankfully and watched her push

her way on to the crowded tram before I began to walk to my bus-stop.

I did not know, now that I thought of it, what young men were like. I had known only one or two young men and those one or two had been vastly different from one another, as Hugh Reid of Cairnton was different from Alasdair Mackay of Achcraggan, as all people, men and women, young and old, seemed to be so vastly different from one another. For the rest of that evening, I envied Margaret Bailey because everything seemed to be so straight for her and she seemed to be so completely certain about everything and so happy in her certainty. It must be splendid, I thought, to be like that but, as I was going to bed, it occurred to me that there was no point in envying Margaret or in wishing to be like her for that could never be and to wish for the impossible was a waste of good living time. I think I have always been a practical sort of creature, uninspired, pedestrian, with a dislike of waste, especially of waste of living time for, even at eighteen, in spite of my general optimism about plenty of tomorrows to come, I had my moments of knowing that eighteen of my three-score-years-and-ten were gone for ever.

* * *

'What sort of morning?' Twice asked when he came in at lunchtime.

'A lot of little odd jobs with my hands while my mind dug about in the past,' I told him.

'Dug what for?'

'I suppose it started by trying to think who this Mrs. Drew could be, but I have got no further with that. Me at Cairnton is a bit like what my friend Freddy said once about himself at Folkestone during the war. It was about that ghastly Pierre Robertson that he said it, now that I think of it. I asked Freddy where he had met Pierre and he said it was during the evacuation from Dunkirk. Freddy was in the navy and Pierre was army and Freddy said: There were a lot of them and only a few of us and they all remember *us*. Well, there was a lot of Cairnton and only one of me and they all remember *me* if that doesn't sound too uppish.'

'You don't remember Mrs. Drew, maybe, but you do remember the oddest things, such as that thing that Freddy said.'

'I remembered it because it seemed to sum up that conceited twerp Pierre. Even as one of a crowd he expected to be remembered individually. Mrs. Drew is not like Pierre. She gave me the impression that she got a gloating pleasure out of knowing about me when I didn't know her from Eve — it was as if she felt one up on me. Very Cairnton. Everybody in Cairnton was always trying to be one up on everybody else. Still, looking back from this distance, it wasn't such a bad place. It was quite interesting when you look back into it. I feel I have never been fair to it. I was unhappy a lot of the time I was there so I buried it deep and wrote it off but now I see that it wasn't so bad after all. It is odd that all this should have started with Lady H., a woman I don't know and probably never will know, when Hugh, whom I have known and liked all these years never turned my mind towards Cairnton.'

'You gave it a bit of thought after we met Annie at the Great House,' Twice said.

'But only the ugly side of it.'

It is difficult to describe the quiet joy I found in being able to sit talking to Twice in this trivial way after that long year when a pool of silence seemed to lie always between us, a pool which, yet, had terrible echoes in its depths when, taking the thermometer from his mouth, I would look at it and say in a falsely bright, almost facetious voice: 'Good! Normal!'

Nowadays, the thermometer and the medical chart had fallen into abeyance and were no longer the dominating factor in our lives. When I looked back, I recognised that, for a whole year, the only moments when Twice and I came together were the few moments, night and morning, when we made the entries on the chart. This sheet of ruled paper had been the only common ground between us. The chart was Doctor Lindsay's guide. From it, he made slight variations in his treatment and I was still aware of its importance but it occurred to me now that the chart had had the sort of importance in our lives that the respiratory system has in the human body. If a man ceases to breathe, he ceases to live but it is only spasmodically and very seldom that men are aware of the act of breathing. In general, men are more aware of walking the dog, putting through a business deal or falling in love than they are of breathing and they seldom think that if they were not breathing they could not walk the dog, put through the deal or fall in love, and this unawareness of the basic factor of physical life is the natural condition of the healthy mental life. Twice and I had unwittingly allowed Doctor Lindsay's chart, which was the symbol of the avoidance of death, to usurp our minds to an unhealthy degree until, with the advent of Lady Hallinzeil, we suddenly found ourselves back on the plane of walking the dog and forgetting that we were breathing. We were not putting through business deals or falling in love, but a great deal of normal life for people in their forties is lived on the pleasant trivial plane of walking the dog.

'Even if no clue emerged about Mrs. Drew,' Twice said, 'I have no doubt that something else did.' He looked at me sidewise. 'Tell me about it. It is all part of that mysterious time before I met you that I am always trying to visualise.'

I found myself telling him about the interview with Margaret Bailey in the Glasgow teashop which had returned to my mind with such clarity, a clarity that recalled not only Margaret Bailey, but the fat woman with the absurd hat at the next table and the smell of damp warm clothing that hung like a miasma in the air of the overcrowded room.

'That girl, I think, is one of the factors in what may be regarded as my loose attitude to the formal marriage tie,' I said. 'She was inside a rosy cocoon of bliss, protected by the fossilised dogma of the marriage ceremony, and I had a horrid vision of the grey reality, that she was going to turn into one more harassed Cairnton housewife. Going home in the bus, my mind was all prickly and gritty as if, mentally, I were chewing fossils.'

Twice clenched his teeth and screwed up his face. 'Some of your similes set my teeth on edge,' he said, 'but talking of the marriage ceremony, it needs something a lot more live and elastic and less brittle than a fossil to stand up to what life can do to a marriage. And yet, some sort of dogma about it is desirable. All last year, one of the things that worried me most was that you and I weren't legally married. It is very subtle and hardly a reasonable thing and terribly difficult to explain, but I felt that I had done you a shameful injury by going and getting ill. I felt that when you came away with me, you had come without warning that such a thing might happen. The marriage service provides for it — in sickness and in health — and you will notice that the sickness is mentioned first. I had this haunting feeling of guilt that by getting ill, I had cheated, had broken faith in some way, had done something that wasn't in our agreement.'

'But, Twice —' I began and paused, realising that what I was about to say was not true. I had been about to say that any woman in her senses must know that illness is one of

135

life's main hazards but, at the time that Twice and I decided to make our life together, I had never even thought of such a thing. No thought of this hazard had ever entered my head and that was partly why the illness, when it did come, had caused such a mental upheaval, I could see now. I had been able to see the grey gritty reality that lay before Margaret Bailey but although I was much older than she had been when she made her decision to marry, when I made my own decision I had not foreseen any equivalent hazard for myself.

'It may be a delusion I've got,' Twice continued, 'but I think all of last year would have been much easier if the actual contract of marriage had been between us. In other words —' he smiled, 'it is much harder work to be what people call "lovers" or have what is called a "free liaison" than it is to be respectably married — that is if you want to make a success of the thing and give it some permanency.'

It was strange to hear of these things that had been passing through the mind of Twice in the course of that long year when he sat inside his own silence, his eyes fixed on the distance where the hills met the sky. It was alarming, too, to realise that he could be thinking of things so intimate to both of us and that I should be totally unaware of the nature of his thoughts. I had been too engrossed in my own misery, I saw now, to try to imagine what was passing through the mind of Twice and, because I felt guilty, I said: 'If you had had your way, I suppose we would have been respectably married by now.'

Twice's first wife, whom he had married when he was very young, was a Roman Catholic and the marriage had broken down within the first week. She refused to live with him but she also refused to divorce him and Twice had allowed this situation to drift along for some fifteen years, until he and I met.

Since I had spoken, I had become conscious of a strain

in myself, strain born of the knowledge that this was a conversation of which Doctor Lindsay would not approve but, in spite of this, I felt that, now that the subject had been raised, it would have to be discussed.

It may seem strange that, after my decision to make my life with Twice, we had dismissed this fact of our non-marriage almost entirely, largely, I was now realising, because of my own attitude that further discussion of a decision that had long ago been taken and acted upon was a waste of time. It was being borne in on me now, however, that our unconventional way of life seemed to have worried Twice much more than it had ever worried me and I was conscious of a spurt of something like irritation at this worry of his. It seemed to argue a difference between us that I did not want to admit, that he should set more store than I did by the letter of the law and, this apart, it made me impatient that he should complicate a complicated situation still further by dwelling on an aspect of it that could not be amended or that could be amended only at the cost of a great deal of trouble and expense and the amendment that would be achieved would be, in my view, a mere empty conforming to convention which would have no real bearing on the relationship beween us.

However, whether Doctor Lindsay would approve or not, I decided that since Twice had been worrying about all this the best thing I could do was to state my own position as clearly and even as brutally as I could and it was with a calm deliberateness that I continued: 'I was the one who considered that respectability cost too much in hard cash when you started enquiring into that annulment business and frankly, during this last year, I am glad that we had the cash in the bank instead of a marriage certificate. You can't pay for medical treatment with a marriage certificate.'

There were times, times when I felt forced to step into the open and say things like this, when I felt that I was almost a reincarnation of my grandmother, times when I could feel a hard materialistic realism jutting through the surface of my mind as the hard grey schist outcropped among the wine-coloured heather and the soft green moss of the Reachfar moor. And, at these times, I had a consciousness of breaking through the vision that Twice held of me. It was only at these times that I became aware that he saw me as a person of more malleable nature and less ruthless than I felt myself to be, but the awareness was invariably accompanied by an urge to free him of these delusions which, I felt, he cherished about me and although now I began in apologetic tones: 'I am afraid I am a much more lawless and ruthless proposition than you are, Twice,' I went on to say firmly: 'for I do not think that the knowledge that a marriage certificate was tucked away in a drawer would have helped me. No. It wouldn't have helped to know that I had promised publicly to love and cherish you and cleave to you in sickness. In fact, I think the marriage certificate would have taken on the character of written evidence of failure and I was conscious enough of failure already without having it confirmed in writing.'

He was looking at me with his brows drawn down, frowning as he tried to understand. 'Failure?' he repeated.

'Yes.' I spoke the word almost impatiently. 'All the time, I was conscious of having failed you in some way. This was the only reason I could see for your withdrawal from me. The relationship between us seemed to have broken down and the only reason for it must be some failure on my part. I suppose that is egotistical but that is how I saw it.'

He sat staring at the floor, frowning, thinking very deeply, but he did not speak and I, wishing to dismiss the whole subject to the long past where I felt it belonged, went on more lightly: 'Now, though, I see that there were so many factors that my mind simply bogged down among them and I took a sort of refuge in the thought of failure and stopped trying to think any further.'

He looked up and smiled at me. 'To blame the failure, if that is what it was, entirely on yourself can hardly be described as egotistical,' he said. 'It is rather the opposite. It was highly unselfish, it seems to me.'

'Everything is double-sided,' I said, 'and I am aware of being over-supplied with ego. It seems that I always impute everything — success or failure — to me-glorious-me. The truth is, as I said, that my mind was bogged down. I wasn't thinking rationally about any of it.'

'I don't think my mind was bogged down, as you put it,' he said. 'I think mine dissolved into a sloshy sloppy puddle. However, maybe it is starting to set again. You see, all last year, I couldn't see why you stayed with me, quite honestly. I couldn't see what you got out of it. Everything of benefit seemed to be towards *me*. It is a queer thing. It never occurred to me that you could still love me — in sickness. I knew I still loved *you*, that I was utterly dependent on you, that I would probably die if you left me, and yet I couldn't see why you stayed.'

'But *you* stayed with me when I was ill!'

'I don't remember thinking of that.'

'You must have been thinking in a very queer way.'

'I was. I think now that I was thinking with my head and not with my heart, as it were.' He smiled. 'Maybe it was because they were so persistent about the resting of my heart. Maybe the drugs had something to do with it, even. But that is the best way I can describe it. It was as if my brain had got detached from the rest of me and thought in strictly factual terms on its own, like a machine that had no blood in it. Then, that day at the end of

November, it was as if a warm current suddenly flowed into my brain. I suddenly saw you not just as somebody I loved and was dependent on, but as somebody who loved *me*. That was the thing I lost sight of. It seems impossible and unforgivable but it is true. I suppose one is bound to get a bit unbalanced if one is pretty sick, with all the drugs and stuff, and one feels so isolated, too.'

'It seems to me that your brain got the upper hand of your heart for a bit. After all, it is your heart that is weak and your brain took a mean advantage. Brains are mean things at the best of times. Hearts, even weak ones, are better things than brains. Maybe it would be better if everybody had fossilised brains. They would get into less trouble.'

'They would be happier,' Twice said. 'Idiots are the happiest people in the world, I have been told.'

'Would you say Lady H. is happy?' I asked.

'Not particularly. She doesn't strike one as being either happy or unhappy. Why? Do you think she is an idiot?'

'No,' I said, 'but I should say she is fairly fossilised, wouldn't you?'

PART FOUR

THE next morning there was a letter in my mail from Hugh Reid which began: 'My dear Janet, you will be beginning to think that I am organising an old Cairntonians reunion for you in St. Jago when I tell you that I met Kathleen Malone and her manager Michael Curtis at a dinner the other night — the dinner if you are interested was in celebration of Sir Charles Acton's seventy-fifth birthday. Kathleen and Curtis are just off to the States where she has engagements in Boston, New York, and Philadelphia and after that she intends to take her annual holiday. She was thinking of Nassau this year but when I said you were in St. Jago and that it was a holiday playground now too, she seemed to be quite keen on the idea. If she comes to your island, it won't be until about the middle of April. You will find her as charming as ever she was, in spite of her aura of greatness and greatness of a different sort extends to her figure. She is very amusing with her constant battle against her appetite and her weight. I am glad that you and Lady Hallinzeil are seeing a bit of one another. You are probably quite right when you say she is homesick. I thought this sudden decision of hers to go abroad was oddly out of character. That was partly why I wrote to you about her in the first place. At that time, of course, I thought that she was going alone and I was astonished to hear that Mrs. Drew was with her. I thought she had left the service of the family last year. It does not surprise me that you do not like her much. I have not seen much of her, but she does not look very attractive. I hope that Twice is continuing to be sensible about physical exertion. It must be a very difficult adjustment for him but, knowing him, I feel that he will stick his teeth in and have a good try. It cannot have been an easy time for you, either, for in these cases an actual mutation of personality, even, can occur and this has to be met by an adjustment on the side of the partner. If there is anything that you think I can tell you that will be of help in any way, please ask, but I am sure that you and Twice will come through as well as any couple and better than many. I ought to have mentioned that I gave Kathleen your address and told her of your influence with some of the hotel people so you may hear from her — '

Hugh's description of Mrs. Drew as 'not very attractive' amused me very much, and Mrs. Drew looked considerably less attractive to me now than she did when I wrote to Hugh after my first visit to Lady Hallinzeil, but I dismissed her from my mind in preference to thoughts of Kathleen for a prospect of a visit from her was a very attractive one, although a little frightening because of her importance as an artist.

Everyone has his or her own way, I suppose, of separating and grading people in the mind. It is not a question of the judgment that is implied in the division of people into sheep and goats but more a question of categorising. Some people I have met make a first breaking-down, for instance, into rich and poor, my friend Monica's first division is into what she calls 'the quick and dead of heart' and I have often accused Twice of dividing people into 'engineers and the rest'. My own first breakdown is into 'artists and ordinary people', because artists are the only people who can induce in me any sense of awe, any tendency to walk on spiritual tiptoe. They seem to me to stand out from and away and above ordinary humanity as the spire of a cathedral rises above the roofs of a town or as a noble ship sailing down an estuary stands away in magnificent adventurous loneliness.

Thus the prospect of meeting Kathleen again was at the same time enticing and frightening for, having known her for many years now only as a disembodied voice that emerged in majesty from Twice's record-player — our most expensive and luxurious household god — I think I had built up in my mind a vision of a creature not of this earth, a vision vaguely connected with my childhood ideas of the seraphim. It was what Hugh would call a 'matter of adjustment' to strip her in my mind of the halo and great, white curving wings and see her as a middle-aged woman who fought a constant battle against her weight, but, logically, I could see that this would be the cross of Kathleen's life for she had always loved sweets and when I had last seen her, several years ago, she was already growing portly.

*   *   *

In 1938 I was twenty-eight years old and earning my living as a private secretary in London. Like many of the young people of my generation, it seems to me now that I was a very light-hearted thoughtless creature, for I do not remember thinking of myself as having any past or any future. I read a great deal and could lose myself on Melville's high seas or in Jane Austen's drawing-rooms at will but I do not remember thinking of anything very much in personal terms of my own life except what I would wear that evening, whether I could afford the hat I had seen in that shop window or why Jack Martin, who was quite intelligent about lots of things and worked in the foreign exchange part of a bank and was a very good dancer, was such a bore with his pride in the fact that he had never read a work of fiction. I think I gave a fair amount of not very concentrated thought to Jack Martin and Alan Stewart and sundry other young men of my acquaintance for, at twenty-five to twenty-eight years old, I was beginning to consider the matrimonial question with what little seriousness I could muster, which was not a great deal.

I lived in a little flat in the basement of my employer's house which meant that I had only to go upstairs to work each morning and I had my own entrance through a gate in some railings, then down some stone steps to a small paved area and in through a narrow green door to a largish room which was both bedroom and living-room. In addition to this, I had a very small bathroom and an even smaller kitchen and I was extremely happy and carefree.

The young men of my acquaintance were the only snags in the effortless flow of my life from day to day, for at times I imagined myself in love with one or another of them. At other times, one or another of them would express a desire to go to bed with me or even marry me and all this was very unsettling because, invariably, when these relationships reached this certain point of the bed or marriage, I would suddenly realise that although Jack danced well, I could not live with a man who took pride in never having read a book and that although it was fun to go for days in the country or to Rugby matches with Colin, I would never dream of going to bed with him. When these moments of crisis came along, I had a cowardly, dishonest, but quite effective way of getting over them. I picked a quarrel with the young man in question, came to a dramatic and final parting with him and then retired to my basement, telling myself in a theatrical way that I was finished with all that nonsense and would henceforth devote my spare time to higher things — the arts, for instance. Then, for about a month or so, I would be seen — if anyone were interested to observe me — at exhibitions of pictures, in cheap seats at concerts, in the galleries of theatres and at the cinemas where French films were shown until, one evening, on my art-sated way home, I would encounter some acquaintance who would suggest a drink at some club over which I would meet a new young man and the whole performance would begin all over again. It is difficult to believe that I lived this way for several years and more difficult still to believe with certainty that I was not unique. There were literally thousands of us, all over Britain, who lived in much this manner in the thirties' decade and I have often thought that we were waiting, subconsciously, for the dawn of the 3rd of September 1939. We were not unaware of what was happening in Abyssinia, Spain, Italy and Germany. I think we knew that violence was building up just over the horizon but we also knew that there was nothing we could do about it. Not yet. So we hopped about, hither and yon, chattering and twittering and fluttering our wings like so many street sparrows before a thunderstorm.

It was in the course of one of these periods between boy-friend and boy-friend, when I was affecting a life of the arts, that I looked through the theatre column of my newspaper and saw the name Kathleen Malone in very small print at the bottom of an opera advertisement and decided in my light-headed way that it could not possibly be Kathleen Malone from Cairnton but, because it was a sort of omen and I had never seen *Tosca* staged anyway, I would go so far as to buy a stall if one was available for that evening.

A stall was available, it was indeed Kathleen Malone from Cairnton who was singing a minor part, and I then did something that I had never done before and which seemed like an adventurous excursion into the unknown, I sent a note round to her during the interval—a note written on the dismembered envelope of a letter from my

147

father. I did not really expect any reaction to my note. My awe of the arts set in now. Kathleen, I believed, singing as one of this illustrious company, would have no interest in Janet Sandison, private secretary, whom she had not seen or heard of in about ten years, but at the second interval the programme girl handed me back my own note with: 'Come round at the end. K.' scrawled at the bottom in very bad writing.

I remember very little of the remainder of *Tosca* except the terrible scream of the heroine as she hurled herself from the ramparts, so excited was I at suddenly turning into one of these enviable people who knew someone 'on the stage' and were invited to 'go round after', but when I did make my way round to the stage door and in along the bleak passage to the bleaker room that Kathleen shared with three other women, the glamour disappeared. It did not matter, however, for there was Kathleen, a little fatter than she had been at Number Two Row, much more self-possessed and very very pleased to see me.

We did not talk much while she changed and removed her make-up for the other women were there and I was conscious of a queer constraint in the atmosphere which at the time I could not account for, but which later I came to think was born of the watchful jealousy on the part of three members of a fiercely competitive profession for a fourth who, even in that time in their sight, probably had the mark of her future upon her. In the cold foggy alley beyond the stage door, I said: 'Where shall we go? Would you like a meal?'

Kathleen pulled her coat collar round her throat. 'Come back with me for supper,' she said. 'It's just off Gerrard Street. Not far. I live at Violetta's when I am in London.'

We began to walk along the alley to the street. 'Violetta's? You mean Violetta Cervi?'

'Who else? Didn't you know she was in London?'

'No.'

'She has been here since she got married five years ago. She married Mario Antonelli — Antonelli's restaurant, you know. He was a sort of second cousin of hers or something.'

'I'll love to see her again. How is she?'

'Just the same. Laughs and sings all the time in spite of everything.'

'In spite of what?'

'Mario died a year after they were married.'

'Oh, poor Violetta!'

'She is all right, you know. Sometimes I wonder about Violetta. I wonder if she ever feels anything very much, but you can't help liking her. And she is so kind.'

'She was always kind. It was the main thing about her. That and being so pretty.'

'She is still pretty and warm and gay. But for going home to Violetta's, I think I'd go dotty.'

'It is a hard sort of life, yours, Kathleen, isn't it?' I ventured, remembering the bleak room and the three women.

'Pretty rough. But I wouldn't do anything else. We turn down here. It will be a fairly rowdy full house tonight, being Saturday but after supper we can go to my room.'

'Other people besides you stay with Violetta then?'

'It's a boarding-house. Sometimes I wonder if it isn't a brothel. When Mario died, the place came to Violetta but her brothers-in-law run the restaurant now and she has turned the three top floors into a boarding-house. She doesn't have to take in lodgers, but Violetta loves to be surrounded with people. They are nearly all theatricals and sometimes there is a circus crowd, acrobats they are, but none of *them* are here just now. They are up in the Midlands. Here we are.'

I was completely fascinated, for this was a new side of London to me. We went in from the pavement through a narrow doorway beside the restaurant which had 'Antonelli's' written in gilt on its windows and up a long flight of stone stairs, whereupon Kathleen produced a key that admitted us through another door to another flight of stairs, wooden this time and laid with brown linoleum. At the top of this, another door led into an untidy hallway which was full of macintoshes and sundry items of clothing and pervaded by a strong and savoury odour in which garlic was the dominant. It reminded me of the smell in the house above the Café Firenze. From a room on the right came the sound of many voices, most of them foreign in accent, which also brought back to me on a wave out of the past the sound that used to emerge from the big dining-room above the café in Cairnton.

'Violetta!' Kathleen called, digging me in the ribs with her elbow. 'Don't say anything. Violetta!'

The door on the right opened, Violetta came out on a burst of laughter from inside and pulled the door behind her.

'I brought a friend for supper,' Kathleen said.

'Of course. Of course,' said Violetta, looking at me and smiling. She was about to turn away towards what was obviously the kitchen when she hesitated, the smile faded from her pretty face under the dark curls and then it returned again, widening and brightening into a gay radiant warmth. 'Janet-a! Janet Sandison! Oh, Janet, I am so happy!'

With the swift flight of a bird, she was upon me, taking me utterly by surprise for, in the Cairnton days, she had been as undemonstrative as all Cairnton people were. It was strange to be folded in this warm soft embrace and kissed on both cheeks while the dark curls brushed my forehead and even now I can remember the rose-fresh clean scent that emanated from her, overcoming for a second the smell of cooking and garlic.

She began to help me to take off my coat, talking and laughing and interrupting herself to give orders to the man and woman in her kitchen as she did so, and I remember vividly the quick thought in my mind that I would find this sort of fussing from any other woman I knew rather objectionable, for I still had the solitary stand-offish apartness and physical independence of people that had been in me as a child. But from Violetta it was not objectionable because it was a natural gift with her and she did it well so that in the simple taking of my coat from me, the hanging of it on a hook and then the patting into place of the collar of my dress she managed to convey a warm cosseting welcome that drew me to her and made me feel — the only fitting word I can use is — beloved.

After the meal in the noisy dining-room, Violetta suggested that Kathleen and I go with her up to her flat to have a glass of wine although it was now long past midnight. Despite the fact that I was often, in those days, out dancing at night-clubs until two and three in the morning, this sitting up late, drinking light-red wine with Kathleen and Violetta, had a new and entrancing element of what, in those days, I called 'the Bohemian' in it.

When we left the dining-room, we went up another flight of linoleum-covered stairs, round a corner and then up still another flight which brought us to a short landing with a single door opening from it and from the other end of this landing another flight of stairs led downwards into the darkness. One had a feeling of being detached utterly from the street below, from London, even from the earth. When Violetta opened the door and we went inside, I discovered that we were in what had been originally the attics for all the walls sloped a little towards the ceilings at the top but they were attics converted into a most luxurious flat. The sitting-room, into which Violetta led us, had originally been three rooms and it was L-shaped, furnished with a few good pieces, a few comfortable chairs, had a very beautiful Dutch flower picture above the fireplace and a small grand piano in the short part of the L. I can remember even the dark apricot velvet of the curtains, so astonished was I to come upon this room above, first, the raffish restaurant on the street level and then the shabby boarding-house on the intervening floors. I looked at the piano.

'Do you still play and sing, Violetta?' I asked.

She looked up from the wine she was pouring from a straw-covered flask and laughed. 'Let us be truthful, Janet. I never could sing very much. But sometimes I hum a little and play a little to amuse myself. But that is better,' and she indicated the big radiogram that stood in one corner.

We spent a happy hour or two, talking about Cairnton and the time that had passed since then and I remember thinking that, although Violetta had been married and widowed within that ten years, she was the one of us on whom time had left least mark. Behind the eyes of Kathleen great secret depths had formed, depths which seemed to hold more sorrow than joy and, now and again, as we talked she would suddenly seem to be rapt away from Violetta and me, lost in some distant place of the mind or soul where we could not follow and where she did not want us to follow. Kathleen was and is an artist of the dedicated sort, but at that time I did not know that such people live in two worlds and that they begrudge a little the time they have to spend in the, to them, trifling world which is my natural and only habitat.

Violetta was the exact antithesis of her friend Kathleen in this respect, however. She was very gaily of the every-day world. She seemed to have fluttered through the years between Cairnton and London, while Kathleen had been making her early strivings, with the gay inconsequence of a butterfly in a flower garden and in contrast to the withdrawn air of Kathleen, she seemed to exude a happy urgency of the here and now, as a butterfly over a flower bed in high summer seems to be the utmost symbol of all flowers and all summers. She had the engaging gift of out-giving, of lively interest in the smallest detail of what one was telling her as, when I spoke of my employer, she said: 'Fat or thin? Bald or lots of hair?' as if it were important to her that she must visualise him exactly. She did not speak at all of herself, except to make dismissive replies to questions as she had done about her singing and playing by nodding at the radiogram but when Kathleen was telling me of her sojourn in Milan, it was Violetta who broke in and with vital, loving, laughing interest began to summarise for me Kathleen's career in a way that Kathleen herself could never have done. In a similar way and with a similar loving interest, she told me about her boarders and how the little actress who had sat at a far corner of the table had a young man who was pining with love for her.

'Silly little Celia,' Violetta said. 'She thinks that one day she will be a Dame of Empire playing Lady Macbeth, but she won't. She should marry Fred and have a bungalow on a bypass and babies. One day she will.'

The thing that struck me most forcibly was that Violetta was so much wiser than Kathleen or me, although we were all very close to the same age. Kathleen knew a vast amount about music and I knew a great deal about all sorts of unimportant trifles of everyday living which made me hold Kathleen in respect as a person of much greater potential than myself. But I felt that Kathleen, born with the specific gift of her voice, had striven for the specialised knowledge which she now possessed and I knew that I myself was an ungifted, light-minded, unintelligent nonentity, but Violetta seemed to have been born with some age-old wisdom and a love of life itself which, down the years, had grown and burgeoned until, now, Kathleen and I were like two innocent children, sitting at her feet but warm in the sunshine of this love of hers.

When I left them to go back to my basement, I left in a flurry of invitations from Violetta to come and see her at any time and I did, on two occasions, go back to the little side street in Soho but, both times, I was told that she was away for the weekend. After that, another boy-friend intervened in my life and in the way that can happen so easily in a city like London and more easily still to someone with a head as giddy as I had in those days, I did not ever see Violetta again, just as, in all this time in London, I had never seen Hugh Reid although he was in the city for several long periods while I lived and worked there.

Kathleen, however, I did see fairly frequently during about three months following our meeting at the theatre, for she seemed to enjoy spending quiet spells during the day in my basement. Often I would come down at four or five o'clock when my employer released me, to find that she had let herself in with the key I had lent her and I remember that, one evening, walking with her part of the way to her theatre, I complained of having called for the second time at Violetta's and having been disappointed.

'That's nothing,' Kathleen said. 'Sometimes I don't see her for weeks and I live there.'

'Oh.'

'She has a tremendous number of friends, and she is very busy too.'

'Yes, she must be with all the boarders and everything,' I said. But after that I did not speak of Violetta to Kathleen again for I formed the idea, from Kathleen's repressive attitude, that she resented a little my 'butting in' on this friendship of hers.

That night, in the room with the apricot velvet curtains, I had been aware of a deep intimacy between these two, an intimacy which had been between them at school in the Cairnton days and which had developed still more down the years. It was almost a mother-and-child sort of bond, with Violetta as the watchful loving mother to the gifted sad-eyed Kathleen, a bond which I could understand, especially from Kathleen's point of view, for in the course of that one evening I myself had felt drawn to Violetta in a childlike trustful way as the very young and uncertain are drawn to the old and sure.

But, although it was of Kathleen that I saw the most, it was of Violetta that I thought most for she had all the fascination for me of the anomaly and mystery. She was the one of us who looked youngest, yet she was the wisest. She was the one of us who had been most sheltered by money and home-life from the outer world, yet she knew more of it than we did. She was the one of us who seemed to flutter through life with the least thought and conscious effort and yet she had mastered life in a way that we had not. These were all things that I 'felt' about Violetta but they were felt with an inner certainty that hardened them into an actual knowing.

In September of 1939 my flutterings about London came to an end, as so many other more important activities came to an end. I joined the Women's Auxiliary Air Force which sent me first to the east coast and then to an intelligence unit in Buckinghamshire and in the great world upheaval I lost all trace of Kathleen, Violetta, and many other people. Of some, like so many of us, I lost trace for ever in the most final way of all.

What I am about to write now may, at first, look like a pointless digression, but it is not. It is an attempt to say what I mean. There are two points in literature which have always attracted much critical comment. One is that

155

Jane Austen was writing during the time of the Napoleonic Wars and yet never mentions the wars. The other is that E. M. Forster, without warning of any kind, suddenly opens a chapter with the sentence: 'Gerald died that afternoon.' The non-mention by Jane Austen and the short sentence by E. M. Forster portray in a curious way the place of the 1939–1945 war in my life. For me, the war was six years of life suspended, when little of personal importance was mentioned and in 1945, when it ended, I was thirty-five years old, my life going into its afternoon, an afternoon in which many whom I had known in the morning were already dead.

I think that those of us who, like myself, were nearly thirty when this war began, were not affected by it as was the generation that was plunged into the earlier war that began in 1914. This first war had burst upon an astonished world, but people of my age could remember it and people are never astonished a second time in precisely the same way. And the later war did not burst upon the world. We, of my generation, unwittingly allowed the world to roll steadily and inevitably towards it and when it began we became aware that to be unwitting is not to be unguilty. In the armed forces it is a maxim that 'ignorance is no excuse' for any dereliction of duty, the implication being that within the framework of the service the last detail of every duty is somewhere laid down and in 1939, I, probably in common with many of my age, suffered a blighting moment of truth when I recognised that my ignorance of the trends of the last ten years was no excuse. European events had been laying down clearly that the world was rushing towards war, but I had taken no notice. Guilt came upon me and numbed me to everything except a certain endurance, six years of the sort of guilt that one does not want to remember. And so I do not mention the war very often but there is always in my mind the guilt and the knowledge of the bald fact that 'Gerald died that afternoon'.

During the war the people whom I admired most and envied most were those who used their artistic gifts of various kinds to bring a little light and sparkle into the dull uniform monotony of the lives of the rest of us. I admired the courage of the men at sea, on land and in the air, but I did not envy them their attributes. Given the choice, I would not have chosen to be like them for, even although I was involved in the war myself, fighting as a very small unit in a very small way, I was grateful at the back of my mind that my fighting potential was so limited, for there is a moral question of right or wrong about the whole business of war. In a cowardly way, I took refuge in the fact that I was 'fighting, but not very much'. About the arts, however, there is no moral question in my mind. The arts anywhere, at any time cannot be wrong and, in a grey tin hut in time of war, a manifestation of the arts has a rightness so strong and overpowering that it seems to be the only rightness in a totally wrong world. Feeling like this, I suppose it was natural that I was, among other things, a loud-voiced member of the Entertainments and Amenities Committee of my officers' mess for five long years. This was the link that brought Kathleen Malone into my orbit for a single evening late in 1944 when, with another singer and one or two musicians, she came to entertain us for an evening.

We lived in long, low, tin huts, divided into small single rooms which, architecturally, reminded me of the miners' rows on the Ither Side o' the Brig at Cairnton, especially when, on cold dark nights, I walked along the fifty yards of muddy path to the ablutions block in my macintosh carrying my towel, soap, and toothbrush in an old shopping bag. In summer, though, our hutted township was pleasanter than the miners' rows for the huts were built

157

for reasons of camouflage, in the deep green shade of a beech wood where, in spring, the violets and primroses grew about our doorsteps and where, in summer, we threw our shoes and other odds and ends out of the windows at the nightingales in order that we might have a little peace to sleep.

We of the Entertainments Committee always shared out the visiting artists among us for the more private side of hospitality and Kathleen and her party arrived shortly after I came off duty at four in the afternoon so, after a cup of tea in the mess, she and I had a good two hours together in my little room before the early meal prior to the concert.

I found it a satisfactory thing that Kathleen always seemed to ride the crest of the wave of national calamity. She had helped her brothers to success during the General Strike of 1926 and it was during the war of 1939–1945 that she made her own mark on the musical world so that, when it ended, she was waiting, at the peak of her powers, for that world to come to her feet which it duly did.

Some special gift has an aura that hangs about its owner and this aura, this confidence of power, was very marked in Kathleen as she sat in my one canvas chair beside the fire of fallen beech branches in the little black stove, while I sat on my bed.

'And you have had four years of this, Janet?' she asked, looking round at the tin walls which were sweating a little with the heat from the fire.

'It isn't all that bad, you know. The work is interesting. It is one of the biggest officer strengths in the country and a lot of my colleagues are very gifted and interesting people and we are near enough to London to get some of the best entertainment, like tonight.'

'A month of this would kill me.'

158

'But you don't have to do it, and there are lots of us who can do it without turning a hair. Different backs for different burdens, you know. How are your people?'

'Mam and Paw are marvellous. Clan got them moved out to a cottage near Balfron when the Clydeside bombing started and they are still there. Mam went down the hill a lot after Terry was lost.'

'Terry? Lost?'

Kathleen nodded. 'At sea last spring. Mike was killed in North Africa in 1942.'

'Kathleen, I am sorry. And where are Clan and Pete?'

'Clan is a prisoner in Italy but Pete is here in England — R.A.F. but not operational. He hates it but I am glad he is not fit to fly. If anything happened to Pete it would kill Mam.'

'He always was her sort of special one, wasn't he?'

She smiled. 'She would never admit it, but he was.'

We talked for a bit of Cairnton and Cairnton people, but all this was very far away for Kathleen had been out of touch with the place for almost as long as I had, ever since 1930 when the boys had moved their parents and their home from Number Two Row to Glasgow as Clancy, so long ago, had promised they would do.

'I say,' I said then, 'do you know anything about Violetta? I was in London about a year ago meeting a naval chum of mine called Freddie Firmantle — I think you met him once at my basement — and when we were looking for a place to eat, I suddenly thought of Antonelli's. We went round there but there's nothing but an enormous bomb-hole.'

'I know. That happened fairly early in the blitz but they had shut up shop by then anyway. The place was a fire station or something. Violetta is all right. Violetta is always all right. She is in a big old farm-house in Shropshire with fifty kids from an orphanage in Liverpool and six or seven nuns that look after them. I stay with her whenever I get up that way.'

'And how *is* she?'

'The same as ever. She doesn't look a day older except that she is getting a little fat like me, only with her it's round the behind instead of round the chest.'

'And just as pretty?'

'Prettier, if anything.'

'Prettiness isn't really the right word for what Violetta has,' I said, 'and it isn't beauty either. It's a tremendous warmth and liveliness and gaiety. I am surprised that she hasn't married again by now.'

'It isn't for want of men asking her to marry them. My brother Clan was one of them — Clan was dotty about her when he was in London before the war. Remember in the Cairnton days how you and I thought Violetta was a terrific flirt and all that? It was all nonsense, I think. We had a story-book or opera conception of a beautiful Italian girl — I know I had — I saw her as a sort of Puccini soprano, a *Traviata*, maybe. It's all rubbish. I don't think Violetta cares a hoot about men.'

'They cared about her, anyway. Remember the Café Firenze, with them all ogling her from the booths along the wall and all the scandalous stories of rich young followers in large racing-cars?'

'I know, but none of it made any impression on Violetta. I don't think even Mario Antonelli meant much to her. I think that was a sort of family political marriage. They were related and he was very wealthy. I think money was more important than most other things to those Italians who came over here at the end of last century and the importance of it is bred into their children. There is one thing, though. It is a pity that Violetta did not have any children before Mario died. She adores children.'

'She is something of a child herself still,' I said, 'or she was that time I saw her in Soho before the war. Yet, at the same time, I remember thinking how wise she was. In many ways, she looked like a pretty, happy, care-free child and yet behind it all there was this air of wisdom, as if she had been born with it and hadn't had to acquire it the hard way, by growing up, as you and I have had to do.'

'I know what you mean,' Kathleen agreed. 'She is wise, and she is also very clever in a business way as all the Cervis are. Mario left her a lot of money but she has got a lot more now. Violetta even understands about stocks and shares!' Kathleen's voice was protesting. 'When I think of that, I find myself standing in awe of her. I can't count a pound of silver, Janet. If it wasn't for Michael Curtis — he is my accompanist, the tall dark man, you know — I'd never have a penny, but Michael manages me as well. But going back to Violetta, she maintains these orphanage children in Shropshire entirely, you know. Ever since Mario died, she has worked for children's charities and since this war started she has worked harder than ever. The children she has up there are children who lost their parents in the bombing of Liverpool and some who were orphans before — her special lot, as she calls them — but she is interested in goodness knows how many orphanages and spends a lot of money on them.'

'The older I get the more I look at people and the queerer they become. On the face of it, you would never have said that Violetta would turn into an earnest lady sitting on the boards of orphanages.'

'The thing is she isn't an earnest lady to look at her on the face of it,' said Kathleen. 'She just looks very much as she always did, pretty and young and gay, but she is far more interested in orphanages than in men.' She put her head on one side. 'And talking of that, why aren't *you* married?'

'Probably nobody ever asked me.'

'Don't give me that! What happened to all those young men you used to roar around London with? Freddie Firmantle, for instance?'

'Oh, Freddie's married. His wife is in Canada. Good lord, Kathleen, Freddie and I can't do anything together except dance. We still meet and dance when we get a chance. Georgina—his wife—has sense. I think I am going to turn into a spirited spinster. I don't seem to be cut out for this marriage thing.'

'Why not?'

'I can't quite get it straight in my mind. I am sort of scared of it. There's so much claptrap all round it, all this guff about romance and being faithful unto death and all that. Since I took part in this war and observed a little of what goes on among people, I feel that disillusion is lying in wait for every bride at the church door and that a lot of cheated wives are sitting at home right now, looking after the children while their husbands are being gallant at the war, only the gallantry isn't the sort that their wives are thinking about so romantically. I'd have to be terribly sure and certain before I got myself involved in marriage.'

'It's difficult to be sure and certain about anything in this life.'

'That is why I see myself as a spirited spinster,' I told her. 'We were brought up to believe in getting married and setting up house and having children but this thing of human relationships is broader than that. I feel that a relationship has to be a live thing, a thing that grows and develops in order to be satisfactory. The marriage-and-children way is the conventional and easiest way of attaining it, provided the two people do keep growing and adjusting themselves as the years go by and the children and the problems come along but so many people don't. I know so many marriages which have just sunk into a static sort of boredom. I think the way we were brought up is wrong in a way. One was given the impression that after the marriage ceremony it was roses, roses all the way and no further effort was required. I have never been able to look straight at the marriage thing and I am frankly frightened of it. My friend Monica will be along here with your accompanist in a moment — she and I are real friends. We have fun and we stimulate one another and in this place we keep each other sane, I think. At this moment, I wouldn't give her up for all the men in the mess, the whole five hundred of them. And anyway, what about you? Have you never thought of marriage?'

'I am too busy singing,' Kathleen said. 'And I am a bit like you. Men don't mean very much to me. No relationships mean very much to me compared with my relationship with singing, I mean. I suppose it is wrong to be the way I am, Janet, but it seems to be the way I am made. I used to think I sang to earn my living but I don't. I sing just because I have to and I can't do anything else.'

*   *   *

When Twice came in for lunch, I gave him Hugh's letter to read and then said: 'Isn't it wonderful about Kathleen?'

'Marvellous!' His eyes glittered with an enthusiasm that I had not seen for a long time. 'I remember thinking what a wonderful woman you were for knowing Monica when she introduced me to Sir Charles Acton at Prestwick Airport, but Kathleen Malone makes you more wonderful still.'

'Silly ass! Because I canalise — if that's the right word — a couple of musicians in your direction is no reason for hanging a halo on me.'

'Oh, yes, it is. It is one more splendid thing you have added unto me.'

'But I haven't. It's accident.'

'The accidents that pivot around us are like our goods and evils. We have to carry them along with us and be responsible for them, taking praise or blame where they are due, so I am praising you for the accident of knowing Kathleen Malone.'

'You are in far too fizzy and clever a mood for me today. Let us descend from these mountains. You observe that Hugh has no love for Mrs. Drew either?'

'I do. I also notice that Hugh doesn't know what Lady H. is doing here in St. Jago any more than you or I do, so that makes us all quits.'

'The trip was probably a whim,' I said. 'When you are as rich as that you can afford to have transatlantic plane-trip whims, I suppose. Oh, well, there have been times when I have been a little bored with Hugh for wishing her on to us, but now that he has tried to wish Kathleen, I forgive him. The last time I saw her was in 1944. I remember telling her that when the war was over and I stopped being an intelligence officer, I was going to turn into a spirited spinster. I meant it too. That was how it looked at the time. Marriage seemed more and more unlikely.'

'You certainly did turn into a spirited spinster,' Twice said. 'When we first met at Slater's Works, I had never seen a female with so much spirit, if that is the word for it,' he added as an afterthought. 'Do you remember that day we had the row about the girl welder?'

I shook my head. 'No. I remember a bit of an up-and-down about cheese —'

'No. This was later than the cheese affair. I sent a chit into the office telling you to give this girl two weeks' money and pay her off. Her name was Bessie something and you —'

'I remember the girl. She married that fitter called

164

Jimmie Lewis. But she wasn't paid off. She left to get married.'

'You bet she wasn't paid off! You sent for me and told me I didn't want to pay off Bessie, what I wanted to do was pay off that lout Jimmie Lewis. You said you would think more of Jimmie Lewis if he would leave off fitting for half an hour and marry Bessie — that he would neither take her nor leave her alone, you said. Calls himself a man, you said, somebody ought to dot him one.'

'Gosh, I remember. And then you said you were in the engineering and not the matrimonial business —'

'And then you picked up that old desk-blotter and hurled it and it wrapped itself round the ears of the machine-shop foreman who happened to come in through the door.' We sat laughing at one another until Twice said gravely: 'I went out to the fitting-shop and stood staring at Jimmie Lewis until I realised that I was embarrassing the chap. I was wondering if he felt about Bessie as I felt about you and if, like me, he had some encumbrance like Dinah that made him feel tied hand and foot. Neither take her nor leave her alone, you had said and I became conscious of behaving in much the same way about you and that you might be aware of it. Calls himself a man — somebody ought to dot him one, you had said and I felt that you had dotted me one which had made me begin to see that I either ought to clear out altogether or tell you the truth about where I stood. It took me a long time to get around to telling you where I stood but that row was a very important milestone on the Dover Road.'

'The first part of the road was very rough going,' I told him. 'I thought I would never get you. And that is another conventional fallacy — that the male does the pursuing. Men sometimes make an initial gesture but they don't pursue after one chokes them off. But women! *Venus toute entière à sa proie attachée* and all that.'

Twice laughed. 'And look where it has landed you.'

'I am entirely satisfied with where I have landed,' I told him.

He had just gone back to the office that afternoon — it was only a little after two o'clock — when Lady Hallinzeil drove in to Guinea Corner and I was a little uncertain about how to greet her as I wondered what sort of account, if any, she had had of my encounter with Mrs. Drew on the day before. Doors are always open in the tropics and I got up from my writing-table when she walked into the room but before I could say anything at all and before she sat down even she said: 'I understand that Maggie was rather snappy with you yesterday. She is a little naughty sometimes.'

It may have been childish but the light indulgent tone of her voice, as if she were speaking of a child guilty of a lapse in manners, annoyed me. 'She was considerably more than snappy,' I said, moving across the room to sit opposite to her, 'she was extremely offensive and if I did not feel that her sanity may be in question I should be a great deal more annoyed than I am already.'

'Her sanity?' She gave a light laugh. 'Oh, don't be silly, Mrs. Alexander. Maggie may be a little bad-tempered now and again — '

Her smug air irritated me and I was suddenly aware that the temper that used to hurl blotting-pads across the office at Slater's Works was not entirely dead.

'Lady Hallinzeil,' I broke in, 'I have lived long enough to recognise a fit of temper when I see one. You are talking utter nonsense!'

'Really!' she said in a protesting voice, as if nobody had ever spoken to her in such a way before — and probably nobody ever had, when I thought of it — and as if she could barely believe that anybody was speaking to her in such a way now.

'Yes. Really,' I said. 'Lady Hallinzeil, there is something seriously the matter with that woman. I think you should have her medically examined. A sudden transition from England to the tropics doesn't suit everybody, you know, especially in middle age, as Mrs. Drew is.'

She looked at me sadly as if pained that I would not allow her to gloss over Maggie's rudeness, but when I looked back at her with something of the determination I felt, her fairish skin flushed with embarrassment.

'These things are so difficult,' she said peevishly, as if she were being forced to discuss something that was revolting to her, as if she resented this incursion of stern reality and felt it to be unjust. I had never seen her display so much feeling about anything before. 'That is just the trouble,' she added in a near-whisper. 'It *is* her age.'

'There is more to it than that, Lady Hallinzeil,' I said.

The night before I had agreed with Twice that it was as well to leave her in blissful ignorance of Mrs. Drew's failing but now I was less sure of this. I think I resented her attitude that everything was in order if she made a pretty apology and as long as Mrs. Drew did not offend herself in any way. And now, also, I had the impression that her ignorance was partly wilful and most of us have a dislike of ignorance, however blissful, and wish to destroy it.

'She can become a real embarrassment to you if she goes on as she is doing,' I said. 'She was more than snappy to me yesterday. It was a most offensive attack that she made. In my case, it doesn't matter, but some of your friends might think differently. To be honest, when I first saw her I thought she was a rather nasty woman but I think now that that was a harsh judgment for I think she is ill. Tell me, does she drink?'

'Drink?'

'Yes!' I felt impatient as her pretty unintelligent eyes gazed questioningly at me as if I had lapsed into a foreign language that she did not understand. 'Whisky, rum, gin!'

'Of course not! Oh, well, sometimes she asks me for a little brandy when she has a headache, but that is purely as a medicine. What on earth made you ask such a question?'

'It struck me yesterday that she might be under the influence of alcohol.'

She looked at me, as I told Twice later, as if I were a page in a pornographic book that had suddenly been presented to her sight.

'Mrs. Alexander!' she said.

I almost lost my temper completely. 'Well, if it isn't alcohol, she is more than half crazy. She should be seen by a doctor.'

'She doesn't like *you* — that's all it is,' Lady Hallinzeil said.

Now, I maintain that this is something that nobody likes to be told about themselves. It is certainly the sort of thing that I would never say to anyone, but Lady Hallinzeil said it to me as if it were the most normal of conversational remarks.

'I don't particularly like her, either, but I wouldn't behave as she did yesterday!' I snapped.

We were suddenly on a different plane. The light dismissive air had left her.

'If you knew about her life, you wouldn't be so harsh. She has had a very hard sad life.'

Her voice had changed. Some guard between her mind and mine had dropped. She was looking away from me, looking out of the window and her face was less vacant than its norm. It had a faraway look, as if she were thinking back into the long past, a past in which she had wandered, uncertain of her way but, although I felt something pathetic in her, I was still impatient with this blind

168

stupidity of hers that was becoming more and more obvious and which had in it a mulish obstinacy, as stupidity often has.

'I have very little time for people who behave like beasts and then blame it on their sad lives,' I said with angry impatience.

She turned her head and looked at me. 'There has been very little sadness in your life,' she told me. This was said with a sweeping certainty despite the fact that she knew nothing about my life and it further irritated me.

'I certainly haven't found in it any reason to behave to a stranger as Mrs. Drew behaved to me yesterday.'

'You don't understand,' she said.

'No. I don't. If I were told about this sad life I might understand better. Indeed, I ought to know about it because Mrs. Drew seems to hold me in some way responsible.'

'You don't understand,' she repeated and then, as if she were making a great effort to speak of something that was repellent to her, she went on: 'I suppose I had better tell you. Maggie's husband committed suicide two years after they were married — at least it was never proved but Maggie believes it was suicide. He was chauffeur to my father-in-law and he seemed quite deliberately to drive the car into the canal one evening on the way home from Glasgow. There were witnesses. He simply seemed to swerve off the road at high speed, hit a tree and crash through the fence into the canal. It was an unauthorised journey. He should not have been out with the car at all.' She paused and I did not speak but sat waiting. 'It was then that Maggie came to me as nursery-maid. Then, later on, she told me that Drew had never been faithful to her. Maggie found it out. He was always taking one of the cars in the evenings and going off to see this woman in Glasgow.'

She paused again, and again I was silent for I could not think of anything to say. If my sympathy in the case lay anywhere, it lay with the young man, Drew, for it did not seem to me that life with Maggie could have been a bed of roses, even when she was a young bride.

'Maggie has never forgiven that woman,' Lady Hallinzeil went on, looking up at me, 'and I don't blame her.'

'I don't agree with you,' I said bluntly. 'I understand about the tragedy, the shock and the bitterness in Mrs. Drew's mind, but I think it very unhealthy to have nourished and cherished a hatred for this other woman for all these years. After all, in a case of that kind, three people are involved — Mrs. Drew, her husband, and the other woman, as she is always called. As a rule, any blame there is is fairly evenly distributed between all three. Lady Hallinzeil, I still maintain that Mrs. Drew is not entirely sane. A hatred like that carried down over that length of time is enough to make anyone unbalanced. Don't you see that? I honestly think you should have her examined. She can't be good company for you, apart from anything else.'

'Sir Hugh Reid has been talking — writing to you!' she accused me and now she clenched her plump little hands in her lap. 'He doesn't understand! None of you understand. Even my own children don't understand. They can't. They don't know!'

'Know what?'

'About Maggie and me.' Her voice had become very intense but with a great effort she controlled herself. 'Maggie is the best friend I have,' she continued more calmly. 'Maggie is the only real friend I've got. Maggie is kind to me,' she ended.

She had a curious ability for implication in the things that she said, an ability that I had not identified before but now I saw that it had always been there although its nature had eluded me. When I had complained to Twice of the over-perfection of the family relationships of which she had told me, it was really of this elusive quality of implication that I was complaining, for everything she had told me of her family, I now discovered, carried behind it, like a trail of vapour, the implication: 'There was never a family as perfect as mine — never a mother like me.' And now, when she spoke to me the words: 'Maggie is kind to me', there was at once in the air between us a faint plaintive echo of the implied but unspoken words: 'But *you* are not kind to me.' 'Maggie is a little like me in some ways,' she said with a light laugh and paused, clearly indicating that she expected from me a disclaimer that there could possibly be anything in common between a member of Maggie's class and herself, but I did not respond and, with a slightly pained look at me, she went on:

'She is quite a sensitive person. I am very sensitive myself — hypersensitive, you might say — and I know how she feels about my coming here to visit you. She doesn't like it, although I have explained to her that you are a friend of Sir Hugh Reid.'

I did not know what to make of this. I was not sure if the fact that I was a friend of Hugh's made me of the social status to be visited or if Lady Hallinzeil were visiting me as a favour to Hugh, but before I could work it out, she added: 'Of course, Maggie doesn't like Sir Hugh Reid either. She says he was the illegitimate son of a dairymaid by a ploughman but I shouldn't think that is true. Sometimes Maggie exaggerates things.'

'I can assure you that it is perfectly true,' I said.

'Oh,' she said as if, deliberately, I had hurt her feelings very deeply.

I had the impression that she would have preferred that I had not confirmed the truth of Maggie's report of Hugh's parentage because it would have been more comfortable for herself to believe it false, and it seemed, also, that she thought me unreasonable in that, one moment, I accused Maggie of a shocking thing like drunkenness and, the next moment, I 'took sides' with Maggie against herself by saying that Maggie had spoken the truth about Hugh. Silently, she seemed to be asking me to make up my mind on whose side I was, whether I was with Maggie or against her so that she herself would know where she stood and I had a sudden awareness of this woman's lost isolation. She had no real attachment to Maggie and less attachment to me. We were mere figures on the periphery of her life and her person, furnishings of her life and now Maggie and I together had changed Sir Hugh Reid who, as the eminent doctor, had been a rather distinguished piece of furniture, into the illegitimate son of a dairymaid, a piece whose place was not in the drawing-room but in the housemaid's attic. She looked at me for a moment as if, literally, she did not know what to think before a little gleam, strangely spiteful, came into her eyes and she said: 'Maggie says *your* father was a farm worker at Cairn-shaws,' and the air was thick with the implication: '*That* will teach you to take her side about Sir Hugh Reid. If it is true you would prefer that nobody knew it.'

'Yes,' I said. 'He was. He worked at Cairnshaws for six years.'

She looked shocked and startled, as if I had been utterly shameless and then she looked in a wandered way round the elegant Guinea Corner drawing-room, back to me and round the room again, as if she found it impossible to understand how I had travelled from the A of Cairnshaws to the B of this house. I had a desperate flippant urge to say: 'I married frightfully above me, you see' because I felt that this would bring her the relief of complete understanding after her own fashion but I did not say it.

'Life is very strange,' she said next, but, in honesty, I do not think she was referring to my status as hostess of Guinea Corner for her thoughts were obviously turned inwards on herself again.

'Certainly Mrs. Drew makes it more than strange. She can make it quite macabre,' I said with a spiteful return to the subject that I knew she would prefer to drop.

'She is all right with people she likes,' Lady Hallinzeil replied and again it seemed to me that there was the self-satisfied implication: 'She likes me, but she doesn't like you.' This infuriated me and my voice was fairly short and clipped as I said:

'Why Mrs. Drew should dislike me so much, I have no idea. I don't even know who she is.'

'But *she* knows *you*!' and this implied that Mrs. Drew was much much cleverer than I was, and that her cleverness derived from the fact that she was in the service of Lady Hallinzeil.

'I wouldn't say she knows me very well. Nobody in Cairnton knew me very well.'

'*Maggie* knows you and who your friends were and everything. That's why she hates you so much. You were a friend of this awful woman that broke up her marriage.'

The first person to flash into my mind was Annie Black, the Cairnton girl who had taken to prostitution but as far as I knew Annie had broken no marriages and she had never been a friend of mine in the sense that Lady Hallinzeil meant—indeed, she had been rather the reverse.

'What was this woman's name?' I asked.

'Cervi. Violetta Cervi. Her father was the ice-cream man in Cairnton. They had that café in the High Street.'

'Violetta?' I said, trying to gather my scattered wits.

'She was a singer in a dance hall in Glasgow. That's where Drew used to go when he took the car at nights.'

173

'Yes,' I said. 'Yes. Violetta sang with Malone's Minstrels at the Blue Lagoon.'

I was remembering a misty autumn evening when Kathleen and I had walked towards my home from Number Two Row, when Kathleen told me of the men who clustered round Violetta at the Blue Lagoon — the 'toff' in the racing car, the boy Andrews from the Station Road, the fellow from Aucheninch. It was possible that Drew had been one of the many, I supposed.

'How in the world did you come to be friendly with a creature of that sort?' I heard the voice of Lady Hallinzeil ask.

I have never been able to formulate in a neat list the things that make me really angry, the things that cause the simmering fuse to reach the charge with a sharp hiss. Perhaps if I could achieve this I would be more on my guard and lose my temper less often. Today, however, it seemed to me that Lady Hallinzeil had been piling Ossa on Pelion ever since she arrived and in this last question she had cast a slur on someone who, although I had not seen her for fifteen years, had remained in that special compartment of my mind that contains my friends and which seems to be surrounded by an electric fence called 'loyalty' whose wires carry a very high-tension charge. This charge now flared up in a hot white light.

'A creature of *what* sort?' I snapped. 'You seem to have made up your stupid mind that Violetta somehow or another forced this young man Drew to drive into the canal! You seem to think that this Mrs. Drew speaks some sort of gospel! I wasn't in Cairnton at the time and had lost touch with Violetta by then but I'm willing to bet any money to a few small potatoes that she was never in the least interested in this fellow Drew! But I am not surprised if Drew preferred Violetta to that old shrew down at the Peak there for I question very much if she was ever anything other than a shrew. Who was she anyway before she married? I don't know her from a few hundred other of these Cairnton women.'

Lady Hallinzeil looked scared and answered me in a near-mesmerised voice. 'Her name was Bailey — Margaret Bailey. She lived at Aucheninch.'

'Good heavens! I've never spoken to her since I was about ten. Oh, yes, I have. I met her in a Glasgow teashop when I was at university. I might have known that was who she was — Margaret Bailey always *was* an ugly mean-souled bitch!'

'Mrs. Alexander!' she protested, horrified and then, her voice shaking as if she were going to cry, she went on: 'You seem to me to be very hard.'

'I am sorry,' I said. 'I do not mean to be hard. I am really sorry, Lady Hallinzeil. I should not have lost my temper like that but, you see, Violetta Cervi was a friend of mine.' I was thoroughly ashamed of myself now, as I always am after these outbursts. 'Excuse me a moment. I am going to ask Clorinda to bring us some tea.'

I went to the kitchen and then came back, loitering, trying to collect myself, to struggle free of the memories of Cairnton, of Margaret Bailey in the Glasgow teashop and of Violetta in the Café Firenze that were cluttering my mind. I came back into the drawing-room and sat down.

'I am sorry, Lady Hallinzeil. I should not have lost my temper like that and I do not mean to be hard,' I repeated, 'but I have never been able to take a single line of judgment in these eternal-triangle stories. As I said, there are three points where the blame, if blame comes into it, can lie. Surely you can see that life with Margaret Bailey — Mrs. Drew — might not be all that a romantically minded young man might want?'

'I am sure Maggie always did her duty in every way,' she said firmly.

I stared at her for an amazed moment, had an urge to burst into laughter but choked it back. 'But don't you think that duty can be deadly dull, especially if carried out flawlessly?' I asked.

'I don't understand you! You are married yourself and you have one of the happiest homes and one of the best husbands I have ever known —'

'And I can assure you that none of it is based on duty,' I said, as Clorinda put the tea tray between us. 'For pity's sake, Lady Hallinzeil, *you* are married too! You know one doesn't do one's *duty*, as if one were a policewoman or a lavatory attendant!'

She stared at me for a moment. 'I have always tried to do my best,' she said and, to my astonishment, she began to cry, making little hiccupping noises like a small child. 'If only you *knew*!' she sobbed.

While she sat there sobbing, mopping her eyes and looking down at the handkerchief between her hands until her eyes filled with tears again, I felt bitterly ashamed of myself. I felt that I had been insensitive, so engrossed with my own annoyance and indignation about Mrs. Drew and so heated in my defence of my friend Violetta that I had not seen the strain building up in this woman facing me, the strain that had now broken down into this flood of tears. I poured out a cup of tea, went round to put it on the small table beside her chair and then I laid my hand on her shoulder.

'Just sit quietly and have some tea,' I said. 'I am sorry I was harsh about Mrs. — Maggie.'

She dried her eyes, took a sip from her cup, but she did not look at me. 'Maggie and I have a lot in common,' she said. 'You see, in my life too there is another woman, just like it was with Maggie. She has *always* been there, all these years, but I didn't know about her until quite lately. That is why I am here. When I came to know about it, I didn't know what to do. I just got Maggie and came away as soon as Robert went to Australia. *She* is with him. At least I suppose she is.'

'Oh.'

'They are awfully clever about it. There has never been any scandal or anything but she is always there, in the background, where he can be with her when he is not at meetings and things. It has always been like that. When we were married at first and he had to go away on business, I never wanted to go. I don't like to travel but I never thought of anything like this. Then, when I was told about it, it was a terrible shock.'

'Who told you about it?' I asked when she paused.

'Maggie. Last September Maggie found out about it and told me. She had been suspicious of Robert for a long long time.'

'Maggie?' I felt utterly exasperated. 'Lady Hallinzeil, don't you realise that this is probably a fabrication? A horrible fabrication?'

'Oh, no, it isn't,' she said very quietly in contrast to my own vehemence. 'No. It is perfectly true. I asked Robert about it, you see, straight away as soon as Maggie told me and he admitted everything. He was perfectly frank and honest with me. It is all very strange and I don't understand it in the least. I asked him if he wanted a divorce but he said no. In fact, he was very angry at the idea. He made me send Maggie away back to Aucheninch but after he went abroad, I got her to come back to come out here with me. I just don't understand about Robert and this woman,' she repeated, beating her clenched plump hands in her lap. 'Just before he went on this Australian tour, we spoke about it again. He tried to explain it to me — how this thing with this woman is quite apart from me and the children and everything but I don't want anything except Robert and our family and I don't understand why *he* should.'

'It is very difficult to understand,' I said.

'I thought you might be able to explain it to me a little. I have often thought of telling you because you are so clever. Maggie told me about you winning that scholarship and everything. I am not clever. I never went to school or a university. I just had a governess and then I got married. I suppose I am not clever enough for Robert, although he says it isn't like that at all.'

This infantile talk of cleverness was embarrassing and pathetic at the same time. 'I am sure your husband is telling you the truth. Cleverness is nothing to do with it,' I said.

I found her absurdly childish as she grappled so inexpertly with an adult situation, but the childishness sat oddly on her physical aspect of middle-aged maturity.

'And I am far from clever,' I went on. 'Scholarships are not much good for helping one to solve the sort of problems that life throws up. There is one thing I am absolutely certain of, though and that is that Maggie did you the greatest disservice she could when she told you about this. Your husband is still the same man you always have known. You were happy until you learned to see a part of him through the eyes of Maggie Drew, the eyes that spied out this other woman.'

'Yes, I was happy, but it was a fool's paradise, as Maggie says.'

'It was still a paradise,' I argued, 'and paradise, even if it is a slightly foolish one is not to be lightly thrown away.'

But she was not listening to what I said. She was caught within her own thoughts like a squirrel in a cage and could pursue only the circuit of thought that she had been pursuing ever since she had come to this knowledge about her husband. The only difference was that, now, she was thinking aloud to me instead of pursuing the circuit in her own mind, but nothing I could say, I felt, would alter the course of her thinking. I even felt a tremor of sympathy for the husband who had been faced with the task of trying to explain himself and his complex situation to her.

'It helps to talk about this,' she said next. 'You see, until now, only Maggie has known about it and she does go on and on so terribly sometimes. She hates men, you see, even Robert and she gets angry because I simply can't hate Robert. Or sometimes I think I do but I love him, you see. Oh dear, I am being silly.'

'No. You are not. You are not being in the least silly, Lady Hallinzeil,' I said, and I meant it.

'Would you call me Helen? It would feel more natural, talking about all this, if you called me Helen and I called you Janet, like real friends and Sir Hugh said you were one of the best friends he had and we both know Cairnton and everything.' She paused for a moment and then said: 'I sometimes wish I had never found out about Robert and this woman at all.'

She paused again as if she expected me to say something and I could think of nothing to say. Just as she wished that she 'had never found out', I wished that she had never told me for, although she had decided that we were 'friends' now that we were on Christian-name terms, I felt that I had seldom met anyone with whom I had less common ground. She did not seem to see me as a person in my own right which, to an ego like mine, is an insult and there was this constant implication that she knew me at all only because of my links with Hugh Reid and Cairnton, both of which seemed to her to be links of doubtful validity, for Hugh and I belonged to what she thought of as the 'wrong' part of Cairnton. Then, although I do not know why this should be, I find it irritating to feel sorry for someone whom I do not basically like. It seems to me to be a paradoxical position to feel a sort of sympathy for someone and yet, at the same time, to feel active dislike for that person, and I was in this state with this woman now.

'She must be a quite dreadful person when she is willing to live like that,' she said with a sniff.

As there had been all along, since she had begun to confide in me, there was the expectation that I would concur in what she said but I could not do it. I was aware of living 'like that' myself.

'Like what?' I asked.

'In the way she does,' she said snappishly.

'But,' I said, 'that is exactly what we don't know. We don't know how she lives. She may be utterly devoted to Robert, as devoted as you are, you know.'

'But she's not *married* to him!' she protested.

'She could be very devoted in spite of that.'

'I don't see how she could. *I* couldn't be, living in sin like that.'

I busied myself with the pouring of more tea and the lighting of a cigarette before I said: 'But she may be a different sort of woman from you.'

'She certainly is!' she said angrily.

I was now growing very bored, very conscious that I was on the other side of a great gulf from this woman, a gulf across which my ideas could not carry to her and I began to wish that she would simply go away. Indeed, my sympathy was veering more and more towards the erring Robert.

'Adultery is a sin,' she said, 'and that woman is an adulteress.'

I thought of pointing out that adultery is one of these interesting sins that require two people for its accomplishment and that Robert was a sinner too, but I knew that this would not please her and so I said nothing.

'Oh, why should this have happened to *me*?' she cried suddenly with a fresh burst of tears.

Here, I thought, is this question that we all ask. I have

asked it myself about this illness that has overtaken Twice and the only answer is that things happen to everybody, but I felt that it would be of no help to point out to Helen Hallinzeil that she was not the first and would not be the last woman to have an unfaithful husband.

While she sat sobbing and talking incoherently of her own virtues as a faithful wife and devoted mother, I even thought of telling her point-blank that this happy home at Guinea Corner which she envied so much was founded not on a marriage certificate, as she believed, but upon what she called 'sin', but I was restrained by the thought that, instead of making her think differently, it would merely throw her into further confusion. In the words of Reachfar, 'she was too old a tree to be twisted now'; she was too rigidly set in her conventional mould to break through to a different mode of thought. It was ironic that I, to whom convention meant so little, should have been chosen by this woman, of all women, as her confidante.

I had not realised until this time the degree to which Reachfar had its own code of morality and its own code of laws. Its morality had been based on family loyalties and the ties of feeling and, although my grandmother paid loud-voiced lip-service to the established legal and conventional code from day to day, this lip-service died first to a whisper and then to silence when she was confronted by a situation in which the legal or conventional code led to human suffering. And then, very shortly, she turned into a loud-voiced, strong-willed partisan of the transgressor against the code, a partisan who could, in the end, rally the whole district to her banner and to the aid of the transgressor. I could have been no more than seven years old when I had heard her burn up with her wrath the malicious slaverings of a local gossip who was discussing the imminent birth of an illegitimate baby to a girl called Mary Junor.

'You hold your bad tongue, Kirsty Graham,' my grand-mother had said. 'Bad girls don't *have* bairns!'

Now, while Helen Hallinzeil wept and repeated over and over her own virtues and the injustice with which life had dealt with her, I found myself escaping into a memory of how Jock Skinner, the rascal of the Reachfar district, had stolen some cutlery and odds and ends from the army camp before disappearing from the locality with his wife and family. My grandmother, like the rest of the district, had been scandalised by the theft but when Jock's wife, Bella, was traced by the police and had denied all know-ledge of Jock, claiming instead to be the widow of a Robert Lawrie, my grandmother began to laugh.

'Aye,' she said, 'Jock and Bella were well met and real fond of one another in their own way. Bella would never *tell* on him and you have to like her for it, for goodness knows it is not many women that would have been doing with Jock's capers.'

When convention or the legal code and feeling came to loggerheads, my grandmother and, with her, the rest of my family, came down heavily on the side of feeling.

Also, from my earliest days, I had been accustomed to hear my chief mentors, Tom and George, discourse at length upon the absurdity of 'the law' by which they meant the legal code. The law, according to George and Tom, was to be obeyed only 'if reasonable', and they did not consider it to be reasonable, for instance, that the law should forbid them to fish for trout at the estuary of the Reachfar Burn on the shore of the Firth. When I had told my family of Twice's and my intention to make our life together, Tom had stated categorically his view of the law with regard to marriage, a view in which George had con-curred.

'For myself,' Tom had said, 'I have never seen a great deal o' use in folk having these fancy weddings. If two people is going to come together, they will come together whateffer, whether a minister will be speaking words over them or not. And if they are going to part from one another, they will be doing that too. Of course, there is the law and a person would always rather abide by the law when reasonable. But in this case, where this woman in Belfast is apparently not reasonable, that makes the law not reasonable either.'

I was thirty-seven years old when this categoric statement was made but it had been implicit in the attitudes of Tom, George and all my Reachfar family for as long as I could remember and my mind had been conditioned as firmly by Reachfar as Helen Hallinzeil's had been by the attitudes and standards of the people who lived in those Victorian baronial houses on the hills above Cairnton. And so, while she sat opposite to me, weeping and wringing her hands while I thought of these things, the gulf between us seemed to be as wide as the difference between our two lives and as deep as the chasm of years that lay behind us.

'I ought to divorce Robert,' she was saying and I began to pay attention to her again. 'As Maggie says, a person has got to have some pride.'

An old woman, known to Twice and me as Cousin Emmie, once pointed out to me that it is very difficult to be sure of one's own motives and, as I rushed into speech to give my view now, I was not certain whether the view I was giving was my true one or whether I were merely allowing myself to be provoked into giving an opposite view to the horrible Maggie.

'Maggie rubbish!' I said. 'What is the use of depriving yourself of a man you are fond of and creating an upheaval in your family in order to be left with nothing but a little false pride?'

She began to cry again. 'I can't imagine living without

Robert. That is why I came out here, away from home and the family and everything—to see if I could do it. But I don't think I can.'

I felt truly sympathetic towards her now. 'I can't see why you should think of divorce at all,' I said, 'especially when your husband doesn't want it.'

'Maggie says—'

'Oh, damn Maggie! Listen, you must be very important to your husband or he would have gone right away with this woman long ago.'

She raised her pathetic eyes to my face. 'Oh, do you think so?'

'One must think so. You must be very dear to your husband in some particular way.'

'But why must he go to this other person? Other people's husbands don't behave like that.'

'How do you know?' I countered. 'I don't think your situation is unique. There have been plenty of examples of it in history.'

'Oh, history,' she said. 'I meant among people one knows.'

'Well, there was the minister at Cairnton,' I said. 'He had not just one woman—'

'Robert is not a person like that!' she broke in angrily, looking at me like a rather damp angry kitten. 'Maggie says Robert is wicked and horrible, but he isn't.'

'I am sure he isn't,' I said.

Her little outburst of anger in defence of her Robert had pulled her together and as Twice would soon be home and I did not want him to be confronted with a weeping woman, I set upon the topic of Maggie viciously as the best form of distraction.

'Your husband isn't wicked or horrible, but that Maggie is!' I said fiercely, 'and although you don't want to believe it, there is absolutely no doubt that she drinks. She is a

184

habitual boozer and Mr. de Marnay at the hotel can tell you how much gin she is getting through in a week if you don't believe me.'

She stared at me, her pretty faded face looking as if it might fall apart with shocked dismay.

'What? Janet! Oh, Janet, what am I going to do?' she said and broke down into a fresh flood of tears.

'You don't have to do anything,' I said with a new burst of impatience born of her tears for, in the end, we are all selfish and that Twice should come home to a calm household was more important to me than all this woman's troubles. 'Now, do stop crying, Helen. That won't do any good. Maggie probably isn't a bad case of alcoholism as yet or you would have noticed it before now.' But would she? 'She probably got at the bottle yesterday when you were out and then I arrived and she hates me anyway, as you said. Helen, do try to stop crying.'

'But you don't understand,' she wailed. 'Robert is going to be so angry when he gets here and finds Maggie with me. You know I believe he *knew* about this back in September when he sacked her. Robert is so clever about knowing things. He is going to be so angry.'

While she cried a little more, I found myself sympathising with Robert Hallinzeil in his predicted anger on his arrival at the Peak Hotel. Life with Helen, with this combination of hers of the stupid, the obstinate, and the pathetic, I found myself thinking in banal terms, could not be a bed of roses and as this final cliché formed in my mind, I said: 'I didn't know your husband was coming here.'

'Yes. About the middle of April, when he finishes his tour of the United States. When I wrote telling him I had come here for a holiday, he suggested at once that he would meet me here and we would travel home together.'

She had stopped crying now and in her voice there was

that implication, of satisfaction this time, that she had an attentive husband who was calling for her at the end of her little holiday.

'It really is disgusting of Maggie!' she said next with a burst of indignation. 'How dare she behave like that down there with all the hotel people knowing about it and everything? What will they think? And Robert is going to be simply furious.'

There was now, I noticed, nothing about Maggie's hard sad life. It was not some unimportant visitor, such as myself, whom Maggie's naughtiness was now affecting but Helen Hallinzeil. As I said, we are all primarily selfish.

'Stick her on the first plane for home,' I said.

She took thought for a moment and then: 'No. It wouldn't be any use. She would make a scene. I would never get her to go by herself and Robert would find out she had been with me anyhow. No. She can just stay — she is very useful anyhow — and take what she gets when Robert arrives. She deserves it, drinking like that. It's disgusting. Robert said when he sacked her that she isn't a fit companion for me and he was quite right.'

She had now quite got over her fit of tears and sat on, talking happily about how she was looking forward to her husband's arrival and to going home to London to her family. I found it strange to listen to her. It was now as if Robert's unfaithfulness did not exist, as if her tears of the last hour had never been wept and as she prattled on in her light contented voice of the new dresses she was getting anent Robert's arrival and of the presents she was buying to take home to her children and grandchildren, I found it difficult to believe that she had ever wept or that Maggie had ever looked at me through a sheet of flame.

She went away, after all, before Twice came home and when he arrived I was still thinking about her, so that when he said, as usual: 'What sort of afternoon?' I said:

'Lady H. has been here. A least, I *think* she has been here. Sometimes I wonder if she really exists at all.'

'For Pete's sake! She certainly exists if only for the reason that no hallucination could be quite as boring. What's come over you?'

'She is not as boring as you might think. At least, the things that go on around her aren't.'

'What has Mrs. Drew done now? Hit Sashie over the head with a gin bottle?'

'No. It's Lord H. this time. Wait till I get a fresh pot of tea in and I'll make your eyes pop out.'

'What a drama!' he said when I had finished my tale. 'Yet one can't be too surprised. It is almost as if one had expected something like this. She is really an awfully uninteresting sort of woman. And Hallinzeil is obviously rather a brilliant type and these types don't make perfect husbands as a rule—not her sort of perfect anyway. I wonder why he ever married her? Her dullness is no new thing—it has been with her always, I should say. Money, do you suppose?'

'I suppose so. I suppose he married her because she was the right sort of person to marry. She was the Lawson heiress of Torrencraig—that came out in the course of the afternoon. I suppose it was a coal and steel alliance—the Lawsons were coal—only she didn't recognise it for that until last September or so. Actually, I don't think she recognises it as that yet—it was all so well wrapped up in bridal veils and the Voice that breathed o'er Eden. Lord, how she irritates me with her smugness and her self-righteousness and that phoney cocoon that she lives inside. She brings out the very devil in me. I behaved like a perfect heel this afternoon.'

Twice frowned sharply. 'In what way?'

'I told her about Mrs. Drew and the booze and I wish now that I hadn't. I thought at the time that I was telling

her about it to take her mind off Robert and his sins and
stop her crying before you came home but my motives
were more complex than that. I told her partly to make
her sit up and see things as they really are for once and — '
feeling ashamed, I spoke in a low voice ' — I am not sure
but that part of my reason for telling her was to pay off an
old score against Margaret Bailey.'

'Margaret Bailey?' Twice looked puzzled and no
wonder.

'Yes. I forgot to mention that. Mrs. Drew is that
Margaret Bailey I told you about that taught me in the
Sunday School.'

'Good grief!' said Twice. 'It's those texts. No wonder she
is drinking herself dotty.'

I felt as if the greyness of the room off the church hall
were closing round me in all its bitter desolation of that
Sunday long ago.

'I wish I knew why any of us does things but I am sorry
now that I told Lady H. about Maggie's drinking. It didn't
make her see anything more clearly. It only made her
more smug and virtuous than ever and start looking forward to how Robert would tick poor old Maggie off when
he arrived. I could have hit her.' I thought for a moment.
'I have more sympathy for Maggie now than I have for
Lady H.' Twice merely laughed at me. 'I mean it!' I said.
'After all, poor old Maggie has had a hard time of it.
Mind you, I don't believe it was Violetta that made her
husband drive into the canal — that's a lot of nonsense.
Maggie herself is enough to make anybody drive into a
canal, but the way she is is not entirely her fault. Anyway,
her husband did die and it is all so dreary — none of the
texts that she had been trained to believe in coming true
or anything.'

'Lady H.'s texts haven't come true either, if you think of
it,' Twice said.

188

'What texts?' I asked, for my mind was fixed on my own sense of guilt about Maggie.

'I imagine that Thou shalt not commit adultery was one of them.'

'Not half!' I agreed, and after a moment I added: 'She said an extraordinary thing. She said she couldn't love Robert if she weren't married to him. Could anybody who had ever felt anything for anybody say a thing like that?'

'I suppose that it is possible,' Twice said, 'for feeling to be inhibited to the degree where it is active only within the limits of the convention, like birds that have been bred out of generations of caged birds never thinking about flying, you know.' He smiled a little and then echoed the thought that had occurred to myself that afternoon. 'It is ironic that Lady H. should have chosen *you* to confide in about this woman who lives in sin with his lordship.'

I giggled. 'I know. And if you are thinking that her strictures about sin worried me in any way, you could not be more wrong. Indeed, I felt quite the reverse of worried. I felt in an uppitty way that, even although I have no marriage certificate or children or grandchildren to bolster me up, *you* do not need another woman in the background to make life with me bearable. I take it you *have* no other woman in the background?' I asked.

'Yes, seven,' said Twice.

'Just fancy,' I said and continued: 'Actually, the whole conversation between Lady H. and me was absurd. We don't even speak the same language in these matters. It was like when we talked about Cairnton — I knowing the sights and smells of its back alleys and she having seen it only as if from the moon. It isn't a question of one of us being right and the other wrong, it is that we operate by two different sets of values which have been imposed on us by our backgrounds. I see her as a victim of the code that applied in those Victorian chateaux above Cairnton while

I, I suppose, am a victim of what applied at Reachfar. But I don't feel like a victim. I feel that I have been lucky, lucky enough not to fall for all that roses and bridesmaids nonsense. Do you realise I might have married that awful Victor Halloran when I was nineteen? I would have been in Hallinzeil House loony bin by now only Robert made them change its name to Cairnton North.'

'No, you wouldn't,' Twice said. 'You would have run away and have become the mistress of someone rich like Hallinzeil.'

'I doubt it. Mistresses like that have to have what Clorinda calls glammah. I love how she says it — she makes it sound so sticky.'

'This one of Hallinzeil's can't have much of what Clorinda means by glammah by now,' Twice pointed out.

'Actually, she is probably the exact opposite of Lady H. She is probably a large, vulgar, sonsie good-hearted soul, full of common sense and good red blood.' But I felt again the nag of guilt and added: 'I do wish I hadn't let fly about Margaret Bailey — Maggie Drew.' I sighed. 'Sometimes I think it would be better if one had no memory, if everything that happened just disappeared into a black limbo.'

'I'd hate to dispense with *your* memory,' Twice said. 'Life would be much less entertaining. And I shouldn't worry too much about giving away the fact that the woman drinks. If you drink, the time comes when it can't be hidden under a bushel. The Hallinzeils would have found out anyway. As Lady H. said, probably Lord H. knows already. I don't think you have done much harm, Flash.' He grinned at me. 'You have the strangest conscience I know. No worry about what Lady H. calls a life of sin but masses of it about giving the old Drew away.'

'My life of sin is my own but old Maggie is somebody else. And there is this cheap feeling of having done something out of spite. It makes me feel small and stupid and as if I didn't know my own motives, like Lady H.'

'You think she doesn't know her own motives?'

'Oh, lord, no! I don't think she has a clue. I don't think she is aware of having any motives for anything she does. She makes me think of one of these primitive amoebic organisms waving a few blind tentacles about at the bottom of a tank. She was conditioned to get married, love husband, have children, love children, have grand-children, love grandchildren and she has done it all, she thinks, in the proper way and sits back waiting for her reward for duty well done, but the trouble is that she hasn't *done* any of it. It has all just happened to her — the pattern she was bred to expect has carried through and she has been a passive part of it. She hasn't lived — she has let life happen to her and if it wasn't for Maggie telling her about Robert's little nonsense, she would have been per-fectly content with her pattern. She would never have seen a flaw in it any more than one of these amoeba things would see a shark coming along to swallow it up. Gosh, I would rather have Maggie Drew! Maggie at least does something. She takes a grip on life and gives it a bit of a shake and gives Helen H's self-satisfaction a good shake at the same time.'

'I see your point. I must say I would like to be an in-visible audience down there when his lordship arrives,' Twice said, 'He seems to be quite a big shot. I had never heard of him before but you know how it is when a name gets into your life — what you call a palter-ghost. He is mentioned again in the *Engineer* this week. He is high finance and backroom politics and all that. When does he arrive?'

'He does other things in back rooms as well as politics. He is supposed to arrive some time in April.'

'I wonder if we'll get a chance to meet him?'

'Would you like to?'

'I must say I would be interested. Wouldn't you?'

'Only in a morbid way,' I said. 'But if you would like it, darling, we damn well will meet him. After all, I've practically stopped him getting divorced. I haven't really. She never had the slightest intention of divorcing him. The role of the wronged martyr suits her down to the ground and she loves herself in it. I tell you what we'll do! Let's have a dinner party, Twice, to celebrate our birthdays and the glad re-union of the Hallinzeils and everything.'

'Could we, Flash?' He smiled. 'It is a long time since we had a party.'

'I don't see why we shouldn't. It will be all very quiet and sedate and correct with the Hallinzeils there and Doctor Lindsay said a little quiet society would be a good thing.'

'Yes, let's do it. It seems the ideal beginning after our long abstinence. The bloke is an international figure, after all. Gosh, I'm looking forward to it already. He suddenly began to laugh.

'What is so funny?'

'It suddenly occurred to me that since I became a crock and we dropped out of the success swim down to the bottom of the pool, the first thing we see is the rather slimy under-belly of one of the most successful of the swimming fish who is right at the top.'

We began to laugh together.

'It's rather fun,' I said. 'And nobody up above can see our slimy underbelly.'

We laughed a little more.

'Twice,' I said then, 'a year ago I didn't think that you and I would ever sit here and laugh at us sitting here.'

'Neither did I.'

'Well, we are!'

'Funny, isn't it?' he said, and we began to laugh again.

Laughter, sometimes, can be an expression of gratitude and while I laughed I thought again of Lady Hallinzeil. I was not irked or irritated by her now. I was not critical of her in any way. More than anything, I felt grateful to her.

PART FIVE

Now that she had made of me her confidante, Helen Hallinzeil became a more frequent visitor than ever. She came to the house nearly every day and was always a little annoyed or quite obviously bored if anybody else happened to call when she was with me and I spent my days veering round between irritation with her, pity for her, and sheer boredom with her conversation. I think it is true to say that I have a habit of turning myself into a confidante and it is a habit in myself that I find very annoying. I do not intend to become the confidante of people like Helen Hallinzeil. It is something that develops as a natural growth out of my primary inquisitiveness about people and their lives, which in turn has developed out of my detailed study of the members of my own family when I was a child in the remote world of Reachfar.

When I first meet people I seem to display or deploy this inquisitiveness in the form of a sympathetic interest in their affairs but, with many of them, when this leads them on to tell me all their secrets, my inquisitiveness is then satisfied and I begin to wish that they would go away. This is, I know, reprehensible and I am ashamed of it and because I am ashamed I screen it with a façade of more interest and sympathy than ever and this, of course, leads to the situation where the confider calls on me at every opportunity as Helen Hallinzeil was doing now.

Ours was one of these unbalanced relationships. Helen was the confider, I was the confidante. I had almost as complete a picture of her life as it is possible for one person to have of another's life, while she knew nothing but one or two bare facts about mine. She did not even know, for instance, that Twice had ever been ill. She was almost the antithesis, I think, of myself, for she seemed to be quite without curiosity and if she did happen to ask a question, the answer always seemed to convey something that defeated her imagination so that she would take on a mystified, boggled look as if the reply were the last in the world that she had expected. And the curious thing was that there was always an implication that, because the reply was not what she had expected, it conveyed something of which she did not approve.

'I haven't said a word to Maggie yet about her drinking, you know,' she said to me one day. 'In fact I am beginning to wonder if it's true. She seems quite normal to me.'

'As long as she is normal there is no occasion to say anything to her,' I said. 'She probably knows that she went a little far with me that day and has pulled herself together a bit. I am glad to hear that she is all right.'

'I haven't told her yet about Robert coming here to take us home either. I think she thinks I have left him for good, you know. I made a mistake taking Maggie back and bringing her out here after Robert had dismissed her. I have to admit it,' she said in a magnanimous noble way, but when she continued a whine of self-pity came into her voice. 'But it was all such a shock. I was in such a state. I didn't know what to do and I had to talk to somebody and it seemed sensible to talk to Maggie because she knew about everything already and she seemed to be such a devoted soul. Just think of her taking to drink like that! I wonder if it is true? As if I hadn't enough to bear already.'

As I listened to these plaints day after day, my sympathy began to flag, boredom to set in and then I became ashamed of my impatience and lack of sympathy. From this it was only a step to anger with Helen because she was making me ashamed of myself and now and then I would make some snappish response, whereupon she would begin to cry. Then I would feel sorry for her and disgusted with myself and I would begin to sympathise all over again. The plaints would increase in volume and become more self-pitying in tone and the whole vicious cycle would begin all over again. I began to wish very hard for the day that Lord Hallinzeil would arrive and harder still for the day when they would leave for London.

'It is this Why-should-it-happen-to-*me* thing that gets me down,' I complained to Twice. 'We all think that about our misfortunes but I wish she wouldn't keep saying it out loud.'

However, these outbursts of mine took place comparatively seldom and, in the main, Helen and I got along very well. Early in March, on my forty-fifth birthday, as it chanced, the telephone was at last installed in Guinea Corner. I mention this minor event because it had an out-of-proportion effect on my spirits, cheering and comforting me in a manner that was hardly compatible with the arrival of the little black bakelite instrument on the table in the hall. The reason for this excessive joy of mine at the arrival of the telephone was that Twice had first been taken ill some eighteen months before during our summer holiday which we were spending in one of the most isolated places in the island, a little cottage called High Hope away in the mountains. I had spent a dreadful, stark moonlit night there while Twice fought for breath, alone with the half-formed knowledge that he was mortally ill, a night that still came back to haunt me with its terrible isolation even although, at Guinea Corner, I knew that I had friends all around me and a telephone in the estate office only less than a mile away.

The telephone did lighten the burden that Helen

Hallinzeil was becoming to me, however, if burden is not too heavy a word for the confidences and plaints which she heaped upon me for, now, she usually telephoned before she arrived at Guinea Corner and if I felt that my patience might give way that day, I would tell her that I had people coming to tea, in which case she usually stayed away. When Twice came in one day following one of her visits, I burst forth with: 'You know what? I am starting to feel really sorry and to have some affection for that awful old Maggie Drew!'

'You have a flair for filling life with surprise. Why, for pity's sake?'

'It's just the way Helen H. talks about her, saying: It was very foolish of me to make a friend of a person of that class, and: I do wonder if she really drinks? It is too dreadful if it's true, and: Really, I shall be glad when Robert comes and gets rid of her. Twice, I believe she is looking forward to her Robert coming and throwing Maggie out. It is a nasty sort of thing.'

'She is probably full of resentment against Maggie,' Twice said. 'After all, it was Maggie who burst her whole happy balloon in the first place. She probably is looking forward to Maggie getting thrown out on her ear as a sort of vengeance for what has happened to herself.'

'But it's so unfair!'

'Yes. It will be Maggie's turn to say: Why should this happen to me? The music goes round and around — Talking of music — it is less boring than Helen H. — there is no word yet about Kathleen Malone? After all, it is nearly the end of March.'

'Not a word. I am afraid she can't be coming. It *is* disappointing, darling.'

'Very, but let's keep on hoping.'

March turned into April and there was still no news of Kathleen, but Helen Hallinzeil telephoned to tell me that her husband was due to arrive at ten in the morning of the sixteenth and invited Twice and myself to the Peak Hotel for dinner that evening.

'But Twice's birthday is on the seventeenth and we are celebrating it on the sixteenth because it is a Saturday,' I said. 'I was planning a small dinner here and intended to invite you. Won't you both come?'

She accepted the invitation and I went on with my plans, inviting Sir Ian Dulac and his son Edward, who happened to be at home on a visit at the time and Delia Andrews and Isobel Denholm, the two young women who owned the Mount Melody hotel.

'Those two?' Twice questioned when I mentioned the last two names.

'For Edward's sake,' I explained.

'What sort of sake for pity's sake? Why should Edward be interested in a pair of Lesbians?'

'I don't expect him to be interested exactly. I thought they might wake him up a bit.'

'Wake him up to what?'

'Sex,' I said. 'Edward is about thirty now. It is high time he got married or something.'

'Are you suggesting he should marry the combination of Dee and Isobel?'

'Don't be silly.'

Twice drew an impatient breath which, in former days, would have been the precursor of a violent argument.

'Now don't you go getting like that,' I told him.

'But look here, Janet, if you have ideas as tortuous as yours, you have to explain them!'

'It isn't tortuous. It is perfectly simple. When Edward is as unconscious of sex as he appears to be, I thought an injection of it in one of its odder manifestations might make him sit up a bit.'

'The things you can dream up!'

'You don't mind having Dee and Isobel at your party, do you?'

'Oh, lord, no. I'm sort of used to them now. But I don't know what Helen H. may think of that he-man although satin dinner jacket that Isobel wears.'

'She won't even notice it,' I said comfortably. 'Besides, Sir Ian gets no end of a kick out of Dee and Isobel. Dashed amusin' havin' them about the place in a way, he says.'

'Yes. Makes ye feel as if this was Paris more than Paradise, by gad!' said Twice, who could mimic Sir Ian much better than I could.

'Listen, chum,' he went on, 'what if you make Edward sit up to the fact that he is a homosexual instead of a confirmed bachelor?'

'He isn't. Sashie says not and Sashie always knows.'

'You have discussed this with Sashie?'

'Not discussed exactly. I simply asked him once if Edward was a homosexual.'

'Why?'

'Because I wanted to know, of course. Why does one ever ask things?'

'There are times in my life,' Twice said, 'when I feel like spending an evening with Helen H. At least one knows pretty well what she may say or do next.'

Sashie and Don, who knew many of the details of Twice's diet, announced that their birthday gift would be a large turkey from the Peak Hotel freezing chamber and, with the most important part of the meal thus dropped into my lap, the rest of the planning was simple. A week before the birthday there arrived from London my own present for Twice, an album of a complete recording of a requiem mass, with Kathleen Malone singing the contralto part, the best substitute for Kathleen herself that I could offer.

On the morning of Saturday the sixteenth, Twice, while

we were drinking our early tea, said: 'You know what I think?'

'No.'

'If I got my birthday books today, I could have two days of wallowing instead of only one. After all, the party is today. I am quite willing to be forty-five a day early. And it will make me only thirty-eight days younger than you this year instead of thirty-nine.'

All our friends at home invariably sent books for birthdays and Christmas for, apart from their desirability in the book-poor island of St. Jago, they also came in free of customs dues.

'As a matter of fact,' he added thoughtfully, 'I am very pleased and grateful to be forty-five at all.'

I rose from my chair beside his bed, went to the cupboard where I had stored all the parcels, took them to the bed and dumped them there. I then locked myself in the bathroom and had a prolonged cry.

When I went back to the bedroom, confident that I looked completely calm and normal, he looked up at me over the album of the requiem mass which he was holding between his hands and said:

'I am sorry I made you cry, darling.'

'It is because of being glad. Everything is so much better and it has all changed in such a short time, it seems. I am not used to it yet.'

'You have a backlog of crying to do. You didn't cry for a whole year. You spent a whole year being calm and unmoved. You must have a lot of tears stored up inside you by now.'

'And probably a lot of bad temper too,' I said, 'if you think I have to explode regularly. Actually, I think I get rid of the bad temper on Helen H. one way and another.'

'This is a very beautiful present,' Twice said, stroking the cover of the album, 'and thank you very much.'

'I am sorry Kathleen herself hasn't shown up. I suppose she went to Nassau after all.'

'Oh, well, there's always Lord H. I wonder what he'll be like?'

'To me,' I said, 'it doesn't matter. I can only see him as a rescuer who will take Helen off my hands. Lordy, but I am tired of her!'

Twice looked contrite. 'And I was the one who wished her on to you,' he said again.

'Oh, nonsense! I would have to have called on her, really, you know, because of Hugh. It was impossible to think of not doing it when I look back at it now. But that was such a queer time, Twice.'

'Very queer.'

'When I look back at it, it was as if I were afraid to leave the house, as if you would — disappear if I took my attention off you for a moment.'

'I know.'

'It was all wrong. The whole attitude was wrong. I can't say why or exactly what I mean, but it must have been all wrong because I was so terribly unhappy. And you were unhappy too, weren't you?'

'I suppose I was, but I can't think myself back into that state now and I don't want to. As I remember it, I was sort of half-stunned. I couldn't see anything clearly or think anything out properly. You say it was all wrong because we were so unhappy. I don't quite see what you mean there.'

'I am not sure myself, but I feel that that sort of unhappiness comes from being somehow at cross-purposes with oneself, living in your mind in a way that isn't really *your* way. I had got separated from you in my mind. I had come to see you as the patient, as Doctor Lindsay always called you and that is not my true way of seeing you. I have to see you primarily as Twice, the person I love, not as a patient, no matter how ill you are. In fact, I ought to take lessons from Helen H. *She* would never be led into taking anybody else's view of anybody. That is part of the reason why she is incapable of being really unhappy. Like now. It is as if she has quite forgotten what a naughty boy her Robert is because she has made up her mind to forget it. He is her dear husband who is coming here to take care of her and take her back to England and dismiss that horrid Maggie who drinks. That's it. To be perfectly happy all the time, all you need to do is sit inside yourself thinking just exactly what you want to think and not let anybody or anything influence you.'

'And be as dead as those fossils of ours.'

'Yes. I suppose so.'

'Have you ever seen a human brain?' Twice asked.

'No. Why? Have you?'

'I once saw a bit of one in a bottle in a lab. It looked like a grey sponge. When it is inside your head, it is a sponge full of blood, I believe. I bet you a brain with no blood in it and all dried up would look exactly like a fossil or like one of those dried-up sea eggs you find at Golden Beach.'

'This seems an odd sort of conversation for before breakfast,' I said, 'but don't let me stop you. After all, it *is* your birthday.'

'I was just thinking in my roundabout way,' he explained, 'that it is the brain being all soppy with blood from the heart that makes all the trouble.'

We spent the long bright day very quietly, browsing about among the books, reading a line here and there while the record-player played the mass and we would talk for spells between long periods of contented silence. It suddenly came to me that, in the course of these last few months, a new way of life had evolved for us. Before Twice's illness, the day of a birthday celebration like this used to be one long frenzy of preparation for the large and rowdy party in the evening and, when I looked back to those days, it seemed impossible that either of us used to have the energy that we expended. And, in those days, had either of us looked forward into the future, I was sure that we would never have visualised a quiet day like this as a birthday celebration.

'Two years ago,' I said, 'I would never have imagined a birthday like this without lashings of whisky and gin and dozens of people in the house all shouting and roaring. And yet I am much happier and much more my true self just sitting here talking to you than I ever was at any of those boozy parties. They used to happen every week. Somebody was always celebrating something.'

'They are still happening. The office was weighted down with hangovers yesterday after the Bentleys' wedding anniversary.'

'I am so glad I wasn't there,' I said.

Throughout the forenoon the telephone rang at intervals as various friends who had attended the parties in former years gave Twice their greetings and before lunch one or two of the younger members of the engineering staff came in to drink his health, but in the main the house had a quiet, peaceful, secluded feeling, as if we were alone in the world.

'This is somehow being a very nice day,' Twice said after lunch. 'I have a curious feeling of having come through a big dark wood and coming out into the clear and I can't think why. After all, nothing specific has happened.'

'I have had a feeling of uplift myself,' I agreed, 'but I was putting it down to Helen H. going away.'

'No. It is different from that. It is suddenly as if I had got rid of all the regrets for the past and the fears for the future. And "suddenly" is the wrong word. It is more as if I had gone through a process and had reached a point of culmination. I suppose what it really is is that I am much better in health and have accepted the situation in its reality at long last. From where I stand now, I can't see why it should have been so difficult to accept. One has always accepted the principle that if one jumped out of a twentieth-storey window into the street one might not survive, and all I have been asked to do is to accept certain new conditions for survival.'

'I think you are belittling what you have been asked to accept,' I said, 'and, besides, surviving and living are two different things. We survived through last year. Of late, we have begun to live again and it seems to me that living is largely a matter of accepting what happens to one, as we have begun to accept this illness that happened to us.' I paused. 'And that word "happened" doesn't say what I mean,' I then went on irritably. 'This illness wasn't fortuitous or the act of a vengeful god. Remember how I said that a marriage certificate wouldn't pay doctors' bills? That was the result of long consideration. Last year, when I thought over every facet of our life together and, indeed, some facets that never existed at all, the idea occurred to me at one point that this illness might be a divine punishment for sin, the sin of our not being married, but it did not take me long to dismiss that as a lot of atavisic superstitious nonsense born out of those hell-fire sermons I heard in my youth. I do *not* believe in the wrathful Jehovah of the Old Testament who metes out dreadful punishments to little people like us for the little sins we commit. This illness has arisen out of *us*, out of the sort of people we are — or were. That's all.'

'I had a little struggle with Jehovah too,' Twice confessed, 'and that reminds me that I thought of something while you were fiddling about in the kitchen this forenoon. You and I owe Lady H. an apology.'

'What in the world for?' I asked.

'It occurred to me that we have been a bit uppitty and

patronising in all we have said about how she is still en-
cased in the tenets of her youth. I have been a pretty good
case of fossilisation myself in one way and another. You
see, I was always taught explicitly and every other way
that hard work was a virtue in itself and to be a good
mixer and joiner-in at parties and things was a social
grace. You were brought up in much the same way. When
you think of it, we got into just as much trouble by sticking to the tenets of our youth as Helen H. did. It was by
working too hard that I got ill and I didn't help matters by
joining too thoroughly in every boozy party that came
along. It seems to me that the time is about ripe for a
whole new set of rules for living, something that will stress
not the rights and wrongs but the fact that right and
wrong are born out of each other, or are like Siamese twins
joined together back to back, or something. I can't say
what I mean, but I see very clearly that if you stick too
hard by something that is coded as right, it can go into
excess and go sour and turn into wrong in its effect, like in
my case where an excess of zeal to do my duty at my job
turned into a strained heart, not to mention what my
social carry-on at the drunken parties did to my liver.'

'I think I see what you mean.'

'And you are right about this illness arising out of the
sort of people we were. But there is nothing harder to do, it
seems to me, than to look at the mess you have got into
and admit that it is entirely your own fault. It is simpler to
escape into belief in a wrathful Jehovah and I would have
escaped that way if I could, but I didn't find it comfortable
to feel that I was a victim of divine vengeance because, like
you, I don't believe in a god who metes out rewards and
punishments. God is not like a higgler in a market-place,
making bargains. I can put into words not what I believe
in but what I don't, and I certainly don't believe in a cold,
calculating, heartless god — it's a contradiction in terms,

208

dammit! What I believe in is some power that lies at the heart of things and how can such a power be heartless?'

'I don't know what I believe in,' I said, 'except that I am certain that our misfortunes arise out of ourselves and that it is mere cowardice to blame them on the stars or Jehovah. Most of my trouble last year lay in the fact that I looked for an easy way out rather than face my own guilty knowledge that if it hadn't been for me in your life, you would have worked less hard and would have lived less hard.'

'Oh, come now, Flash —'

'It's true,' I said. 'Don't let's run away from it. Being saddled with me made you more ambitious than you were before. The fact that we were not married made you want to do even more for me than ever. And then the other mistake I made was in trying to be clever and efficient and see you as Doctor Lindsay saw you, as the patient instead of as the man I loved. My brain isn't worth one damn and every time I have let it guide me I have landed in a mess, but if I have the guts to follow my heart, I get through every time, through for *me*, I mean. I followed my heart at Ballydendran when I hunted you down through the fitting and machine shops of Slater's Works and it was the best thing I ever did for *me*, but for *you* I am a little doubtful.'

'I am not doubtful at all,' Twice said. 'It is a strange time of day and life to say it but you are the best thing that ever happened to me.' He had been smiling, but he suddenly became very grave. 'But I believe that, harsh as it sounded when you said it, the fact that you happened to me did contribute to my getting ill by making me more ambitious. I am coming more and more to feel that if you are the best thing that happened to me, you have also the potential to be the worst. And if I am the best for you, I am also the worst. This seems to be a law of life. I have come to see humanity as poised always between two opposite poles — the positive pole of good and the negative pole of evil. One's best and one's worst seem to be fatefully linked.'

'It seems so. You have made me happier than I had ever imagined was possible, but you have also been the cause of the starkest unhappiness I have ever known.' I smiled at him. 'But I'll accept the good along with the other and, like you, I have no regrets for the past or fears for the future now.'

'Actually,' he said, 'I do have one regret but it is for something I had no control over anyway so the regret is unreal and invalid. If I hadn't been unconscious at the time they sold Reachfar, if I had known they were selling it, I would have tried to stop it. I would have bought it for us, I mean. I feel you had an unfair deal there, Flash. I don't think anybody except myself — not even George or Tom — knew what that place meant to you and I had to be lying unconscious more or less when they sold it.'

This was something that I still did not want to talk about. Reachfar and all my memories of it had receded to a far corner of my mind — I had pushed it away there by an act of will, I suspected and had placed a ring of taboo round it that would protect me from the pain of its loss. When I was ten years old, my mother died and, perhaps through shock or perhaps by a similar though unconscious act of will, I had succeeded in losing all recollection of the time immediately following her death. For nearly thirty-five years, I had lived with this curious blank in my otherwise fairly complete memory, the blank between the time when she was there as an integral part of my life and the time when she was there no longer. Over the loss of Reachfar, my act of will had been less successful. There was no blank and there was not, either, the transmutation of the beloved in the mind that death can cause. Reachfar had not died, been buried or transmuted and transfigured in my mind. It still existed but it was no longer mine and to think of it or talk about it had not even the barren satisfaction of finality, of the chapter that is closed.

And yet, although I tried not to think of Reachfar, I was haunted by guilt that my refusal to think of it or remember it was ignominious, cowardly and a betrayal of all that the place had meant to me and had given to me. Now, nearly thirty-five years after my mother's death, when the pain of loss had gone and memory had done its healing work of transmutation, I would have liked to be able to recall the days of that spring immediately following her death. This blank in my memory also had, now, an aura of cowardice, of refusal to stay with my mother to the last, of betrayal.

Now, as Twice looked at me so gravely, I found one of my childish incoherent prayers forming in my mind: 'Please, God, help me over this Reachfar thing. Let me get it straightened out!' but there was no response except the rising of the mental spectre of that wrathful Jehovah in whom I did not want to believe, the god who made bargains, the god who had given me my choice between my two loves. I could have Twice or Reachfar, this god seemed to have said, but not both. I had chosen Twice and, seeing it in this way, the loss of Reachfar was something I could never discuss with him. I got up, went to the cigarette box, took out a cigarette and, with my back to him, I said: 'But, Twice, there would have been no point in our buying Reachfar. We have been told that your health would never stand up to the north of Scotland.'

'I would still have bought it,' he said, 'for you. Then it would be there to go back to if anything happened to me.'

I felt now that the final thing had been said between us. Never before, in all the talking we had done, had we faced in words the possibility of this final separation and now that the words had been spoken, there was nothing to do but to turn aside for they marked the point beyond which it was impossible to go. I turned round, went to him and laid my hand on his shoulder.

'Twice,' I said, 'we have to be realistic. If Dad, George and Tom couldn't work Reachfar economically, what would I be able to do with it?' It was easy for me to talk in this 'realistic' way about Reachfar because such talk of it was, for me, unreal, my bond with the place having no footing on the plane that is described as realistic. Talking on this level, I could be fluent and convincing and to remain on this level was the means of getting Twice and myself round this dangerous corner. 'If you are visualising me as an old woman, sitting on top of that hill, like some Granny in her Heilan' Hame with the heather growing in at the door and the weeds as high as my shoulders, you simply don't know me. You do know me, Twice. I am a Highland crofter—a peasant, if you like—in blood and bone and to have that place and not be able to keep it in good working heart and run it as an economic proposition would drive me mad. Don't you see that?'

He was looking less grave and tense and I continued in a different tone: 'Besides, in the course of this last year I have come to see that one *cannot* go back. If Reachfar were ours and if, one day, I went back to it, I honestly don't think it would work, all economic factors apart. I am a different person from the child who played around the fields and the moor. Reachfar itself is a different place with a different relation to me and to the rest of the world. One has to accept that things come to an end—' I made an effort to keep my voice steady '—even Reachfar.' I took a deep breath. 'Even if you died—' there they were, the words clearly spoken and, with a feeling of having gained a subtle yet hard-fought victory, I could go on: 'I might go back to Scotland but I would never try to recapture

Reachfar. I feel there is something cowardly in trying to go back in that way. It is an evasion of things as they are, of life as it is.'

Suddenly, I had a curious sense of light breaking in my mind, very faintly, like the first cold glimmer of a Reachfar dawn and with the light came a premonition that, one day, my incoherent prayer that the Reachfar thing might be straightened out would be answered. But this glimmer of light in that shadowed corner of the mind was only momentary. Twice tilted his head and looked up at me, his eyes very blue and searching, and deep in them I seemed to see a reflection of the shadow in my own mind, the shadow that closed in again around the memory of my lost home. I was glad when the telephone rang once again, breaking the tension and splintering the quiet.

'You answer it,' Twice said. 'Tell them I am having a very happy birthday, thank you,' and I escaped into the hall, away from those searching eyes of his.

'Mrs. Alexander?' said the voice and I had an extraordinary flashing memory of the brass lamp and the picture of the Holy Family in the house in Number Two Row on the Ither Side o' the Brig, while I heard a faint echo of a lovely voice singing: 'Lay my head beneath a rose.'

'Yes,' I said breathlessly, almost afraid.

'This is Kathleen, Kathleen Malone.'

'Kathleen! Where are you?'

'At a place called Mount Melody.'

'When did you get in here?'

'We got into the airport about two. We have just got up to this place.'

'Twice!' I called. 'Excuse me, Kathleen. Twice darling, *happy* birthday! Kathleen Malone is at Mount Melody. Kathleen, please will you come to dinner tonight? It's Twice's — that's my husband — it's Twice's birthday. Please, please come!'

'But how far away are you?'

'Only about fifteen miles. We'll send the car for you. Please come, Kathleen! Please do come. We'll send for you.'

'That's all right. They've got cars here. Of course I'll come. Don't sound so desperate, Janet. What time?'

'Any time, but as soon as you can — dinner's at eight.'

'Fine. By the way, I have a surprise for you. Violetta is travelling with me. Violetta Antonelli — Cervi, you know.'

'Of course I know! Oh, Kathleen, bring Violetta too. This is marvellous.'

'All right. We'll both be with you some time between seven-thirty and eight. Tell me, how are you? How long have you been out here?'

I began to answer her but, after a little, I became aware that I was talking to emptiness. The island telephone system was prone to all sorts of lapses, especially on calls from any distance, with the constant work of the new installations that was in hand so I put down the dead instrument, turned to Twice and hugged him.

'Boy,' I said, 'aren't you having a birthday and a half! Darling, get on that broken-down instrument and see if you can get hold of Mackie and Vickers for tonight. We need two more men. Get anybody you can. I'll have to go and put some water in the soup and make another trifle. God bless Sashie and Don for giving us that great big turkey!'

'Hold on a minute,' Twice said, stopping me in my headlong dash towards the kitchen. 'This Violetta — is she the same one that this old Maggie accuses of having come between her and her husband?'

'Yes. But I am sure she didn't. Why?'

'Mightn't it be awkward, introducing her to Helen H. I mean?'

'Violetta is Mrs. Antonelli as far as Helen H. goes.'

'Still, mightn't she connect things up?' Twice persisted. 'Violettas with a Cairnton connection can't be all that common.'

'Helen H. couldn't connect a rasher of bacon to an egg!' I said impatiently. 'Don't bother me! I've got the food to see to.'

'All right. Have it your own way. But I'd rather not have a fight at the dinner table.'

'There won't be any fight. Maggie practically doesn't exist in Helen's mind now.'

It was an act of Providence, I think, that I had so much to do and so little time to do it in for otherwise I should probably have burst with sheer excitement and joy. My four servants, who were pleased in any case at a party in the house after such long abstinence, responded in their volatile Negro way to this happy excitement of mine and Caleb began to peel more potatoes with a broad grin on his black face while Clorinda took to pieces her already-laid table, put another leaf into it and relaid it and Cookie and old Minna the laundress began to help me with the extra soup. By six-thirty everything was organised, Twice and I were dressed and the whole household, down to Dram our mastiff dog and his friend Charlie, our cat, exuded an air of happy expectation.

The first guests to arrive were Mackie and Vickers, two of the young bachelors who were shift engineers at the sugar factory and who lived along with a third called Christie in what we called 'Bachelors' Bungalow' in a state of comfortable squalor which they were always glad to leave, even at the shortest notice, to have a change of food and drink at another table. Hard after them came Sir Ian and Edward Dulac and then, after a short interval, came the great moment when one of the red cars from Mount Melody Hotel drew up at the door. Dee and Isobel sat in front, Isobel driving, and Violetta was the first to alight

215

from the back, dressed in apricot-coloured chiffon and she looked, to my eyes, quite unchanged since the last time I had seen her in London in 1938. The dark curls still shone without a thread of grey above the warm-coloured cheeks and the brilliant eyes and smile still had the soft gaiety they had had when she was a child, dreaming and humming on the gently swaying swing in the garden behind the Café Firenze. Violetta was a little fatter, that was all, but Kathleen was a different matter. She was enormously fat, bulging out of her dress of some black material, looking like a teetotum balanced on her small feet in high-heeled shoes; the soft outlines of her face had gone, giving place to a curious stern authority that made her a little frightening. A consciousness of power seemed to emanate from her, as soon as her eyes turned upon one, blotting out completely the first impression of the near-ridiculous made by her physical appearance.

Sir Ian and Edward and the two young engineers backed away from her after they had shaken her hand, as children back away from some personage they are made to confront on some occasion of ceremonial, but Twice, who was more or less in a state of trance in this presence, stayed firmly by her side, unable in his enchantment even to be overawed. But if the other men backed away from Kathleen, they drifted towards Violetta as if drawn by silken webs that extended from her on all sides, and by the time the Hallinzeils arrived and we all sat down to dinner, I was so pleased with myself as the hostess of this distinguished well-met company that if anyone had suggested that I entertain royalty at Guinea Corner, I should have said: 'Yes, of course. When?'

At the moment when I presented Violetta to Helen Hallinzeil and her husband, Twice watched very intently and anxiously but they both shook hands with the charming Violetta and there was no flicker of expression in

Helen's face other than its customary amiable inanity. As Violetta moved away and Dee and Isobel came forward, Twice raised his eyebrows slightly at me and I said:

'There we are!' in a comforting way like an old nannie which the Hallinzeils thought was addressed to Dee and Isobel while Twice clenched his teeth at me to indicate that he knew it was addressed to him and meant 'I told you so!' before he moved away in pursuit of Kathleen.

Lord Hallinzeil, who sat on my right at dinner, had what I have always called a 'financial' face, by which I mean that clean-shaven, rather sharp type of face under smooth side-parted hair that is seen so often behind the grilles of banks and in the accounting offices of commercial houses. It is a type of face that, for me, has something of the anonymity of a neat bundle of crisp new banknotes held together by a rubber band and while he talked urbanely of his travels around Australia and the United States, it occurred to me that I had never thought of these bundles of new notes in banks as currency, money which would eventually be taken out of the rubber band and find its way into railway booking-offices, small boys' pockets on birthdays, housewives' handbags and the tills of fish shops. In a similar way, I had never thought of where the neat efficient faces behind the grilles went when the bank closed at night. I had never imagined that well-brushed hair being rumpled on a pillow. It was very interesting to sit here beside this man, listening to him talking in this cool impersonal and, indeed, rather superior way of international affairs and to know that, behind it all, lay a private world that was quite apart from the official façade at the other end of the table, looking happier and more lively than I had ever seen her look, in her new dress of green and pink printed silk.

The centre of the table where Violetta sat was uproariously gay for young Mackie, who was a shy person as a rule, had lost all his inhibitions in the warmth of Violetta's charm so that, at intervals in the solemn discourse of Lord Hallinzeil to myself, there would come a burst of joyous mirth, capped by a bellowing laugh from Sir Ian on my left and his near-shout of 'By Jove! Jolly good!' I felt vaguely that Lord Hallinzeil did not entirely approve of these un-earnest goings-on and, although wishing very much to hear what was being said down there, I tried to give him my full attention and listen with what intelligence I had to what he had to say about the difference between Sydney, Australia and San Francisco, United States of America, although they were both famed for their great bridges. As he kept on saying 'Melbourne, Australia' and 'Chicago — in the States, you know', I felt at first that he was being slightly insulting to my knowledge of world geography, but I comforted myself with the thought that he probably had the idea that all dinner hostesses were exactly like his own wife and uncertain whether Yokohama was a Chinese dish or the county in the deep south of the United States about which a certain number of novels had been written.

We sat on at the table for a very long time, even having the coffee brought in there for it seemed to me a pity to break up the happy group at the centre and Twice's near tête-à-tête with Kathleen at the other end while Edward Dulac coped manfully with Helen, but at about half-past ten we all moved out in the direction of the drawing-room in a large chattering group, where Violetta, her young men, Dee, Isobel, Kathleen and Twice coalesced around the record-player and Sir Ian, Edward and Lord Hallinzeil formed another nucleus in a corner. Helen now asked me to take her upstairs, which I did, and in my bedroom she said: 'We are going back to England tomorrow, Janet. There has been *such* a scene down at the hotel — my nerves are simply in tatters.'

Whatever the condition of her nerves, her voice indicated that she had enjoyed every moment of the scene. 'A scene? Who with?' I asked as if I did not know.

'Robert and Maggie of course! I knew it would happen but I did not think that Robert would be quite so furious. We were to stay for another week, you know, but he won't hear of it. He has made all the arrangements and we leave tomorrow and Maggie is to go straight to Scotland from London Airport. Isn't it awful?' But there was the implication that she was more than pleased about it all.

'It all seems a little melodramatic,' I said.

'My dear, you don't *know* what Robert is like when he is angry and of course Maggie didn't expect him and *she* got into a temper and that made things a hundred times worse. Robert is simply not *used* to people talking back to him.'

In my slight experience of him, I thought, he does not give people much opportunity to talk at all and I hoped that Maggie had been insistent enough to obtain a hearing for what she had to say but I did not say this aloud of course.

Helen had sat herself down in my bedroom and was prepared for one long final heart-to-heart talk between us, wondering how things would go when they were back in London; after all Robert was over fifty now and surely he would settle down and it would be unbearable if he did not, until I said: 'I am sorry you are leaving so suddenly. I have seen so little of Robert. Let's go back downstairs,' whereupon I walked firmly out of the room and Helen had, perforce, to follow me.

Before very long the party began to break up, for Kathleen and Violetta were tired after their air journey, but, although Lord Hallinzeil had had a similar journey which had begun earlier than theirs, he seemed to be impervious to fatigue or any of the other human weaknesses. We were all standing at the end of the longish drawing-room, preparing to move out into the hall when, at the open french window at the other end, an extraordinary apparition burst suddenly upon our sight. Maggie, in her neat dark dress with her neat scraped-back hair, her face dead white and sharply venomous, stood there, a gin bottle in one hand and a torn half-sheet of newspaper in the other. She swayed a little, clutched at the window frame with the hand that held the newspaper so that this fluttered to the floor and, holding the bottle by the neck, she pointed with it at arm's length at us all in an unsteady way, so that its arc covered the whole group while she screamed: 'There she stands, the whore! There she stands!' Her voice was so thick that the sibilants were fluffed to 'sh'. 'But jush wait! The Lord shall shmite — shmite — ' Her voice died away, her eyes rolled and became vacant and she fell forward into the room, the gin bottle hitting the hard old mahogany floor with a loud crash, breaking and leaking what remained of its contents into a little pool beside her head.

'Good gad!' said Sir Ian. 'She's well up on her gin, what? Who is she?'

'Really, Helen!' said Lord Hallinzeil.

'It isn't *my* fault, Robert!' Helen protested on a high wail, and began to cry.

I was transfixed until there was a sudden half-smothered gurgle of laughter from Violetta and then she and Kathleen, followed by the young men, Dee and Isobel withdrew tactfully across the hall to the dining-room while Lord Hallinzeil and Sir Ian dragged the senseless Maggie to her feet and out to the car. Helen was now smothered in tears which I helped her dry while her husband paid off the taxi that had brought Maggie and then made voluble apologies all round before he said: 'Oh, come along, Helen!' in a very impatient voice and took her away.

When their car had driven off, we all gathered again in the drawing-room where Twice, in a mesmerised way, was watching Clorinda and Caleb clear up the remains of Maggie's gin and the broken bottle from the floor.

'Goodness,' he said quietly as we all came in, 'what a birthday this has been!'

'Bless my soul!' said Sir Ian. 'Things are wakenin' up round here at Guinea Corner again!' He turned to Violetta and Kathleen. 'Missis Janet an' Twice weren't always as sedate as they've been tonight, were they, Mackie? But, by Jove, that's the drunkest woman I've seen for a long time.'

'That's enough Sir Ian,' I said repressively when the laughter had subsided. 'It isn't funny. Poor Lord Hallinzeil actually blushed with shame.'

There was another infectious gurgle of warm laughter from Violetta which at once made us all smile.

'I am sorry, Janet,' she said then. 'I know it spoiled your lovely party, but Lord Hallinzeil was being such a stuffed shirt and the unstuffing was absolutely marvellous!'

And once more we all exploded into laughter.

When everybody had gone away and Twice was going to bed, he said: 'You can now take back that uppitty look you gave me when Violetta got past the Hallinzeils' at the start of tonight's proceedings. As soon as that cuddly bundle of love and laughter crossed our threshold, I had a haunted feeling that trouble was not far away.'

I shook down the thermometer and entered his temperature on the chart. 'Okay,' I said, 'I take back the look. The main thing is that none of it seems to have upset you, darling. Your pulse is as steady as a rock. Poor old Maggie. But gosh, didn't she look mad when she appeared at the window? Did you see that light in those eyes of hers?'

'She was mad all right. Lord H. will have to put her into

a home or something. She's not fit to be on the loose. What's this bit of newspaper?'

'Oh, give it here. Maggie was waving that like a banner when she arrived. I wanted to see what was in it.'

The paper was the torn-off back page of the local newspaper, *The Island Sun* and when I spread it out the first thing I saw was a large photograph of Kathleen and Violetta with, underneath, the caption: 'Another distinguished person chooses St. Jago for her vacation. Kathleen Malone, the internationally famous singer, with a friend at her New York hotel. Miss Malone arrives here by air this afternoon.'

'I suppose this is what set Maggie off,' I said. 'I suppose she was referring to Kathleen as well as Violetta. She probably hates her success, being Irish and Roman Catholic and all. In Cairnton you couldn't be Irish and Catholic without being the scarlet woman as well. Poor old Maggie. Well, I am sorry, darling. My past popped up to make a very undignified end to your party.'

'All is forgiven chum,' Twice said. 'Kathleen compensates for everything.'

The next morning my world looked totally different, as if the time since Twice had been taken ill were a play that I had witnessed, a play that had been brought to a dramatic if anticlimactic curtain by the entrance of Maggie with her gin bottle. The memory of Maggie seemed to personify all the dark doubts and distortions of these months, the misery and the loneliness of that separateness, of being locked within the bounds of the self. I felt that I was free and, for the first time since Twice went to hospital, I felt that my world was so happy that I must share it, share it by writing a letter to Tom and George and I was almost impatient for Twice to drive away to the factory for the customary, leisurely Sunday-forenoon chat with his colleagues.

For a long time it had been an effort of sheer duty to write to George and Tom, for to think of them was to think of Reachfar, which was painful, but on this morning there was no shadow of pain in the thought of them and Reachfar lay spread behind them in my mind like a landscape behind the figures in an old portrait and it was a landscape of sunlit splendour. But just as I sat down at my table to begin my letter, I heard Clorinda say: 'Miss Malone, please, mam' and I turned round to see Kathleen in the doorway, more mountainously fat than ever in palegrey linen.

'Kathleen! This is splendid. But isn't Violetta with you? Why not? Is she all right?'

'Yes.' Kathleen's face suddenly seemed very stern and grave as she sat down. 'We decided it would be better if I came alone to try to apologise.'

'Apologise? What for?'

'That awful business last night.'

'But anything awful was entirely the Hallinzeils' business!'

She did not seem to hear me. 'Violetta is simply furious with me, Janet, but, as I said to her, how was I to know that you knew Robert and his wife? If Violetta herself didn't know, how was I to know? Besides, I don't think anybody noticed anything, but you can't convince Violetta of that.'

'Noticed what?' I asked. 'Heavens, nobody could *help* noticing that poor old Margaret Bailey falling like a landslide — she is Margaret Bailey from Aucheninch — maybe you never knew her — falling flat on her face in the middle of us all, but what does it matter? In a way, it served those smug Hallinzeils' right as Violetta said last night. Twice and I have been laughing ourselves sick about it again this morning. What has Violetta got to be angry about?'

Kathleen looked at me solemnly. 'You really mean you didn't notice anything?'

'Notice *what*?'

'I might as well tell you. Violetta thinks you know already. Violetta has been Robert Thomson's — Hallinzeil's — mistress for years, since just after Mario died. My God, Janet, I nearly died last night when they walked into this room. And dinner was absolute murder. I thought Violetta was going to have hysterics any minute and there was Robert glaring down the table and I was stuck opposite to that dead-head of a Helen, simply *waiting* for the balloon to go up. I've never spent such a devil of an evening.'

'Well,' I said, feeling stunned, 'one half of the world never knows how the other half lives. I thought it was a delightful party. Lord H. is a pretty good crasher of a bore, I thought, but I enjoyed every minute of the evening in general. Kathleen, you could knock me down with a feather. What does Violetta see in him?'

'Listen, do you think that Helen noticed anything?'

'That one? Look here, Kathleen Malone, I have no great conceit of myself but if *I* didn't notice anything Helen Hallinzeil certainly didn't!'

Kathleen lay back in her chair and sighed. 'I hope to Heaven you are right.'

'Why? It isn't all that important. Helen knows her Robert is unfaithful. She told me so many times at great length.'

'It is better if she doesn't know who the woman is though. Violetta prefers it that way and so does Robert, I gather.'

'I suppose they are right,' I said. 'Kathleen, what *does* Violetta see in that bloke?'

'Oh, what does anybody see in anybody!' Kathleen said impatiently. 'The truth is that Violetta should have been married to Robert Thomson when they were young. He fell in love with her when she was at the Blue Lagoon. He was in love with her when he married that fool of a Helen. I think the two families fixed the thing up really, the Thomsons and the Lawsons, you know. Anyway, there it was. Then Violetta married Mario, but Mario died and then she became Mrs. Anderson — that's the name she goes by when she and Robert are travelling.'

'Apart from you and me, how many people know about this liaison?'

'Not many. Robert is very good at the stuffed shirt thing as Violetta calls it.'

'How long have you known about it?'

'Since just after Mario died and Robert started to come to the Soho flat. Why?'

I saw again the luxurious L-shaped room, the grand piano, the Dutch flower picture, the apricot velvet curtains.

'You never mentioned it,' I said. 'Rather the reverse. You led me to believe that Violetta wasn't interested in men.'

'Neither she was or is — except Robert. And naturally I didn't mention it. It was a very closely guarded secret in those early days. I became involved because when I was singing in Paris or Milan Violetta could come with me, and Robert would follow, ostensibly on business. But it isn't a love affair any longer. Violetta herself says it is only a habit and I think it is even more of a habit with Robert.'

'Love affairs have a way of turning into habits,' I said, 'until some crisis comes along that either kills them stone dead or revivifies them.'

'Meaning?' Kathleen asked.

'Kathleen,' I began, 'Twice has been terribly sick,' and I found it easy and comforting to tell her many things about

Twice and myself, things that I had never thought of telling Helen Hallinzeil who had been with me almost daily. 'Before he got ill,' I ended, 'Twice and I were more or less a habit with one another. We seldom thought about one another as separate people, you know, as seldom as one looks at one's hand and says: This is my right hand. One is never conscious enough of or grateful enough for one's right hand, I feel, now that this illness has reminded me of it.' I smiled at her. 'I hope last night's carry-on doesn't upset Violetta's affair or do you think it might jerk Hallinzeil into leaving Helen for good? After all, it was Helen who brought Maggie here and quite against his will, too.'

'I don't think Violetta wants that, not at this stage anyway. I believe he would have left Helen back in the beginning but Violetta hesitated because of his children. She feels more deeply about children than anything, even Robert, I think. She gets a lot of money from him for her orphanages.' Kathleen smiled. 'I have sometimes suspected that, nowadays, Violetta loves Robert more for what his money can do for her orphans than for himself.'

'He himself is not eminently lovable,' I agreed. 'He is so utterly the stuffed shirt, but I suppose he was different when he was young.'

'When he was young,' Kathleen said, 'he wasn't a stuffed shirt, but he was a limp rag. If he hadn't been, he would have stuck to Violetta and would never have married Helen.'

'Success story,' I said. 'From Limp Rag to Stuffed Shirt. Oh well, as long as Violetta is happy.'

'She was more miserable this morning than I have ever seen her but, even so, she could not help giggling occasionally. She did not mind last night a bit for herself but she hated it for your sake. And I must say that it will take *me* some time to get over it. These situations just are not my cup of tea. Long ago, I used to be afraid that something of the sort would happen, but it never did until last night, when one had stopped being afraid of it. Violetta joined me in Boston a week ago when Robert left New York for Chicago. She didn't want to come down here at all, knowing that he was going to be at the Peak Hotel, but I persuaded her with the idea of doing nothing much except visit you and so on and got Michael to book us as far from the Peak Hotel as possible. Then we come to see you and the first people we meet are Robert and Helen! Honestly, Janet, you have got a positive genius for trouble. You always had, ever since you set your dog on those kids in Cairnton High Street.'

'Don't go blaming *me*!' I protested. 'I was only trying to have an interesting birthday party for Twice.'

'Well, don't say you didn't get it. He is an extraordinarily nice man but I'll never go through such an evening for him again. Where is he?'

'Up at the sugar factory with his low engineering friends. And anyway, *he* enjoyed his party and to me that is all that matters. He and I have come through a queer year and a half, but I feel that a period ended last night when Maggie fell on the floor with her gin bottle.'

We sat talking of the Cairnton of long ago and, as we talked, I was not aware of the Guinea Corner drawing-room or the tropical garden outside. Nor was I aware of being in the presence of a grossly fat woman who was internationally famous. Much more clear in my mind was the room in Number Two Row where the light from the brass lamp struck the picture of the Holy Family and while I listened to Kathleen's voice, I saw again the pretty little Irish girl who, along with Violetta, sang the Ave Maria in the gay crowded living-room above the Café Firenze.

When Twice's car turned in at the gate, I came back to Guinea Corner and into the presence of Kathleen Malone the diva as if emerging from a dream that was more real than the present reality.

'Hello, darling,' I said to Twice, 'you have a visitor.'

He smiled, a radiant beam of a smile that transfigured his face.

'I couldn't stay away,' Kathleen said after a moment. 'You haven't a piano?'

'No,' Twice said, 'but there is a beauty round at the Great House — Sir Ian's place, you know. You mean you would sing?'

'I have to,' she told him. 'There is a piano at the hotel but there are also hundreds of people. That is a snag about holidays for me. I can't practise among a mass of people. Would Sir Ian mind if Violetta and I came down occasionally?'

'Sir Ian and his old mother would be delighted,' I said.

'How long are you staying?' Twice asked. 'I want to tell them at the office how much leave I am taking. I am not a crowd, am I? May I come to the practices?'

'I think you may and Janet too, if she likes, but Janet has heard lots of practices before.'

'All I ask is this one favour —' I chanted in my voice which resembles a little the noise made by an unhealthy corncrake.

' — Lay my head beneath a rose!' sang Kathleen, ending on a deep belling note that flowed out of the windows and away across the wide valley like a stream of pure gold, and then she laughed, the fat genial laugh of a middle-aged, good-natured Irishwoman.

When she had gone away, after we had arranged for her to practise in the Great House drawing-room on the morrow, I said to Twice: 'There are two Kathleens — the diva and the fat Irishwoman who is what Helen H. would call "common". I am a bit frightened of the diva but I love the common one.'

228

'It is a sort of worship I have got for the diva,' Twice said, 'and it extends to the common one because that body contains that voice.'

'I am beginning to think there are two if not more of everybody,' I said next, and told him about Violetta and the reason for Kathleen's call.

'I have been calling Helen H. fifteen different colours of a fool for having to be told by Maggie that her Robert was carrying on,' I said later, 'but I was taken in myself last night. I didn't notice a thing.'

'Neither did I.'

'Oh, you! You spent the whole evening swimming about in the ambience of Kathleen like a goggle-eyed fish. You couldn't have noticed anything.'

'I did notice that Violetta was a very attractive piece of what you call "carry-on". I never did blame Hallinzeil, but I blame him less now. Poor Helen hasn't got a chance. I have met nastier women but never a duller one.'

'Oh, she wasn't so bad. Quarter to one,' I said. 'Their plane took off at twelve. It is amazing how people you don't like much immediately get nicer the moment their planes take off. Golly, I can see them sitting there, with Maggie in the seat in front, probably, so that she can't get at the gin, Lord H. looking poker-faced and pompous and Helen being all smug about Maggie getting what she deserves for making them look silly last night. I suppose that in her way Helen gets fun out of things like the rest of us. She certainly likes being Lady Hallinzeil, don't you think, in spite of everything? She was a different woman last night. There was none of that pathetic thing about her at all.'

I thought for a moment. 'I say, maybe Helen *has* tumbled to the thing of Violetta now after Maggie's dramatic revelation!'

'I shouldn't think so,' Twice said. 'I should think she was

229

smitten deaf the very second the word "whore" rang through the room. In Helen's world, that word simply isn't used.'

'That's true. We all have different worlds and different things are important in them. I suppose the most important thing for Helen last night was that Maggie behaved disgracefully. Poor old Maggie.'

After lunch, Twice retired with a bundle of his books to lie on his bed and I returned to the letter I had begun to write to George and Tom, but once again I did not go very far with it.

For all these many months since Reachfar had been sold and George and Tom had gone to live with my father and my stepmother in their cottage at Achcraggan, I had avoided all thought of Reachfar. When I wrote home, I kept strictly to news of happenings in St. Jago and did not recall in my letters, as I had been wont to do, past happenings at Reachfar when I was a child and when George and Tom mentioned such memories in their letters to me, I always read over them swiftly, not letting the mind dwell on them, not letting them penetrate. But now, George, Tom, and Reachfar were so near in my mind that it seemed absurd to attempt to write to people who were so close as to be a part of myself. It seemed ridiculous to write telling them of Lord Hallinzeil's sententious maunderings at dinner when they must have heard them as I did or to describe to them the drama of Maggie which they must have seen for themselves. Like the brass lamp and the Holy Family at Cairnton, Reachfar was now very real and present and, almost unconsciously, I left my table and went to lie on the sofa near the window which looked out over the garden. The sunlight slanted in long shafts through the slats of the jalousies into the warm dim room and I found myself in that unreal yet strangely real land that lies between sleep and wakefulness, where place and time become interrelated and cease to exist in their normal dimensions, different places and different times overlying one another, so that the mind is filled with a complex of pictures as if many happenings had all been photographed on a single area of film.

*   *   *

I was seeing this room where I lay and hearing again parts of the many conversations which had taken place between Twice and myself since that day at the end of November when we had begun to talk again, but this seeing of the room and hearing of the talk were superimposed on a picture of the Home Moor at Reachfar and all its sounds of summer, the bees working in the heather, the gurr-gurr of the wood pigeons in the fir trees, the distant rumble of a cart over a stony road.

'I can put into words not what I believe in but what I don't,' came the echo of the voice of Twice, but the scene behind the room shifted now and I was looking up at Reachfar from the shore of the Firth some two miles below.

Seen from here, the house and steading form a row of low buildings that run from east to west along the top of the hill, barely breaking the line between earth and sky, but when the hill is climbed and the buildings are reached, they take on the character of a fortress which presents a sturdy wall to the stormy north, unbroken except for the small window of the scullery and this fortress is protected to east, south, and west by the dark fir trees of the moors.

'God is not like a higgler in a market place, making bargains,' came the echo and now I was inside the house of Reachfar on a stormy winter evening, when all the animals had been fed and were warm and comfortable in stable, byre, and sty. Supper was over and we were all gathered round the fire, my grandfather in his big chair at one side, my mother in her low sewing-chair at the other, my father beside my grandfather, my grandmother and my Aunt Kate beside my mother. In the gap left in the centre of this semi-circle was myself, aged about seven, with Tom on one side and George on the other, a smaller self-contained group within the greater group of my family.

Everybody was busy with something, the women with knitting and sewing, my grandfather and my father with seed and machinery catalogues and George, Tom, and I with a 'clootie rug' we were to make out of rags knotted into the fabric of a very large opened-out sack. We were very inexpert, this being our first attempt at a clootie rug and, as often happens, we were as ambitious as we were inexpert. When my grandmother or my aunt knotted rags into rugs, they were content with a few stripes, a few lozenges and a five-pointed star at the centre for a pattern but not so George, Tom, and I. Our rug was bigger and was going to be much better than any rug ever made at Reachfar. Part of our material was three pairs of worn-out brown tweed trousers and Tom had had the brilliant idea that these could be turned into a portrait of Betsy, the plough mare. George had then contributed the notion that what was left of my outgrown red coat would be enough to make a horse-shoe in each corner of the rectangle while Aunt Kate's old green costume, I said, would make the grass on which Betsy would stand and my mother's old blue skirt would make the sky above.

We sat on three stools around a big wooden chest on which the sacking was spread and in which our materials were put away in the daytime and all went well while we cut up and knotted in my grandfather's old grey overcoat to make the frame round the edge. We did this first because, as Tom said: 'The plain bittie round the outside is the most tedious and we should get it done while our blood is up.'

We worked the frame in about two evenings, our blood boiling with enthusiasm to start on the picture of Betsy and the great moment came when I seized the first pair of trousers and began to clip the brown tweed into little strips and all went well again until Tom and George had worked the big blob of brown in the middle of the canvas that was to be Betsy's body. It was when they began to shape her chest, shoulders and neck that the trouble began. 'Dang it, George, man,' said Tom, drawing back and bending a critical eye on the canvas, 'that bittie you've put in there at her shoulder is giving her a sway back like Johnnie Grey-cairn's old Diamond.'

George now drew back, stood up, looked down, frowning. 'Aye. You are right, Tom. That bittie will have to come out.'

As night followed night and bits of Betsy were worked and then pulled out again, my grandmother became more and more impatient. 'You'll never be done at this rate,' she would say, 'and you'll have that canvas in tatters with all your pulling out!'

And my mother would look up from her sewing and say placatingly:

'Never mind them, Granny. They will finish it some time.'

'Dang it!' Tom would say, exasperated. 'You would think that none of the three of us had ever seen a horse!'

'The bliddy thing looks like Jock Scotland's old sow!' said George one night, whereupon my grandmother said sternly: 'Now then, George Reachfar, no more o' that coarse words!'

The trouble lay not in that none of us had ever seen a horse but in that we knew too well what a good Clydesdale looked like.

I was the first to grow bored with the putting in of strips of tweed, the adverse criticism, and the taking of them out again and on the evening when Betsy's neck was being unpicked for about the tenth time, I turned to my mother and said: 'When I was in the Drapery Warehouse buying your thread today, Mother, Mrs. Gilchrist said a queer thing.'

I was aware of gaining the attention of my mother, my grandmother and my aunt. In theory, they did not approve of my eavesdropping at grown-up conversations but, in practice, they had learned that this was something they could not prevent if gossips like Mrs. Gilchrist had not the sense to be discreet in my presence. Also, by the indiscretions of Mrs. Gilchrist and others, I often brought interesting pieces of news home to Reachfar which my grandmother, my aunt and my mother would not otherwise hear.

'It's a wonder that Mrs. Gilchrist's tongue isn't worn as thin as a threepenny bit, the way it's always clapping,' said my grandmother as a sop to her guilt at being about to listen to gossip.

'What did she say, Janet?' my aunt asked, being more forthright than my wily grandmother.

'She said you canna make a silk purse out of a sow's ear.' I could feel disappointment emanate from my grandmother and my aunt. There was little of immediate interest in this old adage. 'What did she mean, Mother? Why should anybody want to make a silk purse out of a sow's ear?'

Before my mother could answer me, Tom threw his rug hook with a clatter on to the top of the wooden chest.

'It's what the whole of the three of us has been wasting our time on for the last fortnight,' he said. 'You canna make a silk purse out of a sow's ear an' you canna make Betsy out of that bliddy ould trooser!'

234

'Now then, Tom Reachfar —' my grandmother began but my mother, smiling, broke in with: 'So you have found that out at last, Tom?'

George now also put down his hook. 'I doubt so,' he said. 'It has taken us a good while to find it out, but Tom is quite right.' He began to fill his pipe and looked at Tom and me. 'They say that a hard lesson is one you never forget so maybe Tom and me will mind on a lesson for once. Well, if we canna make Betsy, what can we make?'

I now became interested in the rug again. The thing had come out of the doldrums and was open to suggestion and progress.

'Mrs. Gilchrist,' I said, 'has a tea cosy with a house and a lady in a crinoline dress on it.'

'No leddies,' said Tom firmly. 'If we canna make Betsy, God knows we canna make leddies.'

'It has got to be something that we can use this brown dollop of Betsy's body for,' said George. 'We are not going to take all that out again.'

'The house on the tea cosy is brown,' I said. 'We'll make a house. We'll make *Reachfar* House!' My enthusiasm dissolved. 'But Reachfar here isn't brown.'

'It could be brown on your rug, Janet,' my mother said. 'White or light grey wouldn't be practical on a rug. We would have to be washing it all the time. And then across the bottom on the grass you could write the word Reachfar so that everybody would know what house it was.'

'Write it?'

'Yes. You can work letters in your rags just like any other pattern — printed letters, you know.'

Tom, George and I looked at one another. There was no doubt that my mother was the one that had sense. We should have asked for her advice about the rug in the first place. She could always think of things that would interest George, Tom and me.

With our blood up again, we set to work and by the time the first spears of the snowdrops were poking through the black earth of the garden, we had Reachfar portrayed in brown, with its light-grey windows, its green-painted door, its dark-grey, slated roof, and black smoke trailing from the eastern chimney across a cloudless blue sky. In each corner round about it, within the dark-grey frame, there was a red horse-shoe and at the bottom edge, picked out on the green grass in large yellow letters was the word 'REACH-FAR'.

When winter finally withdrew away over the Firth and the hills to the north, the spring-cleaning was done and on the Sunday morning before the others got up, George and Tom and I picked up the old rag rug that needed washing and a rest after its winter of hard work and put down our new one in front of the hearth.

'I must say it looks not bad,' said Tom, 'not bad at all.'

'If we could have made Betsy, it would have looked better,' said George.

I was delighted with the rug, would not hear a word against it and did not at all wish to remember our high-flown failure.

'George Reachfar,' I said in my grandmother's sternest voice, 'you know fine that you canna make a silk purse out of a sow's ear.'

'God is not like a higgler in a market place, making bargains.'

'You canna make a silk purse out of a sow's ear.'

'One has to accept that things come to an end,' came the confused echoes in my mind as the scene shifted again. I knew that the clock was striking 'one, two, three' but it was not the Guinea Corner clock that I heard. It was the clock with the spray of roses under the dial that sat on the mantel at Reachfar and it did not chime 'one, two, three' as on other days. It said: 'Dead, dead, dead.'

Dead, dead, dead. Five days ago, I had had my tenth birthday and today was the day of my mother's funeral. I was between George and Tom in my usual place in the family circle but we were all standing and the place where my mother should have been was occupied by the cradle that held my sleeping, newly-born baby brother. In the middle of the floor there were two rows of three chairs, sitting face to face and on them rested the coffin. On the hearth-rug, facing us of the family and the huge concourse of people who crowded the big kitchen and the passage and made the farmyard outside black and sombre, stood the Reverend Roderick Mackenzie, a black shoe on each chimney of the house pictured on the rug, the black-rag smoke trailing away from under his left heel across the blue-rag sky.

He prayed like in church and then took hold of the lapels of his coat and looked at us all with his bright dark eyes as he began to speak but I could not hear any words except 'dead, dead, dead', and I could feel nothing but astonishment that my bunch of celandines should look so brilliant and un-sad, lying on the lid of the brown coffin.

At last the Reverend Roderick paused and I felt the compulsion of his dark glance as he spoke the final words: 'Elizabeth, for us, can never die. When we love, we cannot lose.' He paused again, looked down at the rug on the floor and then looked across the bunch of celandines at the face of my father. 'My friends,' he said, 'let us go now.'

My father took his place at the head of the coffin, my grandfather went abreast with him on the other side and in the same second George and Tom gently squeezed my hands which they had been holding.

'You will stay with Granny and your brother, Janet,' George said in a low voice.

'And make a cup of tea for Granny like a good girl,' said Tom. And then they too stepped forward and took their places at the foot of the coffin. As it was raised on to the four shoulders, a shaft of sharp March sunlight made the yellow celandines glitter like gold and then the house of Reachfar was empty, except for my grandmother and me and the cradle that lay on the floor in the corner where my mother used to sit.

'I can put into words not what I believe in but what I don't.'

'You canna make a silk purse out of a sow's ear,' came the echoes and I was aware of the brilliant afternoon sun moving across the tropical sky, sending a shaft of golden light in through the slit at the side of the blind over the french window. It was as golden as the celandines that grew on the Home Moor of Reachfar.

The Home Moor lay to the south of the house, a flat area of heather and fir trees, full of swampy patches where the butterwort, the sundew, and the wild orchids grow, full of little ponds fringed with marigolds and double butter-cups, full of dry little places where the heather gives way to grey-green grass and the fir trees to junipers which have grown into grotesque unplantlike shapes, some like neatly hewn stone pillars, some roundly squatting like large toad-stools and some near-human and near-animal in shape, like the hobgoblins and fantastic creatures of a story-book world. This moor has a special beauty of its own, an in-timate beauty, as if the very spirit of Reachfar lived here.

The Home Moor was my kingdom as a child. From the time I learned to walk, I wandered in it with my dog, Fly, that wise nursemaid who, when I had left the house and farm-yard behind and hidden by the trees, did not disturb my blissful sense of being alone and utterly lost to the world by telling me that the house and the world were no more than a quarter of a mile away.

When I was five years old I went to school at Achcraggan, which was three and three-quarter miles away on the shore to the north-east, walking there and back by a variety of routes by field paths and stream courses — never by the road if I could help it — but for a long time after I was five I could still lose myself pleasantly among the trees of the Home Moor. The day came, however, when I was nearly seven, when this was no longer so and I remember that day clearly. It was a summer morning and it must have been a Saturday or a day during the school holidays, for I set off with Fly to 'get lost'. This was now a deliberate act for, little as I wanted to know it, the knowledge was in my mind that if I went straight for about a hundred yards into the moor among the trees and turned half right, I would come to what I called the Picnic Pond. In a similar way, I had the knowledge that if, at the same point, I turned half left and walked in that direction for a mile, I would come to the Juniper Place beside the spring. I thrust all this knowledge back and away, ran through the trees, climbed one and looked in a pigeon's nest where I found an addled egg which I broke and examined and then had to run away from the smell and after many turns and twists and long examinations of this flower and that, I looked about me, waiting for the deep thrill of being 'lost' but it did not come. I knew exactly where I was. I knew that just about twenty yards from a big boulder to my right was the open space where the cranberries grew. In the end, I tried walking with my eyes shut and turning about blindly and doing blindfold somersaults but still, every time I opened my eyes, I knew precisely where I was, that the house was that way, that the march between the Home Moor and the Greycairn Moor was that way and that half a mile to the east of where I stood was the spring that fed the Reachfar well. I remember my desolation, my sense of grieved astonishment that I could no longer 'be lost', but I remember no more of that day.

For a short time I avoided the Home Moor, telling myself that it held nothing for me, that it was more fun to poke about in the newt pool in that forbidden place, the Old Quarry or to paddle down the course of the Reachfar Burn from the spring where it rose on the grassy East Moor to its little estuary on the shore of the Firth but in the end I accepted this evil knowledge that I had acquired. I opened my mind to the fact that I now 'knew' the Home Moor and although the knowing still made me feel sad, I comforted myself by telling myself that 'every real grown-up person' like Tom and George 'knew' the Home Moor and that you could not farm Reachfar and graze your sheep properly if you did not 'know' the Home Moor.

'One has to accept that things come to an end.'

Suddenly the shifting visions of time and place — the celandines in the sunlight behind Twice ill in the night at High Hope, the Juniper Place behind my memory of Twice smiling at me that morning, the tall trees above the Reachfar well behind the memory of Twice in the white room at the hospital, the rag rug with Reachfar written on it behind the memory of the arrival of the letters that told me of the sale — suddenly all the visions vanished. I was no longer seeing but hearing, only — hearing fragments of past conversations in that unreal yet strangely real land that lies between sleep and wakefulness, hearing three sets of words sounding together, like the different notes played on three instruments to form a chord.

'I can put into words not what I believe but what I don't.'

'You can't make a silk purse out of a sow's ear.'

'God is not like a higgler in a market place, making bargains.'

The three negative statements went on chiming together, repeating themselves, intertwining themselves in a complex harmony like a peal of bells while in the background my own voice seemed to be saying: 'Accept — end, end, end.'

'I see humanity poised always between two opposite poles,' Twice had said. I heard his voice through the negative statements that jangled on, in ugly dissonance now. Negative — where was the positive pole? And now the noise died, gave way to the soft Hebridean voice of the Reverend Roderick Mackenzie: 'When we love, we cannot lose.'

I became fully awake, sat up and stared out at the brilliant tropical garden under the merciless sun of mid-afternoon but it seemed to be blotted out by a great glaring whiteness on which, strong and stark, as if written in heavy black letters, I saw the words 'Reachfar is mine.' I blinked my eyes, the riotous colour of the garden came into focus but, there in my mind, newly-minted, was the thought: 'The Reachfar I love is mine for always.'

Looking through and beyond this thought, I saw the long months stretching back to that afternoon in the hospital when Twice had seemed to stop breathing and I had prayed: 'Please God, don't let Twice die! I'll give anything, anything, but don't let him die!' It is easier to put into words what one does not believe than what one does. In that moment, when I prayed, I did not believe that a prayer so heartfelt could go unanswered but down those long months, by some distortion of the mind, I had come to look upon God as a higgler in a market place who had made a bargain which exacted from me Reachfar in barter for the life of Twice. I had blinded myself to the fact that Reachfar was mine for ever, enclosed as it was in the silk purse of memory. It was I who had been the higgler in the market place during these long months. It was I who had bartered the silk purse that held Reachfar for the sow's ear of spiritual discontent.

Reachfar, today, was mine more surely than it had ever been for, not five minutes ago, here in the afternoon heat of a tropical island, I had made a clootie rug by its winter fire and had been as lost and happy in its Home Moor as I had ever been as a child when I ran among its fir trees over its springy heather. Reachfar was mine and it would always be mine. It had been given to me on the day that I was born, I had loved it until it had become part of me, I loved it still and as long as that love remained Reachfar would remain mine. It had been given to me and it had not been taken away. I myself had lost it for a time by trying to forget my love for it.

*   *   *

Twice came into the room, put some records on his player and came to stand beside me.

'Sorry,' I said. 'I am crying again, you see. I seem to do little else these days, but it's all right. I am doing it out of happiness again.'

He sat down on the arm of the chair and shook his head from side to side. 'What has made you happy to the point of tears now?' he asked.

'I was thinking about Reachfar.'

He looked down at me, his glance sharpened and he looked again with that genuine 'twice-ness' that Sashie had mentioned long ago and then he said: 'You will never know how glad I am to hear you speak that word in that way.'

'In what way?'

'As you used to speak it — before everything.' He paused

and then went on: 'Ever since it was sold, when something forced you to say the name, like when we spoke of it yesterday, it came out with a harshness in it, not with the old lilt of someone naming a person she loves.'

'It is all right about Reachfar now, Twice. It really is. I had got it all wrong for a long time but it is all right now. I thought I had lost it but I haven't. You can't lose something that is part of you, that is embedded in your heart and that flows in your blood. You can never lose anything you love.' There was a little silence before I continued: 'What an extraordinary thing one's memory is. I remembered my mother's funeral today. I have never remembered it from the day it happened until today. That whole time after she died until just before I went to Cairnton was a blank but today it came back. That was the most lovely spring. The lesser celandines bloomed early but only three were fully out in the last bunch I picked for Mother. She always loved the celandines.'

I told him about the funeral and, some time, I thought, I might tell him, too, of how I had prayed that day in the hospital and of how, when those letters telling of the sale had come, I had thought that God had made a bargain with me but I would not tell him today. As yet, I was too ashamed. Perhaps, even I would never tell him for maybe there are some depths in the mind which should always be kept hidden in the darkness where they belong. I looked up at him.

'This seems to be our weekend for making discoveries, doesn't it? It should have been obvious to me all along that nothing could take away from me what Reachfar is for me but it wasn't. When those letters came from the family saying they had sold it, it was as if I went mad or blind in my mind.'

'Listen,' Twice said, 'what was that text?'

'What text?'

243

'The one the old Drew started on last night before she passed out.'

'Darling, how do I know what she was going to say?'

'Sorry. That is a bit of mental muddle on my part but she has got herself connected in my mind with that text on the card you told me about at the Sunday School.'

'Gracious! I shouldn't be surprised if that is what she *was* going to say last night. She did start off with "The Lord shall smite —" What a queer thing.'

'What was the text?'

'The Lord shall smite thee with madness, and blindness, and astonishment of heart. Deuteronomy, Chapter 28, Verse 28,' I repeated parrot-fashion, thinking of the frenzied woman of the night before and not at all of the words which had lain dead and meaningless in my memory for so long.

'Where are the Bibles?' Twice asked, going to the book-shelf. 'Are they both upstairs? What is the context of that verse?'

'It's one of the curses that follow on disobedience of the Mosaic law,' I said. 'Deuteronomy is a jumble of laws and rewards and curses, mostly curses. It's that wrathful avenging Jehovah of the Old Testament again and I don't want to think about him.'

Twice gave up his search for a Bible and came back to sit beside me again. 'I don't think it is the Lord that smites us with madness or blindness or the botch of Egypt, whatever that may be,' I went on, 'but the botch of Egypt comes into Deuteronomy too. The botch of Egypt caused me a lot of trouble when I was a child, I remember. If a job was badly done, my grandmother always called it a "proper botch" and I thought it very unfair that if somebody had made a botch of Egypt the poor Israelites should have it visited on *them*.'

'The things you think of.'

'I looked up the word "botch" in the dictionary once. I believe there was a sort of pimply suppurating disease called the botch, probably venereal disease — it's a feature of every language to blame venereal disease on another country. And that only removes the whole thing further from my conception of the Lord. I simply don't believe the Almighty would demean Himself to visit punishments of that sort on people. If people get mad or blind or get the botch of Egypt, they bring it on themselves. The reason for it is in themselves somewhere.'

'Madness, blindness, astonishment of heart,' Twice repeated slowly. 'It's odd — the old Jewish fathers had a curious aptitude for hitting nails on the head. All the ills of humanity, practically, could be tabulated under these three heads. Bringing it right home, look at that old woman last night. She was mad with hatred and drink and Helen H. is as blind as a bat about what's going on — '

'And I'll tell you something,' I interrupted. 'Since a year past last August, since that awful night when you got ill up at High Hope, I have been an acute case of astonishment of heart. That is a dead accurate description of what I have been feeling all this time. You got ill, the family sold Reachfar — my brain took in these two facts and coped as best it could but my heart simply stood back in horrified grieved astonishment. It could not understand how these things had happened and it was as if it stopped pumping blood to my brain and pumped up clouds of astonishment instead.'

'I know exactly what you mean,' Twice agreed. 'The psychiatrists talk a lot about disorientation and mutations of personality and so on when people get seriously ill, but they might just as well say that they are smitten with astonishment of the heart and be done with it. It is easy to accept your limitations with your brain but the heart is a tougher proposition. When it stands back astonished like

245

that, there isn't much the brain can do. It can only wait for the heart to get over it and start working normally again — about a year and nine months, in our case.'

'And I have an idea that it might have taken even longer,' I said, 'but for the intervention of Helen H. We have need to be grateful to her and to our other friends from Cairnton.'

PRINTED BY
NORTHUMBERLAND PRESS LIMITED
GATESHEAD